# MISTER DEATH'S
# BLUE-EYED GIRLS

# MARY DOWNING HAHN

## MISTER DEATH'S BLUE-EYED GIRLS

Houghton Mifflin Harcourt
Boston    New York

The text of this book is set in ITC Legacy.
Book design by Sharismar Rodriguez

The Library of Congress has cataloged the hardcover edition as follows:
Hahn, Mary Downing.
Mister Death's blue-eyed girls / by Mary Downing Hahn.
p. cm.
Summary: Narrated from several different perspectives, tells the story of the
1956 murder of two teenaged girls in suburban Baltimore, Maryland.
[1. Coming of age—Fiction. 2. Murder—Fiction. 3. Grief—Fiction.
4. Baltimore (Md.)—History—20th century—Fiction.] I. Title.
PZ7.H1256Mr 2012
[Fic]—dc23
2011025950

ISBN: 978-0-547-76062-9 hardcover
ISBN: 978-0-544-02224-9 paperback

Manufactured in the United States of America
5 2021
4500824879

*To Jim*
*who has encouraged me to write this story since 1980*

# Prologue

HE opens his eyes. It's still dark, way before dawn. He'd willed himself to wake at three a.m., and he's done it. He hadn't dared to set the alarm. What if someone heard it go off? No, he and his brother must leave the house without anyone knowing. Not his family. Not the neighbors.

Without turning on the light, he dresses slowly, carefully—dark shirt, dark pants—then glances at his dim reflection in the mirror. His face looks the same as usual. A pale oval in the shadows, expressionless. The kind of face nobody remembers.

He smiles at himself. The man you meet at the top of the stairs, that's who he is: the man who isn't there. The man you should pay attention to, the man you shouldn't offend. Vengeance is mine, sayeth the man who isn't there.

Quietly he opens his kid brother's door. He's still asleep, head under the covers even though it's June and already hot.

He touches his shoulder lightly and whispers, "It's time."

His brother sits up quickly, startled. Has he forgotten what they're going to do today?

"Get dressed," he says in a low voice.

His brother hunches his shoulders and looks up at him—a kid. Still a kid. Always the baby.

"You can't back out," he whispers. "We're brothers. A team."

"I been thinking," his brother says. "I'm not so sure . . ."

His brother is scared. He can almost smell it on his breath and in his sweat. He squeezes his brother's arm until he winces and tries to pull away. He tightens his grip, hurting him, not caring.

"Get up," he mutters. "You gave me your word."

"Yeah, but maybe—"

"Maybe nothing."

His brother looks like he might cry. "They didn't do anything to *me*," he whines.

"What somebody does to me, they do to you. That's what being brothers means." He gives him a yank. "Get dressed."

His brother gets out of bed. He pulls on jeans and a dark T-shirt. Now they look like twins. Neither one worth looking at twice.

Slowly they go downstairs. They hear their father snoring. Their mother mumbles in her sleep. Ordinary, everyday stuff. Nothing unusual. Yet.

In the basement rec room, he goes straight to the stag's head mounted over the TV, a trophy from his father's hunting days. Gently he lifts the rifle from its resting place on the stag's hooves. Nice touch, that—include the hooves so you can display the deer along with the gun that killed him.

He loaded the rifle last night. It's ready to go.

In the kitchen his brother is waiting, tense, still scared. Together they sneak outside into the darkness. The row houses are silent. Not a light anywhere. Not a car to be seen or heard. He and his brother could be the only people in the world, surviving on their own in some kind of science-fiction novel. Not such a bad idea.

They cross the road and lose themselves in the park's shadows. They pass swings hanging empty but twirling slowly in the breeze, chains clinking like tiny bells. They pass the sliding board, a sheet of silver in the darkness; the jungle gym, the rec center, a barbecue grill, picnic tables. To their left is the baseball diamond. And the lake. To their right is the woods.

They go to the right, slipping through the trees like Indians, their tennis shoes as silent as moccasins. They cross a small bridge over a creek. The water gurgles. A frog croaks. The water smells of mud and dead weeds.

They stop about ten feet from the bridge, at the foot of a maple tree with low limbs perfect for climbing. Holding the rifle carefully, he scrambles from branch to branch, up into the leaves.

"Can you see me?" he whispers to his brother.

"No." His brother peers up into the tree. "You want me to climb up there, too?"

"We talked about this yesterday. Hide in the bushes. When you hear the gun, come running. I'll need you to help me then."

His brother looks around uneasily. He's still scared. "It's so dark," he says. "Why can't I stay with you?"

He scowls down at him, frightening him even more with the fierceness of his face. "You'd better not ruin this."

Stinking with fear, his brother backs away toward the lake. "I won't mess up," he says in a shaky voice. "I'll help you like I promised."

He watches his brother disappear into the shadows. For a while he hears him crashing through the undergrowth. He sighs. His brother is a loser. Not as smart as he is, not as quick. Slow and clumsy and as nervous as a girl—that about sums it up.

At last the woods are silent again. Except for the birds. They're waking up and singing like they're auditioning for a Disney cartoon. So damn optimistic. So cheerful. So happy to be alive. They get on his nerves. He aims the rifle at a mockingbird on a nearby branch. Fingers the trigger. Doesn't pull it, though. Not because he doesn't want to.

He leans his head against the tree trunk and breathes in the smell of damp woods. It's like when he was little and his father took him hunting and they waited in a tree for a deer to step out of the bushes. Patience, it takes patience.

## PART ONE

# The Day Before

# Party in the Park

## NORA

DESPITE the summer heat, I'm sprawled on my bed, radio turned up loud to get the full benefit of Little Richard singing "Tutti Frutti." Dad's not home from work and Mom's outside hanging up the wash, so there's nobody to scream "Turn that radio down!"

The window fan blows warm air on my face. I close my eyes and drift off into a daydream about Don Appleton, a boy in my art class. I've loved him since eighth grade. Not that he knows it. Not that he loves me. Anyway . . .

The car radio blasts "Tutti Frutti," and the wind blows through my hair. Don smiles at me as he slides one arm around my shoulder, and I move closer to him, till I'm practically sitting in his lap. The way Cheryl rides with Buddy, her hand on his thigh. He kisses me and someone blows a horn at us. "You're so pretty," he whispers. "I really like you."

Up ahead is the frozen custard stand. Peggy Turner—Don's real-life girlfriend—is there with her friends. They all stare. They can't believe Don is with me. Right in front of them, he kisses me again, and then he—

"Nora, phone!" my little brother hollers up the steps. "Phone!"

Jolted out of my daydream, I holler back, "Who is it?" I'm too hot to move.

"I don't know," he yells. "Some girl."

Dull from the heat, I go downstairs and take the phone from Billy.

It's Ellie. "A bunch of kids are getting together in the park tonight," she says. "Can you come?"

My mood suddenly improves. "Sure," I say.

"Sleep over at my house," she says. "We'll walk to school together tomorrow. Last day! Yay!"

"Who's coming?" I cross my fingers and hope Ellie will say Don, Don will be there. Which is silly, because he isn't in the same crowd. Don's on the basketball team. He dates cheerleaders and majorettes. He lives in Dulaney Park, the rich part of town. I got Mom to drive me by his house last Halloween, just to see what it looked like. I was scared he might see me, so I crouched on the floor and peeked out the car window. His house was all lit up. Some trick-or-treaters were ringing the doorbell, and I told Mom to drive on in case Don came to the door.

"All the kids will be there," Ellie says. "Paul, Gary, Charlie, Cheryl, and lots more. You know how our neighborhood is."

"More exciting than mine, that's for sure." As I speak, I see Mr. and Mrs. Clements drift past our house, their little dog trailing behind them. They're old. Their dog is old. Old houses, old people—I guess they go together. Not a person on our block is under forty except Billy and me. Boring, boring, boring.

Ellie lives a mile away on the other side of Elmgrove, in Evergreen Acres. It used to be woods when I was little. Block after block, street after street of row houses built after the war for veterans and their families.

Everybody's young there, even parents. Most of the dads fought in Europe and Africa and all those islands in the Pacific. My dad was too old for the draft, but Ellie's father was in the navy. Joined up after Pearl Harbor, the first guy in his town, he told me.

And the kids there—dozens of them, from babies to teenagers. Bikes and wagons and sandboxes in every yard, hopscotch games drawn on the sidewalks, toys scattered on front steps, baby carriages and strollers on porches, ball games in the street, dances in the rec center, souped-up cars with loud radios. It's never boring on Ellie's street.

After dinner, I toss what I need into my overnight case, kiss Mom, make a face at Billy, and follow Dad to the old Buick parked in the driveway. He grumbles about driving me over there, but I'm thinking he doesn't really mind because he can have a beer with his buddies at the Starlight on the way home.

When we're near Ellie's house, I tell Dad, "Just let me out at the corner of Thirty-Third and Madison. Then you won't have to bother with turning around and all."

He glances at me and nods. I hope he hasn't guessed how much the old Buick embarrasses me. Not only is it out of style, but it has dents on the side and the paint is faded and dull. Inside, the drab ceiling liner sags and the upholstery is torn and frayed. The scratchy old army blanket covering the back seat is disgusting. In the heat, it smells like dust.

Worst of all, the radio's broken. If my parents ever think I'm responsible enough to get my driver's license, I can't possibly take my friends anywhere in a car that doesn't have a radio.

The thing is, Dad's an automobile mechanic. Not that you'd guess it. He's English, and he has a posh accent to prove it. Most people think he's a college professor at Towson State. Sometimes I let them go on thinking that.

Anyway, he keeps the Buick running like a top—to quote him. What does he care what the car looks like? What's important is the engine.

"Here?" Dad pulls over on the shoulder and stops.

I open the door, eager to escape before anyone sees me getting out of the car. "That's Ellie's house right there, three doors down." I point at the brick row houses, each with its own small yard and its own chain-link fence. Where I wished we lived instead of in a poky old bungalow down at the wrong end of Becker Street, two doors up from the train tracks.

Ellie's waiting at the door, ready to go. Like me, she's wearing short shorts, a sleeveless blouse, and scuffed white Keds. Her red hair is pulled back in a curly ponytail. "Dump your stuff in the hall," she says. "The rec center just opened."

Mrs. O'Brien sticks her head out of the kitchen and smiles. "Good to see you, Nora."

"You, too." I smile at Ellie's mother. She's dark-haired and sweet-faced, younger than Mom and fun to be around. Best of all, she makes me feel welcome. Special, even. Ellie's friend. Catholic like Ellie. Not the kind of girl you worry about. A nice girl.

In other words, a boring girl. A flat-chested, tall, skinny girl. Not the kind to sneak out or smoke or be a bad influence.

"Gary's bringing his records," Ellie tells me as we leave the house. "He's got *everything*—Fats Domino, Little Richar[d], and Lee, the Platters, Chuck Berry, Bill Haley, the Crew-Cu[ts], Doggett."

We cut across the ball field to the rec center, a low cinderblock building backing up to the woods. In the daytime, it's a summer camp for little kids who sit at picnic tables and weave misshapen potholders on little metal frames, string beads on string, squish clay into lopsided bowls—the same old boring craft projects I hated when I was little. The kind of stuff adults think is creative.

At seven thirty, the sun is low enough to cast long shadows across the grass. The rec center's white walls reflect the sky's pink light. I hear the Penguins singing "Earth Angel." The song transforms the hot, dusty park into a place where a boy could fall in love with you—or break your heart.

"Oh, no. Look who's here." Ellie grabs my arm and points at the parking lot beside the rec center. Buddy's sitting on the hood of his old black Ford, smoking a cigarette. Hair smoothed back into a perfect ducktail, white T-shirt with the sleeves rolled up to hold a pack of Luckies, Levi's low on the hips, motorcycle boots even though he doesn't have a motorcycle. A cool cat, that's how he sees himself. Short and skinny and weasel-faced, that's how Ellie and I see him.

"Why's he hanging around here?" I ask. "I thought all the graduates went to Ocean City the minute they got rid of their caps and gowns. It's what I'm doing next year." I picture myself lying on the beach, getting a good tan. A boy walks toward me—Don, of course, by himself for once. He sees me, he smiles, he—

Ellie says, "I hope he's not planning to start something with Cheryl."

with him at least a month ago," I say. "I thought
~~een them."

~~r head. "For her, but not for him. He calls her all
~~t talk to him, she tells him to stop calling her,
~~ing it. Her parents won't let him near the house,
so ne parks his car down the street and watches for her to come
out. She won't go anywhere unless Bobbi Jo or I go with her."

"I didn't know that." I'm thinking how much in love they used
to be, always together—CherylandBuddy, BuddyandCheryl. I'd
seen their names carved on a tree in the park and scratched in
cement on a new sidewalk. I'd thought then it was true love, it
would last forever.

"There's lots you don't know, Nora." Ellie drops her voice to a
whisper, her eyes widen. "Remember that black eye she had last
April? Buddy did that."

I stare at Ellie, horrified. "She's never told me anything
like that."

"She walks to school with me almost every day now. She tells
me stuff then." Ellie pauses. "Actually, I wasn't supposed to tell
anybody about the black eye. So don't mention it, okay?"

I glance at Buddy, still lounging by his car. "I hate him." And I
really do. I feel my hatred, I taste it, dark and bitter.

"Me too." Ellie's voice rises. We stand there and glare at
Buddy.

He turns his head, sees us, and waves. He doesn't know what
we know. We look the other way and pretend not to notice him.

Behind us, we hear Cheryl calling, "Wait up!" She's with Bobbi
Jo, Ellie's neighbor. They run to catch us, backlit by the setting
sun, one a little taller than the other, both blond, Cheryl's hair in a

long ponytail, Bobbi Jo's short and curly. They're both wearing white shorts and blue shirts. I can't help noticing that Cheryl's shorts are tighter and shorter than Bobbi Jo's. Her blouse is also cut much lower, lots lower than I'd dare wear. But then, I don't have as much on top as she has. They're both wearing too much bright red lipstick. Cheryl's idea, I think.

While we're waiting, I avoid looking at Buddy. "I thought this was a get-together for our class," I whisper to Ellie. "Bobbi Jo doesn't even go to Eastern—plus she's only fourteen."

Ellie looks surprised. "Don't you like Bobbi Jo?"

"Of course I like her. It's just that . . ." Honestly, it's just that when Bobbi Jo's around, boys notice her, not me. But I'm not about to admit that to anybody.

Cheryl slings her arms around Ellie and me. "Hey, you all." She's wearing enough perfume to knock you over.

"*He's* here," Ellie hisses, not looking in Buddy's direction.

"Damn, damn, damn." Cheryl glances at Buddy, still sitting on the hood of his car, still smoking, still watching us. "I was hoping he wouldn't come."

Buddy doesn't move, but he stares hard at Cheryl. Some of his friends have joined him. Like Buddy, they wear tight Levi's and white T-shirts. Vincent, Chip, and Gene. My father would never let me date guys like them. Not that I'd want to. Their droopy eyes and curled lips scare me.

With an eye on us, Vincent says something to Buddy and laughs. Buddy doesn't even smile. He just keeps watching Cheryl. It's creepy the way he looks at her with that cigarette hanging out of one side of his mouth, like he thinks he's Marlon Brando or something.

"He's going to ruin everything," Cheryl says. "I hate him."

"We won't let him near you," Bobbi Jo says.

"We'll be your bodyguards," Ellie says.

"Or to be more exact," I add, "your *Buddy* guards."

We laugh, draw closer together, and walk toward the rec center, arms linked. We're a gang, all four of us. Buddy and his friends aren't going to ruin our fun.

But maybe it won't be fun. Maybe it'll be like all the other parties. Everyone will dance except me. I'll be the wallflower, hiding in the girls' room trying not to cry, wishing I was home, wishing I hadn't come. My mood plunges, I feel like leaving now, before anything bad happens. But of course I can't leave. What would the others think? I have to stay even if I end up crying in the girls' room.

Gary stands by the record player. He's got a stack of forty-fives ready to go. At school he's the guy who runs the movie projector in science class. He sets up the microphone when it's needed. He does sound effects for school plays. I wonder if he ever feels like I do. Maybe he's just pretending to like being the disc jockey while the other kids dance.

A few couples are slow dancing to "Unchained Melody," one of my pretend songs for Don. Slow and dreamy and romantic. Perfect for slow dancing. I dedicated it to him once on a late-night radio show: "To Don from a secret admirer."

When the disc jockey read what I'd written, I almost died of mortification. What if Don guessed I was his secret admirer? I was scared to go to school the next day, but he acted the same as always, kidding me about the picture I was painting in art class. "A masterpiece! But wait, is this horse crippled?"

Nora—a nice kid, but who likes nice kids?

I watch the couples hold each other tight, swaying slowly as if they're dancing underwater. As if they'll die if they're separated. Cheryl and Buddy used to dance like that at parties in Ellie's basement rec room. Not anymore.

At least they'd been in love. Maybe it didn't last long, but still . . .

"Hey, Nora." Ellie nudges me. "Let's get a soda."

The four of us head to the cooler. We don't want to stand around looking like we're waiting for someone to ask us to dance. There aren't many boys here yet, and the ones who are here have partners. Or, like Buddy and his friends, they're leaning against their cars, smoking and watching the scene.

"I thought there'd be lots more kids," Bobbi Jo says, obviously disappointed.

Cheryl looks around and shrugs. "It's early."

Before we finish our sodas, kids start arriving. Cars pull into the parking lot, radios blaring. Doors slam. The concrete floor fills with dancers, jitterbugging now to "Maybelline."

That's when Ralph Stewart shows up. What's he doing here? He's from Don's neighborhood, a basketball player, a big wheel, not the type to hang out in our part of town. I crane my neck, hoping to see Don follow him in, but it's just Ralph. He stands there, scanning the crowd.

"Oh my God," Cheryl whispers. "He came! I asked him, but I didn't think he'd really come." Her face is red. I can almost hear her heart beating faster.

I glance at Ellie. She doesn't look surprised. This must be another secret they shared walking to school.

With a big grin, Ralph saunters over, takes Cheryl's hand, and leads her into the crowd of dancers. Cheryl laughs, tosses her ponytail, moves fast, hips shaking. Ralph matches her every move. He's so cute, I think. Maybe not as cute as Don, but almost. How does Cheryl get boys to like her? What's the secret? Will I ever figure it out?

Suddenly Buddy's beside me lighting a cigarette, his eyes focused on Cheryl and Ralph. "What the hell is Ralph Stewart doing here?"

He asks like it's my fault, like I should apologize. My face burns and I shrug. "How should I know?"

"Cheryl invited him." Bobbi Jo leans past me and grins at Buddy. "They're dating, if you want to know."

I stare at Bobbi Jo. I thought Ralph was going steady with Sally Smith. She wears his ring around her neck. I've seen it. Suddenly I feel like I'm not really part of Ellie's neighborhood. I don't live here, I don't walk to school with Cheryl, she doesn't tell me her secrets.

I glance at Ellie. She's shaking her head, sending signals to shut up, but Bobbi Jo ignores her.

"Cheryl thinks he's going to ask her to go steady tonight," she tells Buddy. "He might even give her his class ring."

"What do you know about it?" Buddy sneers. "You should be home playing with dolls or something."

Bobbi Jo's face turns red. "I'm almost fifteen," she says. "I know plenty."

"Don't make me laugh." Buddy starts to walk away just as "Maybelline" ends and Wild Bill Doggett comes on with "Honky Tonk." The music has a deep dark driving rhythm that you feel inside. You want to dance, and not just ordinary jitterbug—you want to use your body in strange new ways. Twist and sway and move your hips. I can't explain the effect it has on me—it's almost scary.

I wish I had the nerve to go out there and dance like Cheryl and Ralph—not exactly the dirty boogie, but pretty close. At the junior prom, a bunch of wild kids from Holly Court got thrown out of the gym for doing it. The look on the chaperones' faces was really funny. You'd have thought it was the end of the world.

Boys whistle and shout as Cheryl boogies. She shoots a look at Buddy like she's taunting him. Making sure he notices her short shorts and tan legs and low-cut top.

"That bitch," Buddy mutters. "Just look at her. I could kill her."

Cheryl whispers something to Ralph. They both look at Buddy and laugh.

"Oh, come on," Ellie says to Buddy. "Don't you ever watch TV? They do stuff like that all the time on the Milt Grant show."

"Not like that, they don't." Without another word, Buddy walks away.

"Honky Tonk" ends, and "Tutti Frutti" starts. Paul asks Ellie to dance and Walt asks Bobbi Jo. That leaves me sitting there by myself as usual. Just as I'm thinking I'll go the girls' room, Charlie shows up. "Come on." He sticks out his hand. "Let's dance."

I take his hand and follow him into the crowd. He's shorter than I am. But he's funny, and I like him the way he likes me—as a friend. Dancing with him is a whole lot better than crying in the girls' room.

"Gary," Charlie shouts, "put on Little Richard next—'Long Tall Sally.'"

As soon as "Tutti Frutti" is over, Gary drops the needle on "Long Tall Sally," and Charlie and I laugh. It's his song for me—he's dedicated it to me more than once on radio show call-ins: "And now, for long tall Nora from short skinny Charlie, here's Little Richard singing 'Long Tall Sally.' "

Ellie thinks Charlie likes me more than he lets on, but I don't believe it. I want him as a friend, not a boyfriend. Someone to have fun with. Besides, I can't imagine kissing a boy shorter than I am.

Charlie spins me in close. "Oooh, baby!"

I laugh and step on his foot. When he spins me, I bump him with my elbow. He does a dirty boogie move and I imitate it. "Oooh, baby," we shout.

By the time the song is over, we're laughing so hard we can't dance. It's dark now. A few couples drift away from the shelter's lights toward their cars, toward the woods. The night air is hot, humid, heavy. An almost full moon has just risen over the dark mass of trees. Somewhere in the shadows a mockingbird sings, almost like a nightingale, I think.

"Unchained Melody" is playing again. I picture myself with Don, dancing, slow and close, his cheek pressed to mine. He'd be singing to me and me alone, his lips pressed to my ear, his breath a tickle on my cheek. Why can't life be the way I want it to be? Just once?

But it's only Charlie I'm with, and we're walking back to the picnic table, talking about chemistry. I'm scared I'm getting a C or even worse and he's telling me not to worry so much.

He's right, I do worry too much. All the time, about everything. Chemistry and math are just little things on my worry scale. I worry about being too tall, too skinny. Sometimes I have weird thoughts and then I think I might be secretly crazy. What if I crack up someday? Lose my mind? Go nuts? What if I end up in Spring Grove Insane Asylum? The people there howl when the moon's full, at least that's what a boy in my math class told me. He should know. He lives on the street that ends at the asylum grounds. There's a big iron gate and a guard in a little booth and a tall fence with spikes. I'd be afraid to live on that street.

Do other people ever worry about the kind of things I worry about? I glance at Charlie. Not him. He's still talking about chemistry and how much trouble he'll be in if Haskins gives him a C.

It's just me. There's something wrong with me, with my brain or something. I might have a tumor, I might die young before I even graduate from high school.

We sit down beside Walt and Bobbi Jo. I try to push the heaviness in my head away. I smile, I laugh, I pretend I'm just like everyone else. The Great Pretender. I'm good at that. Acting normal.

While Gary chooses the next record, Cheryl and Ralph join us. Her face is flushed, her eyes bright. She's holding Ralph's hand.

Over on the other side of the rec center, just where the rec lights meet the dark, Buddy is watching her. He's looking at Cheryl like he hates her.

Cheryl notices Buddy and holds Ralph's hand tighter.

Ralph grins at Bobbi Jo. "Aren't you a little young to be out this late?"

"Less than two years to go and I'll be sixteen," Bobbi Jo says.

"Yeah, but when you're sixteen, we'll be eighteen," Ralph reminds her. "You'll never catch up with us."

"I can pass for sixteen right now," Bobbi Jo says. "I told that cute guy at the Esso station I was sixteen and he believed me. He wants to take me out, but I know what my father would say if he showed up at our front door. He won't let me date." She pouts for a second and then smiles at Ralph.

How I wish I had dimples like hers. But maybe they wouldn't look as cute on me. Maybe my face is the wrong kind for dimples. Too long maybe, too plain.

Ellie and Paul come over. "It's too hot to dance," Ellie says. "Look at my hair, it's all frizzed up and I'm roasting."

"There's a cure for that." Cheryl drops her voice low. "Ralph's got a couple of six-packs of Rolling Rock. We're going over to the playground. Want to come?"

I glance at Ellie. If we get caught with beer, we'll be in a lot of trouble. She looks a little worried, but she says, "Count me in."

Bobbi Jo grins. "Me too."

*Me too, me too, me too . . . I will if you will . . .*

We walk across the baseball field lit by lights from the rec center. Our shadows stretch out toward the woods, long and thin with impossibly small heads.

For maybe the first time in my whole life, I'm doing something really reckless. Beer. The nice kid is going to drink beer. Maybe the nice kid will get drunk. Maybe the nice kid will make out with somebody. Who knows what the nice kid might do on a warm, dark summer night?

# Drinking Beer and Making Out

## NORA

**N**EAR the playground, a bunch of guys are playing pickup basketball. *Thud, thud, thud,* the ball bounces. *Thwang,* it drops through the net. Somebody curses. Somebody laughs.

Buddy joins the boys on the court. Did he follow us across the field? Must have. My arms prickle a little. It scares me to think about him skulking behind us. He's stupid and mean and I don't like him. Don't trust him either. Those squinty eyes of his, that narrow foxy face.

Why can't he just leave Cheryl alone? Can't he see she doesn't like him anymore? She likes Ralph. No, she *loves* Ralph. Anyone can see it in her face, in the way she looks at him. Maybe Ralph's looking at her like that too, but I'm not sure. Boys are harder to read than girls.

Except for Buddy, who still looks like he hates Cheryl. But he used to look at her like he loved her. Which I think he did. But she stopped loving him and that's the problem. It seems to me, if I was ever lucky enough to have a boyfriend, I'd never stop loving him. True love forever. That's all I want. Isn't that what everybody wants?

Before Cheryl sees him, Buddy slips away from the basketball game. Walks up behind her, grabs her arm, forces her to turn toward him, his face close to her face. Close enough to kiss.

Ralph and Paul have gone to get the beer out of the car. Bobbi Jo, Ellie, and I stand there paralyzed. We don't know what to do.

"You cheating little bitch," he mutters. The veins in his neck stand out like cords. His face is red. His hair is in his eyes. He looks wild, crazy, mad enough to do anything. Hit her. Strangle her.

"Get your hands off me." Cheryl doesn't look scared. Just angry. She tries to yank her arm free, but Buddy holds tight.

I look at Ellie and Bobbi Jo. We should do something, say something, but we just stand there like we're watching a play. Not something real.

Suddenly Ralph is there, his hand on Cheryl's other arm. "What the hell's going on?" he asks Buddy. "Let her go."

Buddy's grip on Cheryl tightens. He scowls at Ralph. "Go back to Dulaney where you belong."

Ralph's face reddens. "This is a free country," he says. "I can come here anytime I want."

Buddy lets go of Cheryl and she moves closer to Ralph. "Leave me alone," she says. "Get the hell away from me."

The boys face each other. Ralph's taller than Buddy, but Buddy's arms look strong. He has the look of a guy who knows every dirty trick.

The other kids crowd around them, pushing each other, shouting, egging them on. "Fight!" a boy yells. "Fight!"

The night is turning into a movie, the kind James Dean and Natalie Wood would be in. It excites me in a strange way.

Cheryl looks pleased to be the center of it all. She flips her long blond ponytail this way and that, staring at Buddy as if she's daring him to fight.

Then Charlie steps in between Ralph and Buddy. He's shorter than either of them. Skinnier. His shadow slants across the basketball court.

"Why don't you just forget it?" he asks. "If a fight starts, some nosy SOB in the neighborhood will hear it and call the cops. They're always prowling around here looking for trouble. They'll spot the beer and arrest us all."

Ralph scowls at Buddy. "Just leave Cheryl alone. She's not your girl anymore."

"She can go to hell for all I care." Buddy picks up a beer bottle and turns to his friend Gene. "Let's get outta here."

Followed by a couple of other guys, they walk over to Buddy's car. Before he opens the door, Buddy turns back and shouts at Cheryl, "If you died tomorrow, I wouldn't shed one tear."

Revving the engine, he drives away with a screech of tires that leaves the smell of burning rubber behind. I can hear the old Ford with its rusted-out muffler long after it disappears.

"Nice going, Charlie," Ellie says. "I really thought they were going to fight."

"Me too." Cheryl sounds a little disappointed, I think. She squeezes Ralph's arm. "I was hoping you'd beat the crap out of him."

Ralph laughs and puts his arm around her. "Come on, let's get a beer."

"Good idea," Charlie says. "How about you two?"

Ellie and I look at each other and grin. We're almost seventeen, with one more year of high school, the best year, ahead of us. We're practically old enough to buy beer legally. Well, in five years, actually.

"What about me?" Bobbi Jo asks.

"Wouldn't you rather have Kool-Aid?" Charlie asks.

"I'm not a baby," Bobbi Jo says. "Give me a beer too."

Walt puts his arm around Bobbi Jo. "Aw, let her have one."

Charlie opens the beer and hands us each a bottle of Rolling Rock. Little bottles, not enough beer to make you drunk.

"Just don't tell your father," he says to Bobbi Jo. "I don't want to go to jail."

"Why would I tell him?" Bobbi Jo asks. "I'd be grounded for life. Or sent to a Catholic girls' school in Switzerland."

"Saint Bernard's Academy of Lost Souls?" Charlie asks.

For once I get the joke, but Bobbi Jo doesn't. "No, I think it's Saint Ursula of the Alps or something like that."

The beer has a harsh taste. Sour. I don't really like it, but I pretend to. People say some things are an acquired taste. Beer must be one of them.

Ralph takes beers for himself and Cheryl and hands a bottle to Paul. "Damn," he says. "That's almost the last of it already."

"After we finish these," Paul says, "I'll collect some money and buy a case."

We sit around the table, laughing and talking, remembering funny things from our junior year and making plans for senior year. And after. When we're finally free of public school. Paul and Charlie and Walt are going to hitchhike across the country after we graduate, working odd jobs and seeing places like the Grand Canyon and Old Faithful. They'll be home in time to start college.

Ellie and I have an idea we'll get waitressing jobs in Ocean City and spend the whole summer at the beach. We'll get great tans and save enough money for fall clothes. We'll start college dressed like *Seventeen* models.

Cheryl's uncle has already promised to hire her as a typist in his welding business. Boring, maybe, but she says he'll pay her a good salary. Ralph says he and Don might spend the summer lifeguarding in Bethany Beach.

My mind drifts. Bethany's not far from Ocean City. Maybe Don and Ralph will eat at the restaurant where Ellie and I wait tables. I'll be tan, my hair will look good, Don will ask me to meet him on the boardwalk when I get off work. We'll walk on the beach, wade in the surf, the moon will be full . . .

"You guys will have so much fun," Bobbi Jo says glumly. "All I'll do next summer is babysit bratty kids."

"You need another beer." Ralph hands her one.

When I finish my second bottle, I decide I like the taste after all. I also like the silly feeling I'm getting, a sort of numbed drowsiness that makes me happy and relaxed. My mouth feels funny and I wonder if I'm doing that curly thing with my lip that Daddy does when he's drunk.

"Ellie," I whisper. "Are you drunk?"

She laughs. "I think maybe. How about you?"

"I'm so drunk I can't get up." We both start laughing like this is the funniest thing I've ever said.

Bobbi Jo sees us laughing and joins in. "Me too," she says. "I'm drunk too!"

"You guys are ridiculous." Cheryl gives us a superior look. "Nobody gets drunk on two bottles of Rolling Rock."

"We do," I say. That makes us start laughing again.

Cheryl puts her arms around Ralph and kisses him. "They aren't drunk," she says. "They just think they are."

Ralph laughs. "Let's see you three walk a straight line."

We reel across the basketball court. I'm laughing so hard I keep snorting, which makes me laugh harder and snort more. In a way, I'm play-acting, not really drunk but definitely not my normal self. I feel like I could fly if I tried hard enough. The future is mine, the world is beautiful, and the fireflies in the trees flash a code I can almost understand.

I grab Ellie's hand and she grabs Bobbi Jo's hand and we dance around the basketball court singing an old song we sang when we were kids. "Up in the air, junior birdman." We can't remember the words, and we start laughing again.

"Okay, okay," Charlie shouts. "You're drunk. Or you're crazy. Come on over here, Long Tall Sally. Sit down before you fall down."

"We need more beer," Ralph says.

Paul collects some money and he and Ralph leave for a liquor store on Route 40. The guy there never asks for IDs, Ralph says. He lets you buy anything you can pay for. Simple as that. You just have to know where to go, and Ralph knows—he knows where to go and what to do and what to say. I wish Don was here and I knew what Cheryl knows, so I'd be sexy and he'd fall in love with me.

While they're gone, some other kids from the neighborhood show up. One of them has a portable radio. When Ellie and I hear Shirley and Lee singing "Feels So Good," we sing along. I'm always Shirley, singing high, and Ellie's always Lee, singing low. We have that song down perfectly.

"God, will you two just shut up?" Cheryl says. "You sound like cats in heat or something."

Ellie and I look at her, look at each other, and keep on singing until the song's over. Cheryl isn't the queen of the world. If we want to sing, we will.

Louise Weeks starts jitterbugging with her boyfriend, Harry. They know the Baltimore dance steps, too. Soon we're all dancing, trying to imitate their moves. Since there are more girls than boys, Ellie and I end up dancing together, which is fine when the music's fast and we can twist and twirl and swing and do the dirty boogie.

Cheryl and Bobbi Jo sit at the picnic table, talking. Cheryl's probably telling Bobbi Jo not to get as silly as Ellie and me. The next time I look in their direction, I see a boy leaning over the table, talking to them. It's too dark to see who it is. I hope it's not Buddy.

The song ends, and Pat Boone starts singing "Ain't That a Shame," a really bad steal from Fats Domino. Ellie and I groan. We hate Pat Boone—he's such a goody-goody. We like bad boys, Elvis and Jerry Lee Lewis and the Big Bopper and Little Richard, the baddest of all, with hair a foot tall and long, painted fingernails and crazy ways.

I hear Cheryl laugh and say something to the boy. I can't make out the words but her voice is sharp, nasty-edged. He moves away from her. In a second, the dark woods swallow him up.

Ellie and I go back to the picnic table. Even though it's almost midnight, it's still hot, the air heavy with humidity. Down in the woods, I hear a frog croaking in the creek.

"Who was that guy you were talking to?" Ellie asks Cheryl.

She shrugs. "Some stupid jerk from my history class."

"He wanted Cheryl to dance with him, and when she wouldn't, he started bugging me." Bobbi Jo laughs. "Cheryl called him Crater

Face. She said his clothes were ugly and so was he, and then she told him to get lost." She dissolves in giggles, and Cheryl lights a cigarette.

Still laughing, Bobbi Jo says, "You should've heard Cheryl. That guy won't bother us again."

"It's not my fault he's a faggot," Cheryl says.

"The beer's here," somebody yells.

This time, they hand out National Bo in tall, long-necked bottles. Bigger bottles last longer, I guess.

It's my third beer. I must be drunk. I must be really bad, too. A very bad girl. A juvenile delinquent. Before I know it, I'll be in a home for wayward girls.

We dance again. This time I'm with Charlie, and the Platters are singing "Only You." I let him hold me tight, I feel his body press against me. I don't care that his head is on my shoulder instead of the way it should be, my head on his shoulder.

The next thing I know, I'm letting him kiss me and I like the feel of his lips on mine, even if I have to bend down a little.

Then the song ends. We draw apart and look at each other. Charlie says, "Whew, Long Tall Sally," but for some reason I start laughing. I laugh and laugh. I laugh so hard I'm scared I'm going to wet my pants.

Charlie stares at me like I've hurt his feelings, but then he starts to laugh, too, and everything is okay. We're still friends. Just friends. Even though for just one second I felt the tip of his tongue slip between my teeth.

Ellie and Bobbi Jo surround me. "Do you have to pee?" Bobbi Jo whispers, her beer breath in my ear.

We slip away from Charlie and head for the woods. "Bobbi Jo was scared to go by herself," Ellie says.

I don't say it out loud, but the woods are scary even with three of us. Behind us the playground is washed bright with moonlight, but here between the trees, blackness swallows us up.

Suddenly Bobbi Jo grabs my arm. "What was that?"

"What was what?" I whisper.

She looks over her shoulder at the dark trees. "I thought I heard something."

Now I think I hear it too—a snapping branch, a loud rustle in the underbrush. I shiver and tell myself I'm being stupid. What could happen to us in the park?

"I didn't hear anything," Ellie says.

"I thought somebody was following us," Bobbi Jo says, still scared.

Ellie laughs. "To watch us pee?"

Bobbi Jo and I laugh too. But not as loud as Ellie.

We follow her deeper into the woods and squat down in the bushes near the creek. Although I'm careful, I feel warm pee run down my leg and into my shoe. Ellie loses her balance and topples over with a crash. The three of us laugh so hard we all end up on our backs in the leaves. I pray it's not poison ivy. How would I explain an itchy rash all over my rear end?

"Let's wade in the creek," Bobbi Jo says. We take off our shoes and scramble down the bank. The water is knee-deep and cold. We slosh along, splashing each other and laughing.

"Where did Cheryl go?" Bobbi Jo asks.

Ellie giggles. "The woods with Ralph. Where do you think?"

She catches my eye. "Don't look so shocked," she says. "I saw you kissing Charlie."

I feel myself blush. "Well, I'm not about to go off in the woods with him."

She laughs and makes kissing noises. "Nora and Charlie sitting in a tree," she chants, "k-i-s-s-i-n-g—"

I give her a push and she sits down in the water. Before I can even say I'm sorry, I slip on the mossy stones and splash down beside her. Bobbi Jo laughs and Ellie grabs her ankle and pulls her down with us. The water runs over our legs and cools us off. The buzzy feel of the beer slides away. In the woods, thousands of fireflies blink their lights like magic.

"I think Cheryl is really in love with Ralph," Bobbi Jo says in a dreamy voice.

"We all thought she was in love with Buddy not so long ago," Ellie reminds her.

"Yes, but he didn't deserve her," Bobbi Jo says. "Ralph's different. He's nice. He'd never hit her."

I sit there quietly watching the fireflies and wishing Don liked me the way Ralph likes Cheryl. Why don't I have long blond hair and breasts big enough to see without a magnifying glass?

"I hope I have a boyfriend like Ralph someday," Bobbi Jo whispers into the dark.

"Don't worry," Ellie says. "As cute as you are, you'll have all the boyfriends you could ever want."

Unlike me, I think, unlike me. I try not to envy Bobbi Jo's pretty face and blond curls. Try not to compare my plain face and wispy brown hair, frizzy in the summer heat. My freckles. The funny bump in my nose. My long skinny arms and legs. Why did Charlie kiss me? Why would any boy want to kiss me?

Tired of my own boring thoughts, I stand up and grab one of the grapevines dangling from the trees. Giving my best Tarzan shout, I swing on it. Bobbi Jo and Ellie scramble to their feet and catch vines of their own. Soon the three of us are swinging back and forth like ten-year-olds, whooping and laughing.

Suddenly Bobbi Jo lets go of her vine and stands still in the middle of the creek. "Shh!' she whispers. "Did you hear that?"

Ellie and I drop down beside her. I hear what Bobbi Jo heard, branches rustling, something moving. No mistaking the sound this time. Slow footsteps are moving toward us. I shiver. Someone's out there in the dark, watching us.

"Who's there?" Ellie croaks.

A stone splashes into the water beside her. Then another and another. They're falling all around us.

We scramble to our feet, slipping and sliding, and cling to each other, terrified. Bobbi Jo murmurs, "Hail Mary, full of grace . . ."

"Paul, is that you?" Ellie calls. Her voice shakes. We huddle together in the creek.

Bushes rustle. More stones splash into the water. Someone laughs the laugh of the Shadow and intones, "Who knows what evil lurks in the hearts of men?"

Bobbi Jo starts to cry. "Who is it?" Ellie shouts. "What do you want?"

"The Shadow knows." More laughter. More stones. Branches snapping, leaves stirring.

"This isn't funny!" Ellie yells.

And then they're sliding down the bank, splashing toward us, laughing. Paul first, then Charlie and Walt.

"Don't be mad." Paul puts his arm around Ellie. "Look what we have for you." He presses a bottle of beer into her hand.

Charlie hands me a beer, and Walt offers one to Bobbi Jo.

"You scared us half to death," Bobbi Jo says. She wipes her eyes, brushing away tears.

"Did you think it was the crazy man with the hook?" Charlie twists his body into a menacing shape, his face a lunatic's grimace.

"Or the wild goat man of Baltimore County?" Walt reaches out and grabs Bobbi Jo by the neck.

She pushes him away. "It's not funny!" She sounds like she might cry again.

"Ah, we forgot," Walt says. "Bobbi Jo's just a little girl, scared of the dark." He tries to hug her, but she won't let him near her.

"I'm going home." She throws her beer into the bushes and scrambles out of the creek.

"We'll go with you." Ellie follows her into the woods and I go after them.

Ellie and I drink our beer as we walk. "Chugalug, chugalug," we chant, sashaying back and forth, hips bumping, making Bobbi Jo laugh in spite of herself.

The boys catch up with us. Charlie takes my hand. "Don't be mad, Long Tall Sally," he whispers in my ear, his breath warm and tickly.

"You really scared Bobbi Jo."

"How about you? Did I scare you?"

I shrug and toss my empty beer bottle into the bushes. I was scared, but I don't want to admit it. He'll tease me.

"Elmgrove isn't known for maniacs loose in the woods," he says.

"We're not that far from Spring Grove," I mutter.

The dark trees press in around us. I hear rustling sounds like a person walking carefully, following us, trying not to make any noise. *Snap* goes a twig. I can almost feel someone watching us. Buddy. It must be Buddy looking for Cheryl.

Not quite accidentally, I move closer to Charlie.

He lets go of my hand and slips his arm around me. We walk side by side, his head at my shoulder. Why oh why isn't he taller? Or me shorter? We kiss a few times. It's nice but not like it would be if I loved him.

"What about Cheryl?" Bobbi Jo asks. "Shouldn't we find her and tell her we're leaving?"

Walt shoots a look at Charlie and Paul. They laugh. "I think Cheryl can find her way home without our help."

We stumble across the park, laughing and singing the Eastern High fight song. I throw up in the street and Charlie wipes my face with his T-shirt, which I think is very gallant. He kisses me again even though my breath must stink of beer and vomit.

When the Dawsons' dog starts barking, the boys take off for their houses. "See ya tomorrow," Walt shouts to Bobbi Jo.

"Sleep tight," Charlie hollers. "Don't let the bedbugs bite!"

We wave and watch them disappear around a corner, reeling and holding each other up, pretending to be drunk. I can hear them laughing even when I can't see them. I feel sad all of a sudden, lonely. If only the night could go on and on and never end. If only I was holding Charlie's hand. If only I was kissing him. I think I like him more than I thought.

"Don't forget," Ellie tells Bobbi Jo. "We're leaving for school at eight fifteen. Don't be late!"

"I'll be ready," she says. "I've always wanted to see what Eastern's like inside. No nuns watching you all the time. No priests. I wish my parents would let me go there."

"You won't see much," Ellie says. "All we do is pick up our report cards, hand in our textbooks, pay library fines, that kind of stuff. We'll be out by eleven."

"It's really a waste of time," I say.

"For you, maybe."

Bobbi Jo slips through her front gate. As she opens her front door, I hear her father shout, "Where have you been? Do you know what time it is?" The door slams, but we can still hear him shouting at Bobbi Jo.

"Uh-oh," Ellie whispers. "I hope *my* parents are asleep."

I follow her into the house. The rooms are dark. I hear her father snoring, and I think of my father at my house, snoring beside my sleeping mother, the two of them folded up together in bed, the room dark and still, the house dark and still. My brother asleep or maybe listening to the radio, those late-night stations from far away. Rock-and-roll in New York or Pittsburgh or maybe even Detroit on a clear night. My room lit dimly by moonlight, my bed still made.

For some reason, it scares me to picture my empty room. It's almost like I'm dead and my family is going on without me. I shiver—has someone walked on my grave? What does that expression mean anyway?

"Come *on,*" Ellie urges me. I realize I've stopped halfway up the steps, dreaming in the dark.

We make it to her bedroom without waking anyone. I fall into bed and go to sleep with my fingers pressed against my lips, holding Charlie's kiss there.

# PART TWO

# The Endless Day

# The Last Day of School

## NORA

ELLIE'S alarm clock goes off at seven a.m., but one of us reaches over, turns it off, and falls back asleep. At seven fifty, Ellie's mom wakes us up. "Didn't you hear the alarm?" she asks. "Hurry up, you'll be late!"

We stumble around the bedroom, pulling on crinolines and full skirts, tucking in blouses. buckling cinch belts, searching for socks and our grass-stained Keds. I'm still half asleep, groggy from being up late, drinking beer, and smoking.

For some reason Ellie wants to wear this little pin made of ceramic flowers, but her fingers fumble with the catch. It takes her at least five minutes to get it fastened, partly because her mother keeps calling, "Hurry up, girls, you're going to be late."

We're eating cereal when Cheryl and Bobbi Jo show up.

"You're early," Ellie says. "We're not ready."

"I promised Ralph I'd meet him at school at eight fifteen on the dot," Cheryl says. "Besides, if I leave now, I won't run into Buddy."

"Guess what?" Bobbi Jo asks Ellie and me. "Ralph has this friend he wants me to meet." She smoothes her hair. "I'm telling him I'm sixteen."

I almost choke on my cereal. What if it's Don? What if Ralph is fixing her up with Don? I hate Cheryl, who must have set it up, I hate Ralph, I hate Bobbi Jo. It's not fair, it's just not.

"See you later," Ellie says as Bobbi Jo and Cheryl leave. "Don't forget the picnic. You're bringing the rolls and I'm bringing the hot dogs and Bobbi Jo's mom is making potato salad."

"Who's bringing the soda?" Bobbi Jo asks.

"Paul and Charlie," Ellie says. "Walt's bringing cookies or brownies or something."

"If you see Buddy, tell him I hate him," Cheryl calls from the door.

Mrs. O'Brien looks at us. "Did Cheryl break up with Buddy?'

"A long time ago, Ma," Ellie says. "She has a much nicer boyfriend now."

Mrs. O'Brien takes our empty cereal bowls to the sink. "I'm glad to hear it. I never liked that boy. He has a sneaky look. I'm surprised Cheryl's parents didn't send him packing long ago."

"They tried," Ellie says, "but you know how Cheryl is. She kept seeing him anyway. But not anymore. Now she hates him. And he hates her."

Mrs. O'Brien sighs. "What heartless girls you are." She smiles when she says it, so we know she's joking.

By the time Ellie and I are ready, we have five minutes to get to school. We'll never make it on time. But so what? It's the last day. The last two hours of our junior year. A line from an old grade school jingle runs through my mind: No more classes, no more books, no more teacher's dirty looks.

As we leave the house, I hear a car backfire somewhere close, a series of bangs loud enough to startle me.

Ellie laughs. "How come you're so jumpy?"

"Not enough sleep," I mutter.

We cut across the baseball field, walking slow. It's too hot to walk any faster. On Eastern Avenue, the morning traffic rumbles past. Horns blow.

"What do you think of Cheryl and Ralph?" Ellie asks. We've entered the woods, taking a well-worn path everyone uses to walk to school. The air smells of dew and damp leaves, and the ground is soft and yielding under our feet.

"They seem to really like each other," I say slowly.

Ellie nods. Birds sing in the green leaves overhead and a breeze stirs the air. The day is supposed to be a replay of yesterday, hot and humid with a chance of thunderstorms in the afternoon, but it's cool in the woods.

"But don't you wonder what he sees in Cheryl?" I ask, giving in to my jealousy at last. "He used to go steady with the most popular girl in school. Sally Smith was Junior Prom queen, a cheerleader, too. Why dump her for Cheryl?"

"Maybe Sally dumped him. Maybe he likes the way Cheryl dances." Ellie swings her purse by its long strap. "She was really getting on my nerves last night, acting so superior, like we were dumb kids faking being drunk."

"We were drunk," I say, "but not so drunk we went off in the woods with a boy."

Suddenly neither one of us likes Cheryl. We criticize her clothes, the tight shorts and low-necked blouse she wore last night, the way she danced with Ralph. We're sure she bleaches her hair even though she swears she doesn't. Nobody's a natural blond except Scandinavians.

Ellie says, "Cheryl had a big pimple on her chin this morning, did you notice?"

We laugh and sing the Clearasil song.

"What's so special about Cheryl anyway?" I ask. "Why do boys like her so much? She's not all that pretty. Her teeth are so big she looks like a chipmunk."

We laugh again.

Ellie reminds me of the time Cheryl sneaked out of a slumber party and stayed out all night with Buddy.

I was there. I definitely remember.

"That's why they like her," Ellie says. "She pets and stuff."

What exactly does petting mean, I wonder. Letting a boy touch your breasts or put his hand on your knee, maybe more. Stuff you'd have to confess, that's for sure. But Cheryl's not Catholic, she doesn't have to tell a priest what she does with boys.

"What do you think she was doing with Ralph down in the woods last night?" Ellie asks.

We look at each other, wondering . . .

By now, the trees have closed in around us, silent in the morning coolness, their trunks tall and straight. Slants of sunlight knife down through the leaves and dapple the path.

Ellie tells me about a story she read in *True Romance* magazine. "The girl was a tease. She got a bad reputation and . . ."

While Ellie talks, I glance over my shoulder, suddenly alert to a difference in the silence. A rustling in the leaves, a branch snapping, a sense of being watched, just like last night.

I glance at Ellie. She's fallen silent. Has she noticed something too?

A crow takes sudden flight from a branch. His alarmed cry sets off a chorus of caws from dozens of crows. They all fly up into the air and circle the treetops. A murder of crows, that's what my English teacher calls them—a flock of sparrows, a gaggle of geese, a murder of crows.

"I knew a boy once who had a pet crow," Ellie says. "He taught him to talk. And then some older boy shot him with a BB gun and killed him. It was so sad. Tommy really loved that crow."

"That's horrible." I swing my purse at a bee. "Get away!"

A few minutes later we come to the footbridge. Buddy's leaning against the rail, smoking a cigarette. It must have been his eyes watching us through the trees.

"Have you seen Cheryl?" he asks.

Ellie shakes her head. "She and Bobbi Jo left for school early."

"We overslept," I added. "They didn't want to wait for us."

Neither one of us gives him Cheryl's message. I hate to say it, but he looks so miserable I almost feel sorry for him.

"I wanted give her a ride to school," he says. "I thought maybe if I told her I was sorry, maybe she'd, I mean . . ." He lets the words trail off into a shrug and takes a long drag on his cigarette.

I watch him exhale a thin stream of smoke. My face feels hot with embarrassment. He's pathetic, pitiful, not like he was in the picnic grove. I glance at Ellie. Neither of us says anything.

"You want a ride?" he asks. "You'll be late if you walk."

We look at each other. He's right. Even with a ride we might be late, but not *as* late.

Ellie nods and we follow the path out of the woods and through a field of tall weeds. Buddy's old black Ford is parked at the end of Chester Street. All three of us crowd together in the front seat. I'm in the middle, jammed so close to Buddy our shoulders and arms touch. This is where Cheryl used to sit, I think, with her hand on his knee. I look at his knee and wonder what it's like to put your hand on a boy's knee. And then break up with him.

At first no one says anything. What's there to say that isn't the wrong thing?

But of course, just as he parks the car in the student lot, Buddy says it anyway. Looking past me at Ellie, he asks, "Do I have any chance of getting her back?"

Now my face is surely on fire, and there's a lump in my throat.

I could tell him, but of course I don't. Can't. I hear the pain in his voice. Maybe it wasn't all his fault she dumped him. Maybe she wanted someone better, someone like Ralph, a popular guy, not a nobody like Buddy.

To avoid looking at him, I stare at the blue tassel from his cap, which he's hung on the rearview mirror. No more classes for Buddy, no more books. Lucky him. He's a graduate now, an alumnus. He won't be back in the fall. He won't have to see Cheryl again.

Ellie shakes her head. "She really likes Ralph." There's no sympathy in her voice or the flip of her ponytail. She doesn't like Buddy. Never has. Tough break.

Buddy mutters a word I've seen written on walls but never heard anyone say out loud. Without looking at either of us, he reaches across us and opens our door. "What're you waiting for?" he asks. "The bell's ringing."

Ellie and I get out, me clumsily, my skirt catching on the stick shift. I jerk it free and shut the door. Buddy drives away, screeching the tires the way he did last night.

We agree to meet at the school's main door as soon as we get out of class and head off to our homerooms.

Miss Atkins collects library fines and textbooks. She hands out report cards. I have four Cs—PE, American history, chemistry, and Latin II, which I thought would be easy for me because of being Catholic but boy, was I wrong. I hoped I might get an A in English, but Mr. Smith has given me a B. My only consolation is my usual A in art. No celebration at my house. My mother will ask why I don't try harder, why I'm such an underachiever, why I don't care about my grades. I'm smart, she says, but I don't make an effort. Where will I go in life?

I want to tell her I'm not smart. I want to tell her school is boring. It's meaningless. It doesn't matter. High school is a waste of time. And anyway, what's wrong with a C average? Aren't most people average? Isn't that what average means?

Besides, I want to be an artist. I'm sure artists don't care about grades. Like me, they know high school is just this thing you have to get through. Once you're out, you're free to think and do what you like.

But standing at the double green doors, waiting for Ellie, I feel my insides churn again. I might tune my mother out, but I won't forget what she says. Or maybe it's more like I'll forget the words but not the meaning. I'm lazy, I'm a disappointment, I'll never amount to anything.

Then Ellie's there. Charlie and Paul are with her. So is Ralph. And Don.

I can't say a word, my heart is bumping and thumping and my knees feel funny. Don. Why is Don here?

"I thought Cheryl and Bobbi Jo would be with you," Ellie says to me.

I blush. It sounds like an accusation. What have I done? Why aren't they with me?

"I haven't seen them," I say.

"Cheryl promised to meet me," Ralph says. "Don and I were going to take her and Bobbi Jo to Top's for milk shakes."

So it's true, I think, I was right. He's fixing Bobbi Jo up with Don. I want to say, "Ellie and I can go instead." I try to smile at Don, but the lump in my throat is back and now it's me, not Buddy, I feel sorry for.

"They came by the house this morning," Ellie says, "but we weren't ready and they left without us."

"Where do you think they are?" I ask her, suddenly worried. "They should be here."

"Maybe they decided to skip and go to Horn and Horn for coffee," Ellie says with a shrug. "Cheryl does that sometimes."

Somehow I don't think Ellie's right, not when Cheryl was planning to meet Ralph. She wouldn't stand him up. A whisper of worry runs through my head, but I tell myself nothing could be wrong. What could happen to her and Bobbi Jo between home and school? A twenty-minute walk. Maybe less. And Ellie and me only ten minutes behind them. There must be an explanation.

But worry tugs at me. What if? What if? What if what?

# At Ellie's House

## NORA

RALPH and Don head off to the school parking lot, and we take Chester Road toward the park and the path to Ellie's house. Charlie and Paul walk ahead, comparing their report cards. Ellie and I trail behind. She got straight As, which makes her happy. "If I do well on the college boards next fall," she says, "I'll be sure to get a scholarship to Saint Olaf's."

I nod, still puzzled by her choice of colleges. Saint Olaf's is in Minnesota, where the winters are freezing cold. I'd rather stay here and go to Maryland Institute in Baltimore. My art teacher took us there on a field trip and I loved everything about it, how it smelled and how the students looked with paint on their clothes and how the light slanted in through skylights. And the easels—so many tall easels. It was like being in the woods. I hated to leave.

Mr. Taylor says it's one of the best art schools in the country. The trouble is, it's really, really expensive, and my mother won't let me go. First she says she can't afford it, but more important, I'll meet the wrong sort of people. They'll be a bad influence. I'll get in trouble. What kind of trouble, I asked her once, but she wouldn't say. Which means it has something to do with sex, something she never talks about, only hints at. *Don't let a boy put his hand on your knee.* I think of my bony knees and wonder why a boy would want to put his hand on them. There must be more to it than that.

It's a good thing she doesn't know how much I liked kissing Charlie. What if he puts his hand on my knee? Will I have to confess it? Will I have to confess kissing him last night? Is drinking beer a sin?

Mom says I can major in art at Towson State. No college boards to worry about. Anyone who graduates from a Maryland high school can go there. The tuition's cheap, too. Three hundred a year. I'll be living at home and taking the streetcar, at least an hour each way. Maybe I should have studied harder, taken those boring classes like plane geometry more seriously. Then maybe I could get a scholarship to Maryland Institute.

But truthfully I'm kind of afraid to leave home. What if no one likes me in art school? What if I'm not talented after all? What if the other students draw better than I do? What if I flunk out? What if I lose my virginity?

Towson State isn't nearly as scary, plus I'd still have my room, dinner every night with Mom and Dad and Billy, just like always. What a baby I am. Afraid to leave home.

Ellie pokes me in the side with her elbow. "You haven't heard a word I've said."

"Sorry, I was thinking."

"About what?"

"Oh, I don't know. Nothing interesting." No use talking to Ellie about my worries. She's so smart, ready to go to college and major in physics or something brilliant. Loneliness jabs me like a stitch in my side. Will there ever be a person I can talk to about how I really feel?

"Hey." Charlie turns and looks back. "You girls are really poking along. If you don't hurry up, you'll be late for the picnic."

Ellie laughs. "The picnic's not till noon. It's only ten o'clock."

Since he and Paul are obviously waiting, we hurry to catch up. It's much hotter now. We're at the end of Chester Street. The path dips down through a field and into the woods, still cool but more humid than earlier.

As the trees close in around me, I hear Buddy's car somewhere behind us, probably on Chester Street. I recognize the sound it makes. I picture him driving up one street and down another, smoking a cigarette and looking for Cheryl and Bobbi Jo. Where could they be?

Again, I push away the feeling something's wrong. This is the first day of summer vacation, we're having a picnic, then maybe we'll go to Five Pines swimming pool. Cheryl and Bobbi Jo will turn up with some crazy story. We'll all laugh.

I look at the back of Charlie's head, at his pink ears, at his crew-cut, hair so short I can see his scalp. Did I really kiss him last night? Did I drink three beers or four? Did Ellie and Bobbi Jo and me sit in the creek and sing? Did Ralph and Cheryl go off into the woods and not come back? And the scene with Cheryl and Buddy and Ralph, the anger breathing fire in the air, did that really happen?

The whole night seems like a dream, a story somebody told me. I glance at Ellie. The heat has curled her ponytail. Wisps of hair escape and cluster in ringlets on her neck. She seems far away too. I almost expect her to turn to me and ask if I'd seen the fairies hiding in the trees, casting spells on us like Puck in *Midsummer Night's Dream*. All night we'd wandered through the woods, enchanted, she might say, lost in magic and dreams.

On the bridge, Paul takes out a pack of Luckies. "Anybody want a cig?"

I glance at Ellie and she shrugs why not. When she takes one, I take one. *I will if you will.* We need practice, we need to learn how to inhale.

The four of us sit in a row on the railing and smoke. The night's spell comes back, and I'm convinced the woods are full of magic. I feel eyes watching us, hidden in the deep green. A rustling here, a scurrying there. For some reason, I shiver and breathe in so much smoke that I cough and choke and almost fall into the creek.

Charlie laughs and slaps my back a few times. "Don't fall, Long Tall Sally," he says and puts an arm around my shoulders. "You kissed me last night," he whispers.

I blush. "It must have been the beer," I tell him.

"Maybe you and me should get together with a six-pack every night." He wiggles his eyebrows like Groucho Marx.

I laugh and shake my head, but even while I'm laughing him off, I'm thinking how much I liked kissing Charlie. Or maybe just how much I like kissing.

I finish my cigarette, toss it into the creek, and watch it drift away. Ellie tosses hers after mine and slides off the railing. "We should go," she says. "Cheryl and Bobbi Jo are probably waiting for us at my house."

We're back in the woods again. The path is splashed with sunlight and birds are singing from hidden places in the trees. Ellie is walking with Paul. I'm walking with Charlie. We must look like a mismatched couple. But for once I don't care. I like Charlie. I like him a lot.

Charlie's telling me a funny story about his father coming home drunk one night and going into the wrong row house. "He can't understand why everything seems backward, turned around, like a mirror image of our house with everything in the wrong place. He starts to go up to bed and sees Mr. Evans at the top of the steps, pointing a gun at him and shouting, 'Stop or I'll shoot!'"

Charlie pauses to control his laughter and goes on. "Dad looks at him and says, 'Bob, what the hell are you doing in my house?'"

We're all laughing now. "After that," Charlie says, "Mr. Evans made sure he locked the door before he went to bed."

We come to the edge of the woods and step out into the morning sunlight. The heat hits us in the face. I can almost feel the starch in my crinoline dissolve.

"Whew," Paul says. "It's going to be a scorcher."

"It already *is* a scorcher," Charlie says.

We cross the park, so ordinary in the daylight. A Rolling Rock bottle catches the sunlight, a reminder of last night. Paul picks it up and tosses it in the trash with the others. "We don't want cops thinking kids hang out here and drink beer," he says.

Charlie nods. "They'll start cruising by every night, shining their spotlights, hoping to catch some juvenile delinquents." He looks at me. "And I'll never get another kiss from Long Tall Sally."

We all laugh, but something moves inside me at the thought of kissing Charlie again. Can you be in love with two boys at the same time? Suppose it had been Don I kissed last night? Confused, I turn my head, afraid I'm blushing. I don't want Charlie to know what I'm thinking. Or Ellie either.

At the corner, the boys go their way and we go ours. Charlie shouts, "See ya soon!"

I hope so, I hope so, but I just smile and wave. If I let myself like Charlie, really like him, he'll stop liking me and fall for Bobbi Jo.

At Ellie's house, we expect to see Cheryl and Bobbi Jo perched on the steps waiting to tell us where they've been, grinning, full of secrets, but they aren't there.

Bobbi Jo's little sister Julie is pushing her doll carriage up and down the sidewalk. Ellie asks her if Bobbi Jo's home.

Julie shakes her head. "She's at Cheryl's school."

No, I think, no she's not. Where is she? I look at Ellie. She shakes her head and we go inside. Even with all the windows open and a fan running full blast, it's hot. Mrs. O'Brien is at work and the house has a quiet, empty feel. You can always tell when no one's home.

We go to Ellie's room and strip off our sweaty school clothes, limp and wrinkled from the heat, and put on shorts and sleeveless blouses. Then we search the refrigerator for cold drinks. At my house we'd be lucky to find Kool-Aid, but Mrs. O'Brien always has sodas in the refrigerator. She's left a note on the kitchen table: *Hot dogs and buns for the picnic in the refrigerator. Have fun!*

"Your mom is so sweet," I say.

Ellie smiles. "Most of the time. She has her bad moments."

I must have looked like I didn't believe her, so Ellie laughed. "If we'd waked her up last night and she'd seen the state we were in, she would've killed us both."

We take our sodas down to the basement, where it's cooler. Ellie loads her little record player with forty-fives. We loll around listening to the Platters, the Penguins, Fats Domino, Jerry Lee

Lewis, Elvis, and Little Richard while we read old magazines. In *Life*, we find an article on Grace Kelly's marriage to Prince Rainier, and we wonder what it would be like to marry an old ugly guy and become a princess. Would it be worth it? We don't think so. *Modern Screen* has a story about Eddie Fisher and Debbie Reynolds's honeymoon. He's got a nice voice, we think, but he's not all that good-looking. We find some good photos of James Dean in his last movie, *Giant*, and wish as usual he hadn't died. So unfair that people like him have to die.

Just as we're about to find out who Marilyn Monroe will marry next, we hear sirens. Lots of them. It sounds like they're coming down Ellie's street, passing right by her house.

"What the—?" Ellie stands up and starts toward the stairs. "Somebody's house must be on fire."

I hate the sound of sirens. They cry out danger, they scream bad things are happening, someone's hurt, someone's sick, someone's dying. It's not you this time, but maybe next time it will be.

I follow Ellie upstairs. She opens the front door. Police cars and ambulances are speeding across the park toward the woods, sirens screaming. A fire truck follows them, bouncing over ruts in the ground, kicking up clouds of dust.

Some kids are running after the fire truck. I watch Charlie and Paul and Walt disappear into the woods along with the others, some I know, some I don't. I don't want to go to the park. Something's wrong. I can feel it in my bones.

Bobbi Jo's mother stands at the fence, watching. She holds a toddler on her hip; her other arm encircles Julie. She's so young, I think, almost like a teenager in her short shorts. Not a *mother*

mother like mine in baggy women's jeans with a side zipper. But there's something about the way she's standing there that makes me worry. Tense, watchful, holding her children so close that the little one squirms to free herself.

"Hi, Mrs. Boyd," Ellie calls. "What's going on in the park?"

She turns toward us, her face pale. "Have you seen Bobbi Jo?"

Ellie crosses the lawn and stops at the fence. "Not since this morning. She and Cheryl came to get us, but Nora and I weren't ready so they left for school without us."

Mrs. Boyd turns away. Her eyes follow the flashing lights into the woods. She holds the struggling toddler tighter, pulls Julie closer. "Something's wrong."

To avoid seeing the worry, the fear in Mrs. Boyd's face, I study the grass, already turning brown from the June heat. Her words echo my own thoughts. *Something's wrong.*

"You mean all that?" Ellie gestures at the emergency vehicles disappearing into the woods. "It's probably nothing. A kid playing in the water or something. You know how the firemen and the police are. They overreact to everything."

"Did you see Bobbi Jo at school?" Mrs. Boyd asks.

Ellie hesitates. "No, but—"

"Something's wrong," she says again.

The words are almost a wail this time, a child's cry. Julie puts her thumb in her mouth, her forehead creased. The toddler says, "Down, I want to get down."

My skin prickles and my chest tightens. All of a sudden I want to go home. I want my mother.

But Ellie says, "Don't worry, Mrs. Boyd. Nora and I will go down there and see what it's all about."

"No," I whisper, but Ellie doesn't hear me.

"Come on." She runs across the road, hurrying to meet what's waiting for us. I follow her, not because I want to but because I'm afraid to be left with Mrs. Boyd.

The short dry grass is sharp under my feet and I realize I forgot to put my shoes on. Ellie's barefoot too. We run in a limping way, our feet still tender from months in shoes.

"Ellie," I cry. "Ellie, wait. Don't go down there."

Ellie turns, puzzled. "Why not? How often do we see this kind of action in the park?"

"Mrs. Boyd is right—something's wrong."

We face each other in the blinding heat. Insects buzz. Crows make a racket in the woods. Somewhere a dog barks. Slowly Ellie's eyes widen. She stares at me, her cheeks pale under her freckles.

"You're scaring me," she whispers.

"I'm scared." My voice is tight and small. Sweat trickles down my spine. I take her arm, tug at her. "Let's go back to your house."

"It's Bobbi Jo and Cheryl," Ellie says. "You think something's happened to them."

I nod. My mouth is dry. It's all around us, in the silent trees, in the hot June air. The crows make my head ring with their cries. A murder of crows, a murder . . . Something's wrong, something's not right.

Then we hear them. Kids burst out of the woods, run toward us, shouting, crying.

"Cheryl's *dead!*" a girl screams. "They shot her, they killed her!"

My bones are melting. The trees spin, the world turns upside down. Speechless, Ellie and I cling to each other, hold each other up, afraid to let go.

The kids run around us as if we're trees. I recognize Cheryl's little brother, Davy. They're little, too little for this. Especially Davy. He's Billy's age. Ten. Just ten.

"What about Bobbi Jo?" Ellie shouts after them. "Where's Bobbi Jo?"

Gary comes out of the woods. Paul and Charlie and Walt are behind him. All four are crying.

"Bobbi Jo's dead too," Gary cries. "Somebody shot them both. Killed them. They're dead, both of them. Dead." Tears run down his face.

Ellie grabs my hand. "No," she whispers, "please God, no no no no." Pulling me with her, she runs away from the woods, across the ball field, toward Eastern Avenue.

"Wait," Charlie calls. "Come back."

Ellie doesn't wait, she doesn't stop, she just keeps running and I run too. We don't look back. We cross the park on a diagonal, come out on Eastern Avenue, run uphill. Behind us we hear the sirens again. An ambulance speeds past us, then another. Maybe they're not dead after all, maybe they're being rushed to the hospital, maybe we'll visit them tomorrow, bring them flowers and get well cards.

At the top of the hill we run past the Parkside apartments, a maze of two-story brick buildings, courtyards, and parking lots. We see Buddy's car. He's leaning against the door, looking toward the park. His friend Gene is with him.

"What's wrong with you two?" Buddy asks. "You look like you've seen a ghost."

"If we have, you know whose it is." Ellie's voice is cold with fury.

I stare at her, shocked by her anger.

Buddy looks puzzled. "What are you talking about?"

At the same time, Gene asks us what's going on in the park.

"Ask *him*," Ellie shouts, and pulls me away. Without giving me time to ask why she's acting so strange, she keeps running.

I'm hot, I'm tired, the soles of my feet burn with pain. Most of all, I'm scared and confused. It's as if the whole world has changed. Nothing is what it used to be. It will never be the same again.

# Accused

## BUDDY

I'VE been looking for Cheryl all morning, and here's Ellie acting like I should know what she's talking about when it doesn't even make sense. Shit, how should I know what's going on in the park? Man, it's too hot for this crap.

I glance at Gene. He's still leaning against my car, smoking, his eyes narrowed against the sun, sweating in the heat.

"What the hell's wrong with Ellie?" I ask.

"Females." He shrugs and exhales. "Maybe we should drive down to the park and find out what's going on. Didn't you notice the ambulances and cop cars coming up Eastern Avenue?"

I light a cigarette. "An accident on Route Forty or something. Happens all the time."

There's nothing else to do, so we get in my car and head for the park. Just in case there's something to see. Just in case Cheryl is there. I grip the wheel a little tighter. Who am I kidding? She won't be there. She's gone somewhere with Ralph in that big goddamn fancy convertible he drives. Girls—is that all they want?

When we turn down Thirty-Third Street, we see at least six patrol cars. Cops stand around talking and smoking in front of Bobbi Jo's house. Inside, someone's crying, wailing, almost screaming. I start sweating. Something's wrong, you can feel it everywhere. I see Charlie and Paul and some other guys on the corner, all huddled together.

I park the car and Gene and me walk over there. "What's going on?" I ask Charlie.

They look at me. Their eyes are full of hate. I step back. "What's wrong with you guys?"

Paul hits me hard enough to knock me flat. I sprawl on the ground, too surprised to get up. What the hell's going on, what did I do? I look up at Gene. He's standing there, not doing a thing to help me. I start to get up and Walt spits in my face.

Gene comes to life then and grabs Walt's arm. "Cut it out, you little shit."

I'm no sooner on my feet, ready to fight all of them, when a cop comes up to me. "Harold Novak?" he says.

"Yeah." I give him a look I learned from watching old crime movies on TV, sort of a sneer and a smirk combined. I don't want him thinking I'm the kind of guy who gets knocked down all the time.

"We want to ask you a few questions."

"About what?" I'm getting a little nervous. There's something about the way the cop's looking at me, like I'm dirt under his feet. Scum.

"Get in the car." He takes my arm. I can smell coffee on his breath. His face is red and sweaty. "We're taking you down to the station house."

"What the hell for?" I'm scared shitless now, but damned if I'll show it.

"You know why," Charlie yells. "You goddamn bastard SOB!"

"That's enough, son." Another cop has appeared. He pats Charlie's shoulder. "Go on home now."

The boys back away, muttering and cussing at me. If the cops weren't here they'd jump me, all of them. I can feel their hatred like fire in the air, burning me.

"I haven't done anything," I yell at them, but the cops are leading me away, handcuffing me, shoving me into the back seat of the patrol car. "Why are you doing this? What did I do?" I ask them, but they just look at me like they hate me, like they'd like to beat me.

Out the window, I see the people in Bobbi Jo's neighborhood. Women with their hair in curlers, kids with their mouths open, kids crying, kids shaking their fists at me, Gene standing by my car as confused as I am. It's like a movie you start watching in the middle and you don't know what's going on but you know it's bad.

The driver turns on the siren, the car speeds up. Eastern Avenue flashes by in a blur of traffic getting out of the cops' way.

"What did I do?" I ask them, but they keep the backs of their heads to me. So I sit there, scared out of my mind, trying to figure out what's happened and why everybody thinks I had something to do with it. I hope Bobbi Jo's okay. And Cheryl, too. Christ, where is she?

At the police station, the cops take me into this little room with cinderblock walls painted piss yellow. They tell me to sit in a chair facing a table. One sits across from me and opens a notebook. The other one sits off to one side, just out of my line of sight. He asks the questions. I have to turn my head to look at him.

"State your name," he says.

"Harold Novak."

"State your address."

"Forty-eight fifteen Forty-Third Street, Elmgrove." I want to ask him again why they've brought me here, what do they think I've done, but he doesn't pause between my answer and his next question. Nor does his face ever change. He's got one expression. Grim. One voice. Flat.

"Where were you at eight a.m. this morning?"

I shrug, trying to be nonchalant, getting back into my usual pose. Tough. Scared of nothing. Humphrey Bogart in *Key Largo*. "Driving around, I guess."

"Was anyone with you?"

"No."

"Did anyone see you?"

"Maybe. Probably. It's the last day of school, lots of kids were around. Some of them must of seen me." I shift my position but the chair's seat is hard vinyl and sort of slippery. I feel like I might slide off it. I wish I had a cigarette, but I left the pack in my car.

"Were you looking for anyone in particular?"

I shrug again. I could really use a cigarette. "I wanted to give this girl I know a ride to school."

The two cops look at each other like I've said something important. "What's her name?"

"Cheryl," I say. "Cheryl Miller."

They look at each other again.

"Did you leave your car on Chester Street and go into the park?"

I nod. "I was thinking she'd come along and I could take her to school." It's getting hard to act nonchalant. Something bad has happened. Something to do with Cheryl. I can tell by the heavy silence in the room. I'm sweating now, worried, scared. The guy who's been writing everything down lights a cigarette. I wonder if he'd give me one. Probably not. "Is Cheryl okay? Is this about her?"

Instead of answering me they ask me another question. "Do you own a rifle?"

I'm getting scared now. Really scared. Something's happened. Something bad. I'm pushing stuff away, things I don't want to think about, things I don't want to know.

"Yeah," I say, still trying to be tough, but my voice sounds funny now, kind of squeaky, like it did when I was thirteen. "It's a twenty-two, what they call a cat and rat gun." I stare at the cop even though it makes my neck hurt. Why can't he sit where I can see him better? My heart's beating faster. I wonder if the cops can hear it. If that makes them think I'm guilty of whatever it is that's happened. "What's my twenty-two got to do with this?"

The one sitting across from me says, "We ask the questions. You answer."

"Did you have your rifle with you this morning?" the other one asks.

I shake my head. "No. It's home in my closet. I never take it anywhere unless I'm target shooting."

"Do you shoot a lot?"

"I'm on the rifle team at school. I practice out in the woods. With tin cans and bottles."

"Do you consider yourself a good shot?"

"Yeah, pretty good."

They look at each other again and I start worrying I've let them lead me into saying something I shouldn't have.

The cop takes a deep breath. "Did you hide in the park this morning and wait for Cheryl Miller to come along?"

I shake my head again, really nervous now. "Why are you asking me these questions? What's happened?"

It's bad, I know it is, and it involves Cheryl. Something's happened to her. I want to get out of the police station. I want to get in my car and drive as fast as I can. I want to leave this town. I don't want to hear whatever it is they're about to tell me. If I was a little kid, I'd put my fingers in my ears, I'd shut my eyes, I'd hide under my bed or something.

The one across from me puts down his pen and leans across the table. His breath still smells like coffee. "Don't play dumb. You know why we're questioning you. You know what you did, you cocky little bastard."

The other one starts talking and I have to turn my head back to him. "You took your rifle with you this morning," he says in that flat, grim voice. "You went into the park and hid near the footbridge. You waited for Cheryl Miller. When she and Bobbi Jo Boyd came in sight, you shot them both."

At first what he says makes no sense. You shot them both, you both them shot, shot you them both. The words roll round and round, like cannonballs. Them you both shot, both you shot, you shot them, you shot them both.

I grab the edge of the table to keep myself from sliding off the chair. No, no, no, what kind of lie is this? Cheryl and Bobbi Jo shot? Dead, are they both dead? The piss yellow walls close in on me. They're dead. Dead. It can't be true.

It's like the cop has kicked me in the guts, knocked the breath out of me, killed me. I shake my head, I say, "No, no, no, they can't be dead, no no no I didn't do it, I'd never never never—"

The cop in the chair, the one I can never see right, jumps up and grabs me, shakes me, shoves his big red face into mine. "You lying piece of shit," he yells. "She busted up with you, she had a new boyfriend, you made a scene in the park last night. This morning you got your rifle and you went to the park and you shot them."

I shake my head, I struggle to get myself together, I'm scared I'll piss my pants. He's twisting my arm, he's pulling me off the chair, he's threatening to hit me. All I can do is shake my head. I didn't didn't didn't. I didn't didn't didn't.

"You were seen on the footbridge," the cop shouts. "What did you do with the rifle?"

"Nothing! I didn't have it with me, it's at my house."

"We searched your house," he says. "The rifle's not there. What did you do with it?"

"I didn't do anything with it," I say.

"It's in your car, in the trunk, wrapped up in a blanket," the cop says. "Where you hid it after you killed Cheryl and Bobbi Jo."

"No," I say. "No."

"Tell the truth, son," the one sitting across from me says. His voice is soft now, his face calm. "Admit it. It'll be easier for you."

"I *am* telling the truth." I'm trying so hard to convince them but they don't believe me, they're sure I did it, they're so sure I begin thinking maybe I did do it, maybe I have amnesia, maybe I'm crazy, maybe they'll send me to Spring Grove.

Then I remember something. I lean across the table toward the cop sitting there. I do my best to look him in the goddamn eye. "Wait, wait," I say. "I saw this guy in the woods while I was sitting on the bridge. I didn't think anything of it, it was just a glimpse, but I saw him. Maybe he—maybe, I mean, you know, it could of been him. The one who did it." Even to me it sounds like a lie, something I made up.

The cops look at each other and laugh. "Oh, yeah," the one who sits where I can hardly see him says.

I try to tell them more, but there really isn't any more. I glimpsed a guy in the woods. I couldn't see his face. He was there and then gone like some goddamn Robin Hood. No wonder they don't believe me.

After a lot of yelling and a lot of threats, they take me into a small room with the same piss-colored walls to give me a lie detector test. A guy who looks more like a biology teacher than a cop is in charge now. He puts rubber tubes across my chest and belly to check my breathing, then he attaches little metal plates to my fingers to record how much I sweat, and then he straps something around my arm to record my blood pressure. I keep telling myself he's not going to electrocute me, but I don't trust him. Even though he talks in a soft voice, I know he's not my friend.

First he asks me if I like pizza. Really. That's what he asks. "Yes," I say kind of uncertainly, maybe it's a trick question.

"Is your nickname Buddy?" I answer yes, still suspicious.

"Did you just graduate from Eastern?" I say yes again, but I tense up, wondering when he's going to ask if I did it.

"Did you ever cheat on a test?" My heart speeds up because

cheating might be a killer's trait. But I tell the truth, I say yes even though I want to lie and say I'd never do that. The lines on the chart shoot way up and way down. Does that mean the machine thinks I'm lying?

"Do you know Cheryl Miller?"

"Yes." The lines jiggle up and down even more than before, a bad sign for sure.

Then it comes. "Did you shoot Cheryl Miller and Barbara Josephine Boyd?" He speaks in the soft, sort of hypnotic voice he's used from the start.

It takes me a second to realize Barbara Josephine Boyd is Bobbi Jo. I'm really shaken up, so I take a deep breath and almost say yes because all my other answers have been yes. "No!" I say it louder than I mean to, and the needles jump and twitch and scribble wild crazy lines. Guilty lines, dark and jagged.

The man sighs and says, "Please don't lie, son. The machine knows you're not telling the truth."

I try to breathe normally, I try to relax. "I'm not lying. I didn't shoot them, I didn't." No matter how hard I try to control my voice, it rises. The needles go haywire, jumping and jiggling sharp peaks and valleys all over the roll of paper.

The man looks at me sadly as if I've let him down really bad. He shakes his head. He presses a buzzer. The cops come in.

The big mean one grabs me, twists my arm way up behind my back, manhandles me out of the room and down some steps, and locks me up. "Think about it for a while, you little son of a bitch," he says. "When I come back, you better be ready to confess. We know you did it."

"And here's the thing, Harold," the other one says. "We've got ways to make you talk." He pounds a fist into the palm of his other hand. No Mr. Nice Guy now.

They leave me in the cell. I hear them laughing as they go upstairs. "Sorry little piece of shit," one says.

And it's true. I am, that's all I am now. It's like I've lost myself somewhere. Nothing seems real. Not even me.

Hours pass. No food, nothing to drink. No cigarette. They come back and take me to the interrogation room. They ask the same questions over and over again. I give them the same answers. Sometimes they confuse me and I don't say what I mean to say.

They give me the lie detector test again. Same questions. Same crazy zigzag marks on the paper.

Then I'm in the cell and it's dark out. I lose track of time. I think I've been here a week, but when they finally let me go, it's only been forty-eight hours. They tell me my gun was in my closet just like I said. They say it wasn't the gun the killer used. They say I passed the lie detector test after all. I can go home. They act like it was just a game. No hard feelings, nobody hurt. Just a few questions, a little roughing up, nothing to worry about.

When my mother and father come for me, they act like they don't know me anymore. They're uncomfortable. They don't complain about the way the cops treated me, they don't seem to notice the bruises on my face.

Maybe they think I did it. I tell them I didn't, I tell them I didn't even know what happened until the cops told me.

They don't want to talk about it. My mother says maybe I should spend a few weeks at her brother's farm in West Virginia, a place I hate but which now seems better than Elmgrove.

Reporters surround my dad's car. They point cameras, blind

me with flashbulbs, holler questions. And all the time I'm sitting in the back seat, trying to understand that Cheryl is dead. I will never see her again, never hear her voice, never kiss her.

The cops, my parents, my former friends, they all think I killed her. Me. Buddy Novak, the kid who's always blamed for everything. Cheating on tests, writing cuss words on buildings, loitering, causing trouble, being a bad influence, skipping school, speeding, drinking beer behind the gym. And now this. This. The one thing I haven't done. Would never do.

My arm hurts from being twisted, my face is bruised, my belly aches. I slide down in the seat and hope no one will see me.

---

# Running Home

## NORA

ELLIE finally slows down. She collapses under a tree in someone's yard. It's like she's been shot too. I drop down beside
her. We start crying again. Huge, gulping, suffocating sobs. Sobs
torn from our hearts, from our guts. Sobs that hurt.

Then Ellie is on her feet again. "Come on," she says. Her nose
and upper lip are covered with snot, her eyes are swollen.

"Where are we going?" I ask.

"Your house." Ellie wipes her nose on the back of her hand. "I
don't know where else to go. Mom's at work. And Mrs. Boyd—how
can I face her? Oh, God, oh, God, oh, God." She hides her face in
her hands. Tears seep through her fingers, run down her face, and
drip on her blouse. She sits down again and so do I. Grass scratches
the backs of my bare legs. I don't think I can run anymore. Or walk.
Or even stand up. My bones have dissolved.

How could this happen? Something this bad? This horrible?
This unreal? You read about murder in the paper, you hear about
it on TV, a man killed in a robbery, a woman strangled by her husband. Someone stabbed, someone beaten, someone shot. Murder
happens far away, in cities or desolate places. It happens to strang-

ers and you say how sad, how awful, and then a commercial comes on and that's that, you forget. You watch *I Love Lucy* and laugh, you watch *Gunsmoke* and Matt Dillon catches the killer before the show is over. You go up to bed before the news comes on to remind you of the woman's body found in an alley. You fall asleep in your safe little house, and you know all your friends are sleeping in their safe little houses and you'll see them at school tomorrow. And you forget the woman in the alley who will never sleep in her safe little house again.

But not this. You won't forget this. It will be a part of you forever. This day . . . this day will never end.

I glance at Ellie. She's soaked with sweat, and tears are running down her face again. Cars, trucks, buses whiz past. I hear a blast of music from a convertible. A girl rides by on a bike, stares at us, glances back every now and then.

Finally I ask Ellie why she was so mad at Buddy.

She wipes her nose with the back of her hand. "Don't you know?"

"Know what?" Fear nibbles at me.

"He killed them," she says in a dull, heavy voice.

"Buddy?" I shake my head. "He couldn't have. Not Buddy. It was someone else, a stranger, a crazy man."

"You saw him on the bridge," she says. "He must have done it just before we came along."

"No, not someone we know, Ellie." It makes it so much worse. Horrible, even. "Not someone we go to school with."

"He did it. I *know* he did."

"How do you know?"

Ellie thumps her chest. "Here, I know it *here*." She scrubs her eyes with the back of her fist. "Let's go. He won't find us at your house."

My legs go weak again. This is not something I'd thought of. "You think he's looking for us?"

"We saw him on the bridge. We saw the fight they got into, we heard him say he'd kill her."

"But he wouldn't kill *us*."

"We're witnesses, Nora."

I find myself thinking about mysteries—books, movies. What were the three things? Motive, means, and opportunity, yeah, that's it. Buddy had a motive, he had an opportunity, but did he have the means? "Does he have a gun?" I ask Ellie.

"Cheryl told me he has a rifle. They used to go down in the woods and shoot tin cans for target practice. She saw him kill a squirrel once. After that she wouldn't go shooting with him. She can't stand seeing an animal hurt."

"He could have shot *us* this morning," I whisper.

"There were some tenth-graders coming along behind us," she says. "They probably saved our lives."

"But suppose," I say, "suppose we hadn't overslept and we'd all walked to school together like we planned. We'd all be dead. All four of us."

"Oh, God," Ellie whispers. "Oh, God."

I try not to think of Ellie and me dying in the park with Cheryl and Bobbi Jo. No one should be dead. Not them, not us.

By now we're crossing the trolley tracks, only two blocks from my house. I glance behind me, almost expecting to see Buddy's old black Ford coming after us. My street is empty except for my brother's friend Jeff, riding his bike in slow, lazy loops.

The sun beats on our heads and shoulders, and the sidewalk scorches our bare soles. It's hard to think straight. Nothing feels real. I'm lost in a nightmare. I'll never be safe again. Death is everywhere—behind every tree, around every corner. How have I escaped him for so long?

The car isn't in the driveway. Just when I really, really need her, Mom has gone someplace. How can she not be here?

Ellie follows me to the kitchen. I open the refrigerator and find a pitcher of cherry Kool-Aid. I get the ice tray and pry out enough cubes for two glasses. Then, despite the heat up there, we climb the stairs to my room.

While my old table fan whirs and creaks, we gulp down Kool-Aid and then suck on the ice cubes.

"Should we call the police and tell them about Buddy?" Ellie asks.

"I don't know." The idea of talking to a policeman scares me.

Ellie bites her fingernail. It's the first time I've ever seen her do that. "They were only ten minutes ahead of us," she says. "*Ten minutes.* And we didn't hear a thing. Or see a thing. How can that be?"

"No," I say. "We heard those bangs—remember? We thought it was a car backfiring."

She pauses, thinks, gnaws harder on her fingernail. "You think it was the gun?" she whispers.

I notice how tightly I'm holding my glass. My whole body is tense, both inside and out. I try to relax but I can't. It's like gym when the PE teachers make us lie on the floor in our ugly blue gym suits and tell us to relax inch by inch from the toes up. As soon as I'd move from my toes to my ankles, my toes would tense up again. I never made it past my hips.

"What should we do?" Ellie asks.

Usually I'm the one who asks that question. "I don't know."

Just then I hear the back door open and close. For a moment I freeze, terrified Buddy has tracked us down.

Mom calls, "Nora, are you up there?" Without waiting for an answer she runs up the stairs.

She stares at us, one hand pressed to her heart. "Oh, thank God, thank God." She gathers me in her arms as if I'm five years old and hugs me so tightly I think my ribs might break.

"Two girls were murdered in the park this morning, I just heard it on the radio. They didn't release their names. I was so scared." Mom hugs Ellie, too. "I'm so relieved, so relieved." She's almost in tears herself.

"We were there, Mom, we were there just after it happened." I'm sobbing hysterically, clinging to her, soaking her blouse with tears and snot. "We saw the police cars and the ambulances. It was horrible."

With one arm around me and the other around Ellie, Mom tries to comfort us. "They've taken a boy in for questioning," she tells us, "but they haven't identified him."

"It's Buddy," Ellie says. "He did it, I know he did."

Mom looks puzzled so we try to explain, stumbling over words, interrupting each other, correcting each other. "Well," she says, "if you're right, I hope they keep him in jail, where he can't hurt anyone else."

The phone begins to ring and Mom hurries off to answer it. "Ellie," she calls, "it's your mother."

I run downstairs with Ellie. I can tell from what she tells her mother that Mrs. O'Brien heard the same news story and is just as scared as Mom was.

"We're all right, Mom," Ellie insists. "We're all right. No, I'm not crying, I'm okay, just scared, that's all, and—and—and . . ." Ellie does cry then. "Why did it happen, Mommy? Why did they have to die?"

Mom holds me tight. "Poor babies," she whispers. "Poor, poor babies."

Does she mean Ellie and me? Or Bobbi Jo and Cheryl? Or all four of us?

Mrs. O'Brien comes for Ellie. Ellie and I hug each other. How can I bear to let her go? "See you tomorrow" is meaningless. It's tempting fate to say it.

"Mommy, I'm so scared," Ellie sobs. "I saw him on the bridge. He was there, so close to where, to where . . . where they were. He must have done it just before we got there. He could have killed us but he didn't have the gun, he must have hidden it in the bushes, he might come after us and shoot us later."

"Buddy's still at the police station," Mrs. O'Brien tells Ellie. "I hear they plan to keep him as long as they can. They're looking for the murder weapon. As soon as they find it . . ."

She strokes Ellie's hair. "Nothing will happen to you, sweetie. Your dad and I won't let you come to any harm."

I don't believe her. Mrs. Boyd couldn't keep Bobbi Jo safe. Mrs. Miller couldn't keep Cheryl safe. Danger is here, there, everywhere. Death strikes without warning on warm summer mornings as well as in the dark of night.

Finally Mrs. O'Brien and my mother pry Ellie and me apart.

I go to the car with her. "Be careful," I beg her. "If you see him, run."

I stand in the street and wave until she's out of sight, then I go inside, climb the stairs to my room, sit on my bed, and stare out my window at the house next door. My head is a jumble of unfinished thoughts, unanswered questions, bits and pieces of songs, images of last night—Cheryl and Ralph dancing, Bobbi Jo and Ellie and me in the creek, the stones falling in the water, the Shadow's laugh . . . and Charlie. Charlie and me.

# Later the Same Day

## NORA

BILLY'S voice wakes me from a nap. I'm hot, grumpy. Dizzy from the heat. For a moment I don't remember what happened. Then it hits me like a punch in the stomach and I see the park and the kids running toward Ellie and me, crying, shouting.

"Hey, Mom," Billy is shouting downstairs. "Did you hear about those girls getting killed in the park? I wonder if Nora knows them. One of them went to Eastern. I bet she—"

Mom says something in a low voice. Billy bellows, "Really? She was *there*?"

Mom says more. "But I want to talk to her," Billy says.

"Not now, I said!" This time Mom speaks loudly enough for me to hear every word. "Let her rest. If she feels like talking to you later, she will. Otherwise, leave her alone. She's very upset."

I lie back on the bed and close my eyes. Thank you, Mom.

My thoughts drift back to the party. I see Cheryl with Ralph, her blond hair catching the last of the summer sunlight. I hear Buddy say he could kill her. I see the hatred in his eyes, I hear him say, "If you died tomorrow, I wouldn't shed one tear." I smell rubber burning as he speeds out of the parking lot. I see him on the bridge, cigarette dangling from his lower lip. I see his knee next to mine in his car, I see him at the top of the hill on Eastern Avenue. I think of the picnic we were supposed to have, the hot dogs and soda and potato chips, all of us there, planning our summer.

I glance at the Baby Ben clock on my nightstand. Five thirty. This time yesterday, none of this had happened. While we were making our plans, Death was making his plans.

I roll over and shut my eyes. I'm so tired. The soles of my feet hurt, my throat is raw from crying, my eyes burn. Later I'll take a bath, wash my hair, put some lotion on my feet, but not now, not yet. I just want to sleep.

I sink like a stone to the bottom of my mind, to a place so dark, there are no memories. No dreams. Nothing.

Hours later, I wake up. It's dark. Mom is leaning over me. "Are you hungry? I saved some dinner for you."

I shake my head. I'm not hungry. I don't want anything to eat. "How long have I been asleep?"

"It's almost ten."

When I sit up, my head feels light. My feet hurt. My legs are weak. I'm sick, I think, too sick to get out of bed, too sick to do anything for myself. "Can I have something to drink?"

Mom hands me a glass of iced tea. "I thought you'd want this."

I take it gratefully and drink it all.

"Would you like to talk about it?" Mom asks. She looks worried.

"Why did it happen?" I ask. "Why?"

Mom sighs and sits on the bed beside me. Gently she runs one finger up and down the inside of my arm, something she did to help me sleep when I was little. It comforts me.

"They were just kids," I say. "They didn't do anything. Why did they have to die?"

"I'm sure God has a reason." Mom's voice is low. She doesn't believe what she's saying. I can hear the lie.

I'm tempted to say she's not fooling me. I know a lie when I hear one. But what's the point? She's just saying what people always say. Maybe she really believes it. Maybe she just wants to believe it. *God has a plan. There's a reason for everything.* Maybe that comforts her. Why doesn't it comfort me?

I sit up straighter, look her in the eye. "Why does God let horrible things happen to people?"

She tucks a frizzle of hair behind my ear, but before she can say anything I let more words tumble out of my mouth. It's as if everything I've never said out loud has broken loose. "If He's so powerful, why does He let wars happen and earthquakes and floods and fires and car crashes and plane crashes and cancer—"

"Hush." Mom strokes my arm again. "I know how upset and sad you are, but don't let it affect your faith. Maybe you should talk to a priest. Someone with more knowledge than I have."

I nod. Yes, maybe I should do that, maybe I will. Priests must know the answers to questions like mine. That's why they're priests.

"It's on the ten o'clock news," Billy shouts from downstairs. "They're talking to people in the neighborhood."

Mom stands up. "Do you want to see what they have to say?"

I shake my head and turn my back. I don't want to see any pictures or hear any newsmen talking about Cheryl and Bobbi Jo.

The phone rings. Billy shouts, "Nora, it's Ellie."

I go downstairs. From the living room I hear a newscaster saying, "It's hard to believe something like this could happen in a peaceful suburban park."

Without listening to more or taking a look at the TV screen, I drag the phone into the bathroom and shut the door.

"It's me," Ellie says. Her voice is hoarse and low. "Did you watch the news on TV?"

"No," I whisper.

"Me either."

We sit there connected by the telephone line, not speaking, just breathing.

Ellie breaks the silence. "The police are interviewing everybody who was at the party last night," she tells me. "Why don't you come over tomorrow? We can be together when they come to my house."

I hesitate. How can I tell Ellie I never want to come to her house again? I don't want to see Mrs. Boyd. I don't want to see the park. I want to go to some place I've never been, a place where nobody's friends are murdered.

"What's wrong?" Ellie whispers in her sad, croaky voice. "Don't you want to come?"

I swallow hard. I grip the receiver. My chest is so tight, I wonder if I'm about to have a heart attack. "I, um, I um, I mean I . . ." I wrap the telephone cord around my neck and wonder if it's possible to strangle yourself.

"Nora, please come," Ellie begs. "I don't know what to do. I feel like I'm going crazy or something, like I could scream and scream and scream."

I test the cord, pulling it a little tighter, but when it starts choking me, I let it go. "Me too. I feel the same way." It's true. Nothing will ever be normal again. Not me. Not Ellie. Not the Boyds or the Millers. Not Charlie or Paul or Walt.

"So will you come?" Ellie asks.

I nod slowly. "Yes," I say. "Yes. I'll come."

"About ten?"

"Yes."

We sit silently again, breathing into the phone. Before, we've always had so much to talk about, interrupting each other, laughing, making jokes. Now I can't think of what to say. And neither can she.

"It's awful here," Ellie says at last. "I can hear the Boyds crying right through the wall. Even Mr. Boyd. I heard Mrs. Boyd say, 'If only I hadn't let her walk to school with Cheryl. She didn't have any reason to go. Why didn't I say no?' Then Mr. Boyd said, 'You couldn't have known.' It was just like they were in our house."

Ellie pauses, blows her nose, draws a deep breath. "I tried watching TV but then the news came on and it's the big story. Reporters are all over the place, knocking on doors, asking questions. Even now, even when it's dark. They wanted to talk to the Boyds but Mr. Boyd slammed the door in their faces. So did my father. Oh, why did it happen, Nora, why?"

I clutch the phone tighter. I don't know what to say.

"How could Buddy have done it?" Ellie's voice rises. "Why didn't God stop him, kill him or something before he could . . ."

"I hate him, I hate, I hate him." I'm not sure if I'm talking about Buddy or God.

"I wish he was dead." Ellie's voice sinks to a whisper. "If I had a gun, I'd shoot him."

"Me too. He deserves to die like they did." I picture Cheryl and Bobbi Jo walking across the ball field, swinging their purses. What had they been talking about? Probably the party. Maybe Cheryl was telling Bobbi Jo that Ralph wants to fix her up with somebody, they'll go to Top's Drive-In and have milk shakes so thick, you can't suck them through a straw.

Then they come to the woods. The path is shady, narrow, winding through the trees. Birds sing. There's no warning, no time to run. *Bang, bang. bang.* And they're gone, just like that. Life is over. Done. Finished. *Bang.*

"I'm so scared," Ellie whispers. "I can't stop thinking we could be dead too. That stupid pin saved our lives."

I press the cold metal receiver against my ear and remember Ellie fumbling with the flower pin. Such a little thing.

Dead, we could be dead. Dead. Dead. I let the word roll round in my head, hoping it will lose its meaning, become a sound signifying nothing. Dead, dead, dead. I can't make it lose its meaning. It's a dark hole in the world.

Just then Billy knocks on the bathroom door. "Hey, I need to get in there."

I tell Ellie I'll see her tomorrow and hang up. When I open the bathroom door, I get a dirty look from Billy.

"Just because something bad happened doesn't mean you can stay in the bathroom all night," he says in his whiny half-changed stupid boy voice.

I ignore him and go up to my room. I lie in bed in the dark and think about Cheryl and Bobbi Jo. What's it like to die? Does it hurt? Do you know what's happening? Where are they now? Are they in heaven? Or are they just gone?

# Nora's Dream

IT'S dark and Ellie and I are in the woods, down by the stream. Moonlight puddles the shadows with splashes of silver. We look up and just where the moon shines brightest we see Cheryl and Bobbi Jo. They're wearing what they'd had on when they stopped at Ellie's house before . . . before they— And they're covered with blood, their skin, their hair, their clothes, and they come closer, so close we can see the bullet holes. And they say together, "It was Buddy, he killed us, he killed us, don't let him say he didn't. He did it, he shot us, and now we're dead."

They're holding hands and they're crying. Ellie reaches out to Bobbi Jo, but they step back, fading slowly into the shadows.

"Tell the police, make them believe you" is the last thing they say.

## PART THREE

# Nothing Will Ever Be the Same

# The Long Way to Ellie's House

## NORA

I WAKE up shaking. My heart pounds. This isn't the kind of dream where you say *Thank God it's not true.* Not this time. This time the dream is true. Cheryl and Bobbi Jo are dead. And I have to go to Ellie's house and be interviewed by the police.

The sun shines through the white ruffled curtains. It slants across the flowered wallpaper and lingers on the collection of china dogs I've kept on my bureau since I was little, the blue Eastern High pennant tacked to my wall, posters from school dances nobody asked me to, pictures cut from movie magazines. A picture of Jesus hangs between James Dean and Elvis Presley. He's pointing to his heart, which glows under his robe. His face is long and sad, his hand graceful.

Why didn't he stop Buddy?

My closet door is open and I see my clothes, skirts and blouses and dresses all crammed together, a crinoline peeking out, belts and shoes on the floor. My bureau drawers are stuffed with underwear and socks and pajamas and jeans and shorts, my diary hidden among them, buried deep. My desk is littered with art supplies and drawing tablets and a stack of paperback mysteries.

The clothes I wore yesterday lie in a heap on the floor. I'll never wear them again.

Everything looks like it belongs to someone else, a girl I don't know anymore, a stranger.

I smell coffee and bacon and glance at my clock. Ten of nine. Mom must have fixed breakfast for me. Daddy's at work. Billy's probably outside, celebrating summer with his friends, riding bikes or playing in the woods, the kind of stuff I used to do.

I get up slowly, as stiff as an old lady, and pull on a pair of shorts and a blouse. I look for my sneakers and remember I left them at Ellie's. Under my bed, I find a pair of old white moccasins. Not much better than going barefoot, but they'll have to do. The soles of my feet are still sore from yesterday.

I take my seat at the kitchen table, and Mom puts a plate of scrambled eggs and bacon in front of me. I look at it as if it's food from outer space.

"Eat," Mom says gently. "You didn't have dinner last night. Or lunch either."

"I'm not hungry." I stare at the food. Cheryl and Bobbi Jo will never eat anything again.

"Please, Nora." Mom's hand is on my shoulder, her face is sad. "I know how hard this is for you, but you have to eat."

I nod and pick up my fork. You are not dead, I tell myself. Your mother is right. You have to eat.

The eggs are moist, a little runny, and the bacon's limp and greasy, the way I like it. But not today. It's an effort to chew and swallow without gagging. Mom stands by the sink watching me, so I eat. Her worry washes over me like cold rain.

I choke down my vitamin pill with orange juice and glance at the clock, a black cat with a long tail that swings back and forth. *Tick tock tick.* I won it when the new shopping center opened a few years back. I'd been hoping for the fancy Schwinn bike, but Mom was pleased with the clock. It keeps good time, she says. It's almost ten already.

"I have to go to Ellie's," I tell Mom. "The police want to question everyone who was at the party."

She stares at me, suddenly tense. "Do you have to?"

"I promised her."

"But your father drove the car to work," she says. "I can't take you."

"It's okay. I've walked plenty of times before." Including yesterday.

"Don't go through the park," she says. "Promise."

I shake my head. I'll never ever go through the park again. "He's still in jail, isn't he?"

She nods and points to the paper she's been reading. Buddy's senior picture stares at me from the front page of the *Morning Sun.* He isn't smiling that smirky smile now, I think.

"He's still a suspect," Mom says, "but he's passed two lie detector tests. I don't know how much longer they can hold him."

I let her hug me and kiss me as if she's scared she'll never see me again. I tell her not to worry, I'll be careful. But I find myself looking back at my house as if I'm memorizing every shingle, the shape of the front porch, the dormer windows, the dogwood tree. As if I'll never see it again. You don't know if you'll come back, do you? You don't know when it's the last time you'll leave home.

Before I've walked a block, sweat is trickling down my back. I feel every pebble through the thin soles of my moccasins.

I pass the shopping center. Mrs. Beale, a woman I babysit for, stops me. "Oh, Nora," she says. "Did you know the girls who were murdered? Such a terrible thing." She's wide-eyed, excited. Something has happened in Elmgrove, we're on the news. TV, newspapers. Police in the park.

I shake my head and study the beaded pattern on my moccasins. "Eastern's a big school," I say. "It's impossible to know everybody."

"So sad," Mrs. Beale says. "They had their whole lives ahead of them. It's tragic, just tragic." Her eyes bore into me as if she knows I'm lying. I must know them. The school's not *that* big.

How can I say yes, I know them? If I did, she'd ask more questions, she'd drill me, then she'd tell all her friends and neighbors what I said: "My babysitter knew those poor girls who were murdered in the park. She says the older one quarreled with her boyfriend. She thinks he killed her and the other girl, a younger girl who didn't even go to Eastern. She started crying while she told me about it. So sad. So tragic, their whole lives ahead of them . . ."

I can hear her voice, see her eyes bright with importance. The others lean toward her, their faces sharp, their lips parted, eager to know more about the murder. Her little girls stand in the hall and listen to things they shouldn't hear.

"Did you see the paper this morning?" Mrs. Beale goes on. "Front-page pictures of the girls and the park with a map showing where the bodies were found. The reporter seems to think the older girl's boyfriend did it. Did you know him? Sonny or Buddy or something? He's in police custody now—they're questioning him about the rifle. It hasn't been found yet."

I shake my head, stunned by the information she's hurling at me. "He's a year ahead of me," I say. "He just graduated."

"His picture chilled my soul," she goes on. "The smirk on his face, the look in his eyes, that awful pompadour. Typical juvenile delinquent, just the sort to kill his girlfriend."

I shift my weight from one foot to the other. I feel the sidewalk's heat through the soles of my moccasins. "I don't know him. I don't know anything about him or what happened."

"Well, take a look at the *Sun*," Mrs. Beale says. "The reporter interviewed lots of people in the neighborhood. Isn't it strange that no one heard the shots? All those houses and not one person called the police, not until that poor little boy's dog found the bodies. To think of something like that happening here. You're just not safe anywhere."

I nod and try to edge away from her. I'm dizzy from the heat.

Mrs. Beale shakes her head and tightens her grip on her purse. "Well, I have errands to run, Nora. You take care, now."

I watch her head for the air-conditioned comfort of Walgreen's drugstore. Then I cut down a side street, hoping not to see anyone else.

All the time I'm walking it's an effort. One foot forward, then the other, block after long hot block. I've never gone to Ellie's without cutting through the park.

I see some kids I know a block ahead. Before they see me, I duck down another side street. This one leads uphill.

The telephone poles smell like the boardwalk in Ocean City.

Creosote, Dad says, a kind of black tarry gunk they use to water-proof wood. I wish I were in Ocean City. I wish I'd been at the beach when all this happened. Then I wouldn't be walking to Ellie's to be interviewed by the police. I'm too young for this. I'm just a kid, a child.

I look at the houses on Tulip Avenue. A long line of brick ramblers, climbing the hill one after another. Each one has a picture window, sometimes to the right of the front door and sometimes to the left. Most have tidy green lawns and flower gardens and little bushes trimmed into balls. I spot garden gnomes, silvery glass globes, a miniature wooden lighthouse, birdhouses on poles, a pink flamingo. A few yards are patches of dirt where kids play with wagons and tricycles and toy trucks.

In art class we studied vanishing point perspective. This street is a perfect example. The houses march into the distance, getting smaller and closer together as the street seems to narrow. If I lived on this street I'd vanish too. When I grow up I'll live in a city, a real city like New York.

*If* I grow up, that is. For the first time I realize not everyone lives to grow up. I mean, I knew that before, but not like I know it now.

Finally I cross Forty-Third Avenue and I'm in Ellie's neighborhood at last. I see news trucks and police cars in the park. I stare at my moccasins and walk fast, head down, and charge through Ellie's gate. I run up her sidewalk, taking care not to look at Bobbi Jo's house. Before I raise my hand to knock, the door opens and Ellie pulls me inside.

"Where have you been? It's past eleven."

"I took the long way. I didn't want to go through the park."

Ellie nods. "I had a horrible dream last night," she whispers.

"I did too." We stare at each other, wide-eyed.

"I dreamed we saw Cheryl and Bobbi Jo in the woods and they told us Buddy killed them." Ellie's eyes fill with tears as she tells me this.

I grab her arms. "I dreamed the exact same thing."

Mrs. O'Brien finds us weeping in each other's arms. We tell her about our dreams and she turns pale. "My grandmother used to tell me stories of the dead coming back in dreams."

She hugs me hard. "Oh, Nora, it's good to see you," she says, and I know she means *I'm so glad you and Ellie aren't dead.*

I cling to her for a moment, taking in the smell of talcum powder and English Lavender soap, a familiar mother smell.

"Sit down," she says. "You must be exhausted."

I watch her fix a tall glass of ice water for me. I drink it so fast, I almost choke.

# The Detectives

## NORA

JUST as I've begun to chew up the ice cubes, there's a loud knock at the door. My heart catapults and I look at Ellie with dread. It has to be the police. We stay in the kitchen and let Mrs. O'Brien go to the door.

Two detectives follow her back to the kitchen. Worried men in dark suits, red-faced from the heat.

Mrs. O'Brien makes room for all five of us at the kitchen table. After the introductions, Lieutenant McCarthy says, "I know this is hard for you girls, but I have to ask you a few questions." His partner, Sergeant Carter, opens a notebook and thumbs to a blank page. Pen in hand, he waits for the interview to begin.

The lieutenant takes our names and addresses and asks us to identify everyone who'd been at the party. The sergeant writes the names down, checking the spelling of each one. Then the lieutenant asks about Buddy. When did we notice he was there? What did he do or say when Ralph showed up and began dancing with Cheryl?

"He was mad," I say. "He didn't like the way they were dancing. He said Cheryl was . . . I mean, he thought she and Ralph were, well . . ." My face is getting hot with embarrassment. The kitchen fan whirs in the window, moving hot air around. I begin sweating. For some reason I feel like I did something against the law myself. And then I remember the beer and realize I did do something against the law.

Ellie says, "They were dancing Baltimore-style—not the dirty boogie, just . . . dancing."

"It made Buddy mad." Suddenly I remember his exact words. "He said he could kill her."

The detectives look at each other. "You're sure he said that?"

I nod. "He was sitting right next to me."

I glance at Ellie and she nods. "Yes, he said that, he said he could kill her, I heard him, too."

"Later," I say, "when him and Ralph almost got into a fight, he said if she died tomorrow he wouldn't care."

Ellie nods her head again. Her ponytail bounces. "I heard that, too."

We go on telling the story of Buddy. "He used to hit her," Ellie says. "He gave her a black eye once. Her parents told him to stay away from her."

"But he was always following her around," I say, "trying to get her to go out with him."

"She was scared to go places by herself," Ellie added. "She hated him, but he wouldn't leave her alone."

The sergeant writes down everything we say, sometimes asking us to repeat something to make sure he has it right.

"Did you see Cheryl or Bobbi Jo talking to anyone else that night?" the lieutenant asks.

"There was a boy," I say, "but I couldn't see his face."

"He was bothering them," Ellie adds.

"Was it Buddy?"

We shake our heads. "Cheryl said it was some guy with pimples, a jerk," Ellie says.

"They got rid of him," I add.

"And you don't know who he was?"

"I'm pretty sure he doesn't live around here," Ellie tells him. "He probably saw us and thought we were having a party or something."

"What time did the party break up?" the lieutenant asks.

I look at Ellie. Neither of us wants to say how late we stayed out. Especially not with Mrs. O'Brien sitting between us. We're also worried about the beer. Suppose Charlie or Paul mentions it? Or Ralph? We're sixteen, five years too young for beer.

"I'm not sure," Ellie says. "I don't have a watch."

The lieutenant looks at me, and I shrug.

He glances at Mrs. O'Brien and she says, "Ellie has a midnight curfew."

The lieutenant turns to Ellie and me. "Did you come home on time?"

"I'm not sure," Ellie says again. "It might have been a little later."

The lieutenant raises his eyebrows. "A little later—does that mean one a.m., two a.m., or . . . ?"

Mrs. O'Brien frowns at Ellie. "I think I heard the front door close around two," she says softly.

He nods. The sergeant writes it down. "That agrees with what Mrs. Boyd told us. She and her husband were waiting up for Bobbi Jo."

I turn my water glass in small circles on the table, making a pattern of wet rings. I remember Bobbi Jo's father yelling at her. He was mad at her on the last night of her life. He must feel terrible. I feel terrible. We shouldn't have drunk beer. We should have gone home when we were supposed to. It wouldn't have changed anything, but at least Bobbi Jo's father wouldn't have shouted at her.

"Where was Buddy all this time?" the lieutenant asks. "Did you see him in the woods or anywhere?"

"I heard noises, not little noises like an animal makes," I said. "Like somebody was hiding in the woods, watching us. You know how you get that feeling? Like you're being watched?" I feel shivery remembering—it must have been Buddy, hiding, watching us, following us. What if he'd had the gun then? Would he have shot all of us?

"But you didn't actually see anyone?" the lieutenant asks.

"Well, no, but I'm sure it was Buddy," I say.

"He's always watching Cheryl," Ellie says. "She hates it."

"How about the next morning?"

We tell him we overslept and when Cheryl and Bobbi Jo showed up we weren't ready to leave, so they went on ahead. And then we both start crying.

The lieutenant waits until we calm down before he asks more questions. After we tell him what time they left and what time we left, he asks if we saw or heard anything out of the ordinary in the woods. "Think carefully," he says. "This is very important."

We look at each other and I remember we were talking about Cheryl, saying nasty things about her, and all the while she was lying dead in the woods just a few feet away. What if she wasn't dead yet and she heard us? In my mind I apologize—I tell Cheryl we didn't mean it, we were just jealous. We're sorry, so so sorry.

Ellie says, "We had a feeling someone was watching us again, but we didn't see anyone and we didn't hear anything." She reaches over and grasps my hand.

"Nothing that sounded like a gunshot?"

"We heard a car backfire," Ellie says. "It was so loud, it scared us."

"Were you in the woods when you heard it?"

"No," I say. "We were cutting across the ball field, near Eastern Avenue."

We look at each other, gripping each other's hand so tightly it hurts. "Was it the gun?" Ellie whispers. "Is that what we heard?"

"It could be," he says. "The time seems right."

"And then we came to the bridge," Ellie says, "and Buddy was sitting on the railing, smoking."

"He asked us if we'd seen Cheryl," I say. "He wanted to give her a ride to school. His car was parked at the end of Chester Street. You know, where the path comes out of the woods."

The lieutenant nods. "How long was this after you heard the car backfire?"

"Five or ten minutes." Ellie's voice shakes. We keep hold of each other's hand.

The lieutenant looks at me. "I'm not sure," I say.

"Then what happened?" the lieutenant asks.

"He gave us a ride to school," I say.

"How did Buddy seem to you?" the lieutenant asks. "Was he upset, angry, worried?"

"He was in a bad mood," Ellie says.

"He was upset about Cheryl," I say. "He wanted her back."

"When I said that wouldn't happen," Ellie puts in, "he practically threw us out of the car."

"He drove away so fast his tires squealed," I add.

Next the lieutenant asks about our walk home from school. Then he wants to know about the sirens and Mrs. Boyd and the kids running out of the woods screaming and crying. Can we remember who we saw? We tell him what we can but it's all kind of vague now, the kids running, the news they shouted, Cheryl's little brother's face. I want to forget it all. Every detail. I want to erase it from history.

"Why did you go all the way to Nora's house?" he asks us. "Why didn't you just come back here?"

"We didn't want to see Mrs. Boyd," Ellie whispers. "We didn't want to tell her what happened."

"And then we saw Buddy," I tell him. "At the top of the hill, by the apartments. He said we looked like we'd seen a ghost. And Ellie said—"

"I said if we saw a ghost, he knew whose it was," she cut in. Her face is red and she's breathing fast. "Because he killed her, I know he did. We both dreamed the same dream last night—Bobbi Jo and Cheryl told us Buddy did it."

Mrs. O'Brien pats Ellie's shoulder, but she shrugs her mother's hand away. Impatient. Near tears again.

"It's true." I lean across the table, imploring him to believe us, to lock Buddy up forever. "The dead come back in dreams." I repeat what Mrs. O'Brien told us. "They tell what happened."

"They tell the truth," Ellie adds. "The dead don't lie."

Lieutenant McCarthy shakes his head. He looks sad, defeated

somehow. I can tell he doesn't believe the dead come back, but maybe he wishes they did. "It's too early to bring charges."

"But Buddy's in jail," Ellie says, "isn't he?" Her voice rises.

"He hasn't been officially charged. We're just questioning him." He gets to his feet and picks up his hat. "Thanks. You girls have been very helpful. If you think of anything else, let us know." He hands us each a card with his name and phone number.

Sergeant Carter closes his notebook with a snap and puts it back into his pocket. Mrs. O'Brien walks to the door with them. I stare at the guns strapped to their belts and wonder if they've ever killed anyone. I picture Buddy escaping from jail and Lieutenant McCarthy shooting him. He should be shot, he should die exactly the way he killed Cheryl and Bobbi Jo.

## MISTER DEATH

HE stands at the living room window, watching what's going on in the park. All day long the police have been there. Yesterday too. Two detectives are standing outside Ellie's house, talking. Dumb as mud, he thinks, both of them, the overweight one and the underweight one. What a pair, the Laurel and Hardy of Baltimore County. He amuses himself for a moment imagining them in a bizarre comic routine involving pratfalls, custard pies, and so on, ending in the big one slapping the little one and saying, "Now look what you made me do."

He wonders what Ellie and her friend told the detectives. What's her name—Nora, the tall one who laughs too loud. She was there the night of the party too. She must have slept at Ellie's that night because they'd walked to school together the next day. He'd watched from his hiding place in the woods. Stupid girls. If they'd been with Cheryl and Bobbi Jo, they'd be dead too.

He wonders if they know that. He wonders if they're scared. He wonders if they think Mister Death will come after them.

He swats the venetian blind cord back and forth and watches

it swing like a hangman's noose. Ellie and Nora are no better than Cheryl and Bobbi Jo, but he hasn't got anything personal against them. Let them sweat it.

Right now the police are draining the lake, looking for the murder weapon. Which is hanging in plain sight on the wall in the basement. Right where it always is.

Yesterday he watched the police use a bulldozer to clear the underbrush so they could search for the rifle near the bridge. The newspaper calls it the picnic grove death scene. They haven't got a clue.

He thought he'd be scared when that kid and his dog found the bodies. But he's not. Just watching the cops proves how smart he is. He took an IQ test in sixth grade and scored in the genius category.

Nobody knows it at Eastern. He keeps to himself and never says a word in class, never does more than enough to get a C. No friends except his brother. At the end of every year, none of his teachers knows his name. One afternoon he bumped into his English teacher at the shopping center, and she looked at him as if he were a stranger. "Excuse me," he said and moved on. Point made. No one notices him. Which is just what he wants. To pass through the world unseen and unremembered.

Today's *Baltimore Sun* lies on the coffee table. The murder is on the front page: GIRLS SHOT IN LOCAL PARK. Yearbook pictures of Cheryl and Bobbi Jo stare at him. Pretty little schoolgirl smiles. So sweet, so innocent, so young.

Bullshit. They got what they deserved.

He thinks of the sheet of notebook paper he left on Cheryl's face. On it, he'd written a slightly altered quote: "and what i want to know is how do you like your blueeyed girls Mister Death."

It's from a poem by E. E. Cummings. He knows it by heart:

Buffalo Bill's
defunct
    who used to
        ride a watersmooth-silver
            stallion
and break onetwothreefourfive pigeonsjustlikethat
                Jesus
he was a handsome man
        and what i want to know is
how do you like your blueeyed boy
Mister Death

Buffalo Bill's eyes were actually brown, but in a famous poster the artist painted his eyes blue because blue eyes were thought to be superior to brown eyes. He wonders if E. E. Cummings knew that.

Now he thinks of himself as Mister Death. He likes the sound of it. A sobriquet, one of his favorite words.

Turning back to the *Sun,* he shakes his head at the girls' faces. "Little did you know when you posed for those pictures they'd be on the *Sun*'s front page. And not because you won a beauty contest."

He's read the article so often, he almost knows it by heart. He's pleased that the reporter called the killer an excellent shot. Hell, he should be. He's been hunting since he was a kid.

He peers down the street. No sign of the detectives. They must be interviewing Ellie's neighbors.

No sign of Ellie or Nora either. They're probably scared to come outside.

Bobbi Jo's little sister is standing at the fence, talking to Mrs. O'Brien. She's crying.

He smiles a bitter smile, one he's practiced in front of his mirror. Tough break, kid. Might as well learn the truth now: Life is solitary, poor, nasty, brutish, and short.

Thomas Hobbes wrote that in *Leviathan*. Hobbes is right. Life is solitary, poor, nasty, brutish, and short.

He toys with the venetian blind cord again. How many kids have read *Leviathan* cover to cover? Or have even heard of Thomas Hobbes? Most of his teachers probably don't know any more about Hobbes than they know about him. The father of modern politics, that's who Hobbes was. He lived in the seventeenth century. He knew Francis Bacon. Maybe even Shakespeare. King Lear probably agreed with Hobbes. Hamlet and Macbeth, too.

It's odd. He'd thought killing Cheryl and Bobbi Jo would be different from killing deer. But it wasn't. They were a little more aware than deer, who know nothing of death, but he saw the same flash of terror in their eyes. As Mister Death, he has the power to take life, and they knew it. Mister Death is merciless. Ask anyone. He hopes they had a second to be sorry for what they'd done.

But he's digressing from the one detail that bothers him. His brother. He hasn't come out of his room since yesterday morning. He's holed up in there, listening to rock-and-roll on a colored music station. He's terrified they'll be arrested.

He's told the little coward that all he has to do is act normal and nothing will happen. But the kid's a wreck. He's going to have to keep his eye on him.

The doorbell rings. It's the two detectives. *Dum de dum dum.* Like Sergeant Friday and his partner. Just the facts, sir.

He's very polite to the detectives, he says what's expected. It's so sad, tragic, girls that young and so on. He tells them he didn't know them, didn't go to the party. He didn't hear anything yesterday morning. He doesn't own a gun, doesn't even know how to shoot one. They don't ask to speak to his brother. Or his parents, who are at work.

They thank him, give him a card with a phone number to call in case he remembers anything later. Yeah, sure, he'll definitely call them.

He watches the detectives walk down the street, probably heading for the Luccis' house to talk to Paul. Paul won't mention seeing him at the party. No one will. It was dark, the girls were the only ones he spoke to. When they laughed at him, scorned him, mocked him, he left. Quietly. The way he'd come, the way he'd entered the woods yesterday.

He's a fader. He disappears into shadows. He wears mental camouflage. He's Mister Death, the man you meet on the stairs. The man who isn't there.

# Night Thoughts

## NORA

I'M alone in my room. In bed even though it's only nine thirty and not quite dark. I want to sleep but I can't.

Everyone else is downstairs watching Sid Caesar. I can hear canned laughter. My parents and Billy laugh too. How can they laugh? How can anyone? I wish they'd shut up. It's all I can do not to open my door and scream at them.

I keep thinking of a poem I read in English class. I don't know why I liked it so much, but I copied the whole thing in my diary so I could read it whenever I wanted to. Maybe I knew someday I'd need that poem.

It's one of the Lucy poems by William Wordsworth, an English Romantic poet who lived in the Lake District, a place I would very much like to see someday if I live long enough to get there. It's supposed to be very beautiful. You can visit the cottage where he lived with his sister Dorothy, and you can take long hikes on the fells like he used to. Of course he's dead now, but unlike Shelley and Keats, he lived to be old and boring. I know all this because I wrote a report on him in tenth grade.

He wrote the poem while he was young, before he got boring. I can say it by heart now:

> A slumber did my spirit seal;
> I had no human fears:
> She seem'd a thing that could not feel
> The touch of earthly years.
> No motion has she now, no force;
> She neither hears nor sees;
> Roll'd round in earth's diurnal course,
> With rocks, and stones, and trees.

That's what it's like to be dead. No motion, no force, you neither speak nor see, you're rolled round, rolled round, you're rolled round and round forever on earth's diurnal course. Not a word about God or heaven, just rocks and stones and trees. Rocks and stones and trees.

Before I got in bed tonight, I tried to draw a picture of Lucy in her grave, but as usual when I'm drawing, I couldn't get what I saw in my head on paper. I tore it up because I was scared Mom would find it and think I was crazy. What kind of person draws dead girls?

The worst thing is—what I can't stop thinking about—the blood. Billy told me about it. The police found blood on the path, their blood in the dust and in the grass where Buddy dragged them. It was in the paper, which I still won't read.

Ellie and I and who knows who else stepped in their blood and never noticed. We walked in it, it was on our shoes, and we didn't know. When I got my sneakers back, I threw them away. Mom found them in the trash and asked why I'd thrown them out, she'd just bought them in May and they were perfectly good. I didn't tell her about the blood, how could I? She'd think I was crazy. I shoved them in the back of my closet, and I wear my old moccasins even though I've worn holes in their soles, holes in my soul.

But the blood, it's like Lady Macbeth, all the perfume in the world. See, the thing is, Ellie and I were talking about Cheryl, we were saying how come Ralph likes her so much—first Buddy, then Ralph? She had a big pimple on her chin this morning, Ellie said, did you notice? and we sang the Clearasil song.

Now I think about the pimple and the bullets and the blood.

We also said she wasn't all that pretty, her teeth were too big, and then I think of the bullets again, of how he shot her in the face.

Why did we talk about her like that?

And why didn't we hear the shots and why didn't we notice the blood and how come Buddy was on the bridge? If he did it, why didn't he hide when he heard us coming? Why didn't he shoot us, too? He could have. If he did it, that is. If he had a gun.

But I remember him sitting there, smoking that cigarette, he didn't look any different, he didn't look like someone who'd just killed two girls.

If he didn't do it, who did? What if the real killer is still out there in the woods? With a *gun*? What if he's outside my house right now, waiting to kill me?

A mockingbird is singing in the holly tree outside my window. Tomorrow a cat could kill him, tomorrow I could die, I could be shot or hit by a car. I could be struck by lightning, I could fall down the stairs and break my neck or fracture my skull, I could drown at the swimming pool. So many ways to die. Poison, suffocation, choking, bleeding, automobile crashes. So many ways, it's a wonder anybody lives to grow up.

I remember an essay we read in tenth grade. A newspaper editor wrote it about his daughter, Mary White. She was riding her horse somewhere in Kansas, and she turned to wave at someone. She hit her head on a tree limb and it knocked her off her horse. She probably never knew what happened. There she was, about my age, riding along, happy and smiling and waving to a friend. And then, just like that, she was dead.

It was the saddest essay in the world. When I read it, I cried and cried because Mary White was a lot like me, a tomboy who didn't want to grow up, and she died on a sunny day in Kansas when Death hid in a tree and took her like he can take anybody anytime, including Cheryl and Bobbi Jo, and why not Ellie and me and whoever else he wants.

I wish I hadn't been at Ellie's house, walking to school and talking about Cheryl and stepping in her blood that we never saw, never knew was there until Billy asked me if I'd seen it. And no I didn't see the blood and yes I must have stepped in it and yes I was jealous of Cheryl because she had blond hair and boyfriends and wanted to fix Bobbi Jo up with Don, the boy I loved even though he thought of me as a nice kid and who likes nice kids? I was someone to tease in art class, not to date.

Why couldn't she have fixed me up with him? But Bobbi Jo was much cuter than me and didn't act silly and immature and goof off and snort through her nose when she laughed and wasn't almost six feet tall and skinny as a broomstick and just about as curvy.

But still alive, every inch of me—at least right now.

But they're not. They're both dead and I have to see them at Hausner's Funeral Parlor tomorrow and go to their funerals the next day, and I don't want to see them, I've never seen a dead person. Or been to a funeral. When my grandmother died, Mom said I shouldn't go to the funeral, I was too sensitive, it would upset me, I'd have bad dreams. Guess what. I had bad dreams anyway.

I don't want them to be dead and I don't want to die and I'm so scared my heart might stop beating right now, which is why I can't lay me down to sleep. I might die before I wake and the Lord my soul will take—but maybe not, maybe he won't want my soul.

The mockingbird keeps singing and my room is hot. I kick off my sheets but then I feel so unprotected lying there and I pull the sheet over my head and curl up small and close my eyes and think of darkness, unending darkness, of rocks and stones and trees, of being caught in the roots, roots holding me tight, rocks and stones pressing against me, and I can't sleep, can't sleep, I think I'm going crazy, I think I *am* crazy, and I start crying and I cry so hard my pillow is wet, and I stop crying and throw the pillow on the floor and the mockingbird keeps singing.

I lie on my back again and stare at the shadows on the ceiling, I lie on my side and stare at the Virgin Mary on my bureau, she stands there, her head down, her arms by her sides. My mother gave her to me one Christmas. I used to pray to her for all sorts of things—Hail, Mary, full of grace, don't let me have impure thoughts, don't let me flunk chemistry, let Don ask me to the junior prom. I passed chemistry but I think that was because Mr. Haskins thought I couldn't help being dumb. The other two prayers she didn't answer.

I can also see the photos I keep in the frame of my mirror, mostly Ellie and me acting silly, some I took at parties at Paul's house, down in the rec room. There's one of Buddy and Cheryl grinning at me, their arms around each other. I should burn that one, I don't want to see it. I should put all the pictures in a shoebox and hide it on a shelf in my closet. They belong to a time that doesn't exist anymore.

Will I ever sleep, will I ever forget the blood, will life ever be the same as before . . . ?

## PART FOUR

# What If He Didn't?

# Just Suppose

## NORA

TWO days before the funeral, the police release Buddy. They held him for forty-eight hours. They gave him two lie detector tests. They questioned him, but he said he didn't do it, he was looking for the girls, that's why he was at the bridge. And he kept on looking for them, driving up and down Forty-Third Street, back and forth between Eastern and the park, looking looking looking.

"And all along, all the time he was *looking*," Ellie says, "he knew exactly where they were. He shot them, he hid them in the bushes, he left them there. How could he do that?"

"How could *anyone*?" I ask. I'm wondering if I should say What if it wasn't Buddy, what if it was somebody else?

We're sitting on my back porch, drinking cherry Kool-Aid and eating Oreos. It's more hot and humid than yesterday—if that's possible. Insects buzz in the maple tree. Mom has gone to the store. Billy is playing with his friends. We're all alone. Just us and our ghosts.

"I can't believe the police let him go," Ellie says. "We saw him on the bridge, he has a gun, he was mad at Cheryl. What more do they need to charge him?" Her voice is bitter.

I wrap my arms around my knees and draw them close to my chest. "Buddy's gun wasn't the same as the murder weapon," I say. "The *Sun* said it was just an air rifle."

Ellie narrows her eyes. She's getting mad, I can tell. "Are you on his side or something?"

"No, of course not." I stumble over my words. "I just don't understand it. No one in his right mind could do something like that and then sit there on the bridge in plain sight, drive us to school—"

"He's crazy," Ellie interrupts. Her mind is made up: Buddy did it, he did it, he killed them. "He should be locked up forever."

I hug my knees tighter. "But he was in my photography class. He signed my yearbook." I lift my head and stare at her so hard, everything behind her goes out of focus, just a green blur of grass and leaves. "What if he didn't do it?"

Just asking the question makes me dizzy. Everyone believes Buddy did it. They want him in jail so they don't have to be scared someone's still out there with a gun. Solve the case, get the killer off the streets, make us safe. *I* want to believe Buddy's guilty for exactly that reason. But he says he didn't do it. What if he's not lying? What if he really was looking for Cheryl and Bobbi Jo? Maybe he wanted to say he was sorry for getting mad, maybe he was still hoping she'd give him another chance. Isn't that what he asked us in the school parking lot?

I remember a picture he took of Cheryl sitting on a picnic table in the park, her jeans rolled just right, wearing her Eastern warm-up jacket with her name embroidered on the front, her blond hair backlit by the sun, flashing a big, toothy smile. It was a good photograph. Buddy had a nice camera, a thirty-five millimeter, he told me, not a Kodak Hawkeye like mine. You need a good lens to take a good picture, he'd told me.

"What do you mean, 'What if he didn't do it'?" My question has shocked Ellie. "We both had the same dream," she reminds me. "Cheryl and Bobbi Jo *told* us Buddy did it. Everyone thinks he did. My parents, the Boyds, the Millers, *everyone.*"

"But what if he didn't?" My voice comes out small and whiny, a kid's voice. "What if it was that guy he says he saw in the woods?"

"Good grief, Nora." Ellie stares at me as if I've lost my mind. "He never saw anyone, he made that up."

I crunch the last piece of ice in my glass. Maybe he did make it up, but I'm thinking of last winter, in Paul's rec room. Buddy's dancing slow, swaying with Cheryl, his arms around her waist, her arms around his neck, their bodies so close you'd think they shared the same heart. The lights are low, the song is "Only You." Cheryl's wearing his class ring on a chain around her neck. He's whispering in her ear, she's smiling.

I'm sitting on the couch drinking a Coke and watching them, wishing I had a boyfriend who'd dance with me like that. Love me like that. The Platters' voices blend. They sing of love and destiny and dreams. My heart aches with loneliness.

That girl smiling in the photograph, that girl kissing Buddy . . . how can she be dead? How could Buddy have killed her?

I start crying again. I can't stand it.

My tears set Ellie off, and she cries too. We're back in that day, that endless day in the park.

## MISTER DEATH

H E reads the morning *Sun.* They've let Buddy go. They think he's innocent after all. Forty-eight hours of questioning and lie detector tests, but no murder weapon. No confession. No witness.

He's never liked Buddy, tough guy with his greased-back duck-tail and Levi's riding low on his skinny hips. Not smart, probably never read a book in his life. He knows the type—a hot rod magazine is his idea of literature. Or the lyrics to something like "Blue Suede Shoes."

No, not lyrics. Words, the words to "Blue Suede Shoes."

He thinks Buddy's not feeling so tough now.

To shake things up, he decides to make an anonymous call to the police. He tells them he saw a teenage boy in the picnic grove that morning firing a rifle, at least ten shots, maybe more. The police ask him to come in and talk to them in person, but he hangs up, amused by his own daring.

The next day the phone call's in the paper: "Though the anonymous tip led to the discovery of a dozen .22 shell casings near a forked tree, police weren't able to get the caller to come in, and they suspect it might have been the killer himself."

He can't help laughing when he reads it.

# The Viewing

## NORA

AFTER a while, Ellie and I get up and go inside. It's four thirty, time for *The Edge of Night*. When I was little, I listened to soap operas if I was sick and felt too bad to read. Most of them were about love and hospitals, but *The Edge of Night* is more like a detective show. It takes place in a small town where crime is an everyday sort of thing. Nancy Drew would have felt right at home in Monticello. At any rate, it's just unrealistic enough to take our minds off our own edge of night.

Ellie's been here all day because she can't stand to be home alone. Her mother dropped her off on her way to work and she's picking us both up on her way to Hausner's Funeral Home for the viewing. Viewing—people enjoy scenic views, they express their views, they change their views, they take dim views, they view the dead.

When the show's over, we go up to my room and peel off our shorts and blouses and change into black skirts and white blouses, what we wear when we sing in glee club. Our bodies are damp with perspiration. Our clothes stick to us.

We hear Mom come home and go to meet her. "Do I look all

right?" I ask Mom. "Is my skirt too tight?" I tug at it, thinking I've drunk too many milk shakes, eaten too many french fries this year. "Should I iron my blouse?"

"You look fine." Mom hugs me.

"My hair, though. It's frizzy. My bangs are too curly."

"Nora, stop thinking about yourself," Mom says.

I blush and look at my feet, sure my white Cuban heels are wrong with my black skirt. Doesn't Mom know how hard this is? I've never been inside Hausner's. I don't even like to walk past it. It sits there like it's waiting for you, a big white house on a green lawn with flower beds and a fountain, right there in plain sight on Delaney Avenue.

It's not a house, though, it's a home, which in this case means a home for the dead. Temporary quarters, a rooming house without bed or board, just a coffin. It's horrible to walk by and know what's in there, who's in there—people who used to walk past just like I walk past. Now I have to go through the door. I have to see what I don't want to see.

A car pulls up out front. Mrs. O'Brien goes into the kitchen to talk to Mom. They both look at Ellie and me from time to time. I can't hear what they're saying, but I know they're glad Ellie and I are here and not at Hausner's. We're safe. Just because Ellie couldn't get her pin fastened. She's wearing it now, I notice. A charm against evil.

In the car, we squeeze into the front seat, Ellie in the middle next to her mother, me by the open window, trying not to think about what the wind is doing to my hair. I remind myself I am not the one who will be viewed.

Mrs. O'Brien makes idle conversation, asking about our day,

commenting on the weather, the hottest summer she can re-member, pointing out a new jewelry shop on Delaney Avenue, wav-ing to someone she knows. Neither Ellie nor I have much to say. I'm aware of how tense my body is, even my fists are clenched. I try to relax, but next to me, her shoulder touching mine, I can feel the same tension in Ellie.

All too soon, Mrs. O'Brien is parking her car in the lot behind Hausner's. It's packed with cars already. Everything from new Buicks to ratty old cars, the kind kids drive. Buddy's black Ford isn't there. I don't think he'd dare to come.

I walk up the brick sidewalk on shaky legs. The fountain splashes. Flower beds line the walk, blooming with bursts of red and yellow. Bees buzz around the blossoms. The lawn is green, freshly cut, not a weed to be seen. Birds sing in the neatly clipped shrubbery. The heat of the day hasn't cooled, but a little breeze ruffles leaves and flowers and bushes, releasing the scent of roses.

"Come on, girls," Mrs. O'Brien says softly. Taking us each by the arm, she leads us gently inside. After the brilliant sunlight, the green grass, the bright flowers, the hall is so dark I can't see for a moment. Everything is quiet. Thick carpet mutes our footsteps. A strange scent fills my nose—funeral flowers and something else. Furniture wax, maybe. Mrs. O'Brien hands Ellie a pen and she writes her name in both books, Cheryl's and Bobbi Jo's.

I take the pen and write my name beneath Ellie's. I remember signing Cheryl's yearbook just last week—*Good luck to a good friend, may you always be as happy as you are now! Don't forget chemistry and how we almost blew up the whole class! See you this summer! Nora.*

How stupid, I think, to have written such a silly thing.

Paul, Charlie, and Walt come in just as I lay the pen down. Sun blind like we were, they almost bump into us. They're wearing suits, white shirts ironed stiff, tightly knotted ties. They look like little boys in someone else's clothes.

We whisper hellos. Mrs. O'Brien gives all three boys a hug. We wait while they write their names in the two books and then we walk down the hall to a sign that says BARBARA JOSEPHINE BOYD and CHERYL LOUISE MILLER. For a moment, I think there's been a mistake. They've put a stranger in the room. Then I realize that Bobbi Jo's real name must be Barbara Josephine. It doesn't suit her.

Through the open door, we see a crowd of people, kids from school, parents from the neighborhood, teachers, strangers. People are crying. The kids look bewildered, stunned. I'm having trouble breathing, I think I might faint, but I allow Mrs. O'Brien to lead me into the room.

Two white coffins stand side by side, almost hidden by flower arrangements. The Boyds and the Millers stand beside their daughters, their faces pale and worn with sorrow. Mrs. O'Brien nudges Ellie and me forward. We speak our regrets to the Boyds and the Millers, our voices low and indistinct, blurred with sadness and uncertainty. Nothing we can say will ever be enough. Nothing we can say will help. Nothing we can say can make anyone feel better.

"We're so sorry, so sorry." My throat closes up. I can't say anything else.

Mrs. Boyd squeezes our hands, so does Mrs. Miller. "Thank you for coming," they both say, speaking in unison as if they've practiced.

Then we pass the coffins. Cheryl on the right, Bobbi Jo on the left. They look at peace, their faces smooth—too smooth, I think later, and wonder how the funeral parlor hid the bullet wounds. Bobbi Jo has a slight frown on her face, just as she had in life when she was puzzled about something. Cheryl has no expression. Their eyes are closed. They have secrets they'll never tell, they know what we don't know. No motion now, no force. They neither hear nor see—but they know, they know.

We back away, Ellie and me. It's not right to look at them too long. Do we expect them to open their eyes and laugh and shout "Fooled you!"? And then Hausner's will bring in a cake and the party will start and the music will play and we'll all dance, even old aunts and uncles and grandparents.

Next to me, a man is talking to another man about an accident that held up traffic on his way home from work. A woman turns to her husband and says, "Don't forget, we have to stop at High's and pick up a quart of milk."

Her husband lights a cigarette and nods. "Do you have enough cheese and bread?"

Ellie and I move away from the smoke, but most of the adults in the room are smoking, so it's useless. It seems disrespectful to smoke and talk about ordinary things like traffic jams and groceries when two dead girls are lying a few feet away in a bower of flowers.

Nearby a group of women compare vacation plans. One's going to Ocean City, another to Atlantic City, a third to the mountains. Don't they realize Bobbi Jo and Cheryl are never going anywhere again?

Just when I think I might start screaming at people to shut up, Charlie grabs my hand. "Come on, let's get out of here."

I look for Ellie. She and Paul are talking to her mother. "But you haven't had dinner," Mrs. O'Brien says.

"It's too hot to eat," Ellie says. "The flowers, they're making me feel sick to my stomach. The smell . . ."

"We'll grab a hamburger if we get hungry," Paul says.

"Don't stay out late," Mrs. O'Brien says.

Outside, I take a deep breath of fresh air. Early evening sunlight stretches across the grass, crisscrossing the lawn with shadows. Birds cartwheel across the sky. A car drives by, leaving a trail of music in the air—"Maybelline." The driver doesn't look at Hausner's, doesn't wonder when he'll be inside mourning someone's death.

We get in Paul's old Plymouth and drive away. I can almost hear Cheryl and Bobbi Jo crying "Wait for us, don't leave us here." I imagine them running along beside the car, their fingers reaching for the door handles, but you can see through them, they can't hold on to anything, they fall behind.

"Where to?" Paul asks.

"Maybe Ellie's not hungry," Charlie says, "but I'm starving. How about Top's Drive-In for a burger?"

"Sounds great to me," Paul says. "Any objections?"

We all agree and head down Route 40. The radio blasts "Midnight Special," summer air blows through the car, and we all try extra hard to act like it's an ordinary evening and we're having a great time. We sing along with the radio, we laugh at Paul and Charlie's dumb jokes. "Why did the little moron tiptoe past the medicine cabinet?" Paul asks. "Because he didn't want to wake the sleeping pills," we all shout. "Why did the little moron drive his car off the cliff?" Charlie asks. "Because he wanted to test his air brakes," we all shout again, laughing like we never heard these jokes a million times, laughing like they're actually funny.

By the time we place our order at Top's Drive-In, Charlie has moved on to sick jokes, like the mother who tells her kid, "Stop running around in circles or I'll nail your other foot to the floor."

After two or three, Paul says, "That's about as funny as a truck-load of dead babies."

We've heard that one, too, but suddenly the jokes aren't funny. We sit there staring at our huge hamburgers and thick shakes and french fries. I'm not hungry after all.

"I can't believe they're dead," Charlie says in a small sad voice.

"Me either," Paul says.

"I keep thinking the phone will ring," Ellie says, "and it will be Bobbi Jo asking me if I want to go to Walgreen's and have a cherry Coke or something."

I feel a disconnection because I didn't really know either girl as well as the others. They all lived in the same neighborhood and saw each other all the time. I live two miles away on the other side of town.

They start reminiscing then, talking about the time Cheryl got stung by a bee on her behind and couldn't sit down for almost a week, and how Bobbi Jo fell through the ice at the lake and Paul and Charlie pulled her out and their jeans froze on the way home, and Cheryl was the best roller skater in their neighborhood and she loved horses and dogs, and Bobbi Jo was scared to climb down from a tree once and they had to get her father to rescue her. And how about the time Cheryl and Nora were lab partners in chemistry, Ellie said, and they forgot to cover their thistle tubes in an experiment and combustible gas escaped into the classroom and everyone had to evacuate.

"Mr. Haskins almost killed us," I say. "We were so embarrassed."

By the time we finish telling stories, we realize we've eaten everything. I guess we were hungry after all. But I feel bad, because even though we were sharing good stories, it was like talking behind their backs. They weren't here to add their opinion. Maybe we had the details wrong. Maybe we left out something important, maybe Bobbi Jo would have said, "Charlie, you said the ice was safe, you swore it was."

On the way home, we drive past Hausner's. The outside lights are off, but a dim light shines in each window. I wonder which one is Cheryl and Bobbi Jo's. I'm glad they're not lying in the dark. Let perpetual light shine on them . . . that's from the Mass, the priest will say it tomorrow.

"Bobbi Jo was afraid of the dark," Ellie says softly. "She couldn't sleep without a night-light."

# The Last Visit

## BUDDY

LATE at night when nobody will see me I drive past the funeral parlor and park a block away just in case somebody recognizes my car. I walk back and sit in the shadows on the front steps. I can smell the roses, which are gray in the moonlight. The grass is gray, the trees are black, and shadows move across the lawn, changing every time the wind blows. Delaney Avenue is deserted, just a strip of gray in the dark. Except for these stupid bugs, crickets or something, making a helluva annoying noise, the night is still. Dead still, you could say.

Behind me is a closed door. I went in there once for my grandmother's viewing and funeral, she wasn't a church type. So I know what it's like. All these rooms, and in each room is a coffin with a dead person inside—a corpse, a stiff—and there are lots of stinking flowers but you smell death anyway.

My grandmother was gray like cement or something, and her mouth was sewed shut and so were her eyes, you could tell if you looked close, and my mother made me look close, she made me kiss her, and she was cold and hard and I hated doing it and I hated my mother for making me do it. I was only seven years old. Just a little kid. I didn't even like my grandmother. She was one mean old lady and never even gave me a kiss when she was alive, so why did I have to kiss her when she was dead?

If I could of gone to the viewing, I would of kissed Cheryl goodbye. I wanted to. I must be crazy for thinking that.

But damn I wanted to see her one last time, she was my girl, I loved her, I loved her more than that SOB Ralph with his stupid basketball team, she would of got tired of him, she would of come back to me like she always did. Or he would of dumped her when he got what he wanted because why else would a guy like him date a girl like Cheryl? He ran with the cheerleaders and the athletes, not girls like Cheryl who took typing and shorthand because she didn't have the money for college.

Why does everybody think I did it? Never, I would never, never never. She was no angel but I loved her. Really and truly. I wanted to marry her.

The thing is, I can see why they might think I did it. Ellie and Nora saw me on the bridge, they spread the word, but why would I have been sitting there if I'd killed them? I would of hid, I would of killed Ellie and Nora, you see what I'm saying?

But who else could of done it? The cops don't know and I don't know. And believe me, I've racked my brain till my head aches trying to come up with the killer. I think back to the party, she went off in the woods with Ralph, I saw her go, but why would he kill her and Bobbi Jo?

And the other guys, the ones that used to be my friends, I can't think of a reason for any of them to do it.

I really did see somebody in the woods but I never got a good look at him. He was off the path, in the bushes, his back was turned.

I figured it was just some guy taking a leak. Now I believe I saw the killer, but I got no idea who he was or what he looked like or if he even had a gun.

I sit here on these hard steps, as close to Cheryl as I'll ever be now, and I can almost hear her saying *I'm sorry, Buddy, I wish I could tell you who killed me and Bobbi Jo.*

Maybe it was a stranger, someone she didn't know, someone she'd never seen before, a crazy man in the woods. Some nut from Spring Grove. It must of been. There's nobody else.

I put my head on my knees and whisper her name over and over again, Cheryl, Cheryl, Cheryl, until it becomes a sound, a whisper of wind, and it isn't her name and she's not dead but at home, sleeping in her bed.

I think of her back in the old days when she was my girl and it's my ring she wears on a chain around her neck and we're in my car, parked on a dead-end street near the lake. It's a cold night and the moon shines on her face, on her long blond hair, and the Platters are singing "The Magic Touch" and we've made out so long the windows are steamed up and we both have the magic touch and it's wonderful wonderful.

Damn it to hell, I love that girl and I want her back and if I find out who took her away from me I'll kill the bastard.

## PART FIVE

# Funerals and Burials and Afterward

# Bobbi Jo's Funeral

## NORA

THE next morning, Mom drives me to St. John the Divine for Bobbi Jo's funeral. Just her and me. Daddy's at work and Billy's afraid to see a dead person. I'm wearing the only other suitable outfit I own, a full purple skirt over a crinoline, a white blouse printed with tiny purple flowers, and my white pumps, slightly run down at the heels and scuffed on the toes. Since it's a Requiem Mass, I'm also wearing a little white straw hat and white gloves.

The first thing I see at the church is the hearse parked at the curb. It's big and black, clean and shiny. The sunlight bounces off the windshield and hurts my eyes. I turn my head. I don't want to think about the hearse. And where it's going.

People go slowly up the church steps and through the doors and they're wearing black and their heads are bowed. My stomach lurches and I feel empty, hollow, like nothing is real.

Mom parks and gets out of the car. "Come on, Nora," she says gently. "It's almost time for Mass to begin."

The church windows are open and the fans whir but nothing helps. It's stifling hot. Bobbi Jo's white coffin is in front of the altar, flanked by dozens of wreaths and sprays of flowers. The organist plays "*Ave Maria*" softly, a song that always makes me cry for something I don't have and don't even know about.

We dip our fingers into the holy water, genuflect, and make the sign of the cross. Even though we're half an hour early, almost all the seats are filled. We find a pew with room for us both and kneel to pray. Mom has her rosary. I hear the beads click. She bends her head. The brim of her hat hides her face.

I try hard to come up with a prayer, but I can't. Instead I stare at Christ hanging on his cross, his body twisted, his wounds bloody, his face racked with pain.

*why did you let them die why did you let it happen what kind of God are you I can't believe in you anymore*

I hold my breath and wait. Surely I'll be struck dead for thinking thoughts like this in church. Nothing happens. He isn't there, he didn't hear, he doesn't care.

Trickles of sweat run down my back. I glance at Mom, still kneeling, still praying. Why can't I believe like I used to? What's wrong with me? I close my eyes so tightly I see blackness like space, the unending empty universe I'm spinning through along with everyone else in this church, in this world, roll'd round, roll'd round, roll'd round on earth's diurnal course, first morning then noon then night, death, eternal darkness, let the perpetual light shine, let the midnight special shine its light on me . . .

That's what goes through my head instead of the prayer I'm trying to say. I'm crazy, bad, possessed by the devil, the priest will try to get rid of him and when that doesn't work they'll lock me up forever in Spring Grove.

Beside me, Mom sits with a sigh. The pew creaks.

I give up on prayer and sit back. Mom pats my hand. What if

she knew her daughter, the one sitting beside her in the purple skirt and the white blouse with the pretty little purple flowers, was thinking about insane asylums instead of praying? But then, how do I know what *she's* thinking? Or anyone else?

What if I stand up right now and say, How can you believe in a God who let this happen? I imagine faces turning to me, pale with shock. I'm scared I'll do it. I hold my hands tightly, I tense my whole body. Keep quiet, I tell myself. Don't move.

And then the priest enters and we kneel while he makes the sign of the cross. I follow the Latin in my missal, the one I was given when I was conformed, I mean *confirmed.* Back when I believed every word, when I thought God watched over us and kept us safe and if we were good—and I tried so hard to be good—we would go to heaven, maybe after a few centuries in purgatory.

"Thanks be to God." My missal translates what the priest says. "In the name of the Father, the Son, and the Holy Spirit. Amen."

Then he clasps his hands against his chest and says in Latin, "I will go in to the Altar of God."

And the altar boys say, "To God, Who giveth joy to my youth."

The joy of my youth is gone, I think. I look around, wondering where Ellie is, wishing we were sitting together. Maybe with her beside me, I'd feel calm, I'd keep my thoughts under control.

The Mass goes on. I let the Latin fade out of hearing, I do not look at my missal. I hear quiet sobs. People cough. Sighs whisper through the church and gather around the silent coffin. A bird flies by the open window, a flash of red feathers against a blue sky.

The choir sings, "Oh, Mother dear, oh pray for me whilst far from heaven and thee, I wander in a fragile barque o'er life's tempestuous sea." It's a mournful hymn, sung slowly. My barque is so fragile, life is so tempestuous, I will sink any minute. I reach out and hold Mom's hand. Her fingers tighten on mine. Protect me, keep me safe, I beg her silently.

The communion line forms. I take my place behind Mom and move forward slowly, head bowed, hands clasped, trying to look devout, trying to believe this really is Christ's blood, Christ's flesh that I am about to receive, trying not to look at Bobbi Jo lying so still in that white coffin, but I can't keep my eyes away. All this going on around you, yet you do not hear or see, roll'd round, roll'd round in eternal light with rocks and stones and saints, forevermore with thy saints because thou art gracious and your sins are forgiven . . .

The priest's words mix silently with mine and I kneel to receive the body and blood of Christ, *in spiritu sanctu*. Even though I am not worthy for the Lord to enter me, I open my mouth and he puts the wafer on my tongue. It sticks to the roof of my mouth and I pry it off gently with my tongue, taking care not chew it, and swallow. Its hard edge presses against my throat, sticking for a moment.

Head down, I walk back to my seat and kneel as I'm expected to, but I still can't pray. I wonder how many of the people are actually praying right now. And the ones who are—do they truly believe anyone is listening? Is it all Let's pretend we believe and maybe it will be true? Like the flying carpet in *Let's Pretend,* the radio show I loved when I was a kid. But I'm not a kid now. And there's no magic carpet. Or happily ever after or life after death or anything but darkness and rocks and stones and trees.

At last the Mass draws to a close and the priest reads my favorite part, the last Gospel according to St. John. I love it because it's so mysterious—you can't completely understand the Word, how it was with God and was God and was there in the beginning and without him was nothing made that has been made. The word is life and life is the light of men and it shines in the darkness.

I find myself thinking about light and darkness and how often those words are used in the Mass, as if everything is a battle between light and dark and life and death and good and evil, and I know that part is true, I believe that. And I feel a little better listening to the familiar words drift through the church like echoes from the past, going back and back and back in time, spoken once by priests who are now dust just as this priest will be and I will be and everyone sitting here will be. The dark will claim us. There's no escape.

## MISTER DEATH

I T'S the day of the funerals. He stands at the window and watches the cars pass his house on their way to the church. At least a dozen, he thinks—no, more than that. They have their headlights on, they drive slowly. As if they can keep those girls here a little longer. Dead is dead.

But wait, who's that? He presses his face against the glass. It's his brother, wearing their father's dark suit, too long in the sleeves, too long in the legs, walking fast, head down, not looking at anyone or anything.

He wants to run after him, stop him, but that would draw too much attention. Better not. Better let him go and hope he doesn't stand up in church and confess. He wouldn't do that, couldn't. If his father hadn't taken the car to work, he'd drive after him, grab him, force him into the car, keep him from going, but he's already out of sight, heading for St. John the Divine at the top of the hill.

He should have done it without his brother. He should have known the little weasel would betray them.

His mother comes up behind him so quietly, he doesn't know

she's there until she touches his arm. He jumps, startled. "What the hell are you doing, sneaking up on me like that?"

She backs away. His brother's mother, all right. Weak, stupid, never standing up to anyone. Let his father beat him half senseless when he was a kid. Never said anything for fear he'd turn on her. God, what a family he has. You think any of them would care if he was the one who was shot instead of the one who did the shooting?

"I'm sorry," she says in that whiny voice of hers. "I didn't mean to—"

"Just leave me alone." To test her, he raises his hand as if he might hit her. She raises an arm to protect herself and backs away. As if that helps when his father is in a fighting mood.

"I just wondered if you want lunch."

He shakes his head, goes to his room, and shuts the door. He pulls a record out and puts it on the turntable. Turns it up as loud as he can. Mozart's *Requiem*. He's in the mood for a requiem, especially this one. It's Mozart's last work; he died before he finished it. He wrote it for himself, thought he'd been poisoned, knew he was dying. Mozart, a genius, a prodigy, dead before his time. When people mourn, they should mourn for great men, not silly little bitches.

# Ball on a Chain

## BUDDY

THE funerals are today. I sit in my car near the Catholic church and watch. I can't go in there, they don't want me, they think I killed her and Cheryl. Besides, I hate Catholics. Idol worshipers, bead mumblers, mackerel snappers, thinking they're the only ones who know the truth about God and Jesus and the Holy Ghost—the biggest nonsense of all. Three Gods in one. One is enough, if you ask me.

Bobbi Jo tried to explain the Holy Ghost once. If I wasn't so sad right now I'd laugh at the memory, her forehead creased, trying to describe something she didn't understand herself. It's the spirit of God, she said, and it's in all of us, helping us do the right thing, be wise, you know? Like when you're taking a test, you pray to the Holy Ghost to help you . . .

Damn, she was a sweet kid.

I look across the street. The priest has come out, swinging some ball on a chain, it's smoking like something's burning inside. I don't know what it is or why he's doing it. Pagan crap. It scares me. I think Bobbi Jo's soul might be inside that ball.

I know that's crazy, but that's how I am now. Crazy. I slept last night under a bush in front of Hausner's because I didn't want Cheryl and Bobbi Jo to be alone in there. What do you think of that? Spring Grove, here I come. They've got a padded cell ready for me. And a matching straitjacket.

Jesus, here's the coffin. Is Bobbi Jo really in that box? I try to imagine her lying still, not laughing and jumping up every five minutes. She was never one to sit around. No, she always had to be doing something. She thought she was so grown up, but I used to see her playing jump rope with her little sister, those blond curls shining in the sun. That laugh—I can still hear it, a kid's laugh. Cute, she was so cute.

Now they're putting her in the hearse. Paul and Charlie are helping. They used to be my friends. We'd ride around in my car, drink some beer, smoke some cigarettes, drag race tough guys from Fullerton, hang out at Top's looking for girls. Now they hate me. Like everybody else in this town.

I see Bobbi Jo's parents on the church steps. They look bad—ashy gray, old. I can't look at them or the little sisters who look so much like Bobbi Jo. I slide down in the seat and grip the wheel and hope no one notices my car. Or me in it, bawling like a kid.

## Bobbi Jo's Funeral Procession

### NORA

WE stand and wait for the recessional. The choir is singing a Latin hymn, and the organ echoes in the church. The priest and the altar boys lead the way, swinging the censer and filling the air with the choking scent of burning incense. The coffin comes next, carried by six pallbearers. Bobbi Jo's Uncle Jim, Mr. O'Brien, and Mr. Farrell from down the street, Charlie and Paul and one of Bobbi Jo's cousins. The men are grim-faced and tense. Charlie and Paul and the cousin are pale and scared. Bobbi Jo's mother and father walk behind the coffin, holding the hands of the two little sisters.

Mom whispers, "The poor woman, she looks like she's about to faint."

My hand seeks hers again, as if it has a life of its own. She squeezes it and I lean against her, comforted by the familiar smell of her, her shampoo, a trace of cologne, and Mum deodorant.

Slowly, pew by pew, the church empties. The Boyds stand at the door and thank people for coming. Mr. Boyd seems to be holding his wife up. Tears run down her face unchecked, as if she doesn't know she's crying. The little sisters squint in the sun and fidget as if they can't quite remember why they're here.

The funeral procession forms. Two policemen on motorcycles lead the way, lights flashing, sirens blaring. So many cars, all with their headlights on, driving slowly down the familiar streets of Elmgrove, passing places we used to go with Cheryl and Bobbi Jo. The drugstore. The movie theater. Woolworth's Five and Dime. The record shop. Top's Drive-In, the swimming pool, the park, the lake, Eastern High School. I look at them all as if I'll never see them again. As if I'm dead too.

The people we pass stop and watch the cars go by, their faces solemn in the summer sunshine. Some whisper to their friends. The friends nod. They know whose funeral this is.

We go through traffic lights all the way down Route 40 and through the black iron gates of New Cathedral Cemetery.

# Bobbi Jo's Burial

## NORA

At the graveyard I find Ellie in the crowd, and we stand together while the priest says more prayers. "May Barbara Josephine's soul and the souls of all the faithful departed rest in peace and let perpetual light shine on them . . ." His voice drones, the words run together, they blend with the breeze blowing through the trees and the birds singing in shady green places.

The coffin rests precariously on canvas straps above the grave. The grass buzzes with insects. Birds sing. Squirrels dart from tree to tree. Pigeons strut and peck at the gravel path. Far off across the lawn, I see another funeral in progress. Thunderheads loom up and cast dark shadows. The breeze rocks the coffin. Down will come baby, coffin and all.

The priest leads us in the Lord's Prayer and blesses us all. *"In nomine Patris, et Filii, et Spiritus Sancti."*

We make the sign of the cross and say amen.

It's time for everyone but the family to leave. With one last look at the coffin, Ellie and I follow our mothers across the grass to the waiting cars.

"Did you notice that strange guy?" Ellie asks.

I shake my head.

"He was over there." She points at a tall oak and we both look closely. He's nowhere to be seen.

"He had on a suit that was way too big," Ellie says. "The sleeves practically covered his fingers and the trouser cuffs dragged on the ground."

"Did you see him at church?"

She shrugs. "He could have been there."

"Maybe he's a cousin or the son of a family friend."

She shakes her head, stares at the place where she saw the boy. "I can't explain it. There was just something creepy about him. Strange. Like he didn't belong here and he knew it and that's why he was kind of hiding behind the tree."

While she's telling me this, thunder rumbles in the distance and the sky gets darker. A little shiver races across my skin. We hurry to catch up with our mothers so we can go on to Cheryl's funeral.

# Sacred to the Memory

## BUDDY

I WAIT until the last car drives away, and then I follow the funeral procession to the graveyard, always keeping a few non-funeral cars between me and the others. I don't want anybody looking out the rear window and seeing me.

New Cathedral Cemetery. I've driven past it but never paid any attention to it. Never have liked cemeteries. Now I'm driving slowly through its tall gates, past this little place that looks like a toll-booth. Since it's Catholic, I expect some priest to be in there with his hand out. But there's just some old guy, keeping an eye on things, I guess.

The cemetery's huge. Tombstones and angels and Catholic crap everywhere. I hate the idea of Bobbi Jo being in this place.

I find a parking place pretty far from the funeral. Like some goddamn thief, I sneak across the lawn, using headstones and trees as cover. It reminds me of playing war when I was a kid. Now it's Elmgrove against me. Don't let them see you, don't let them catch you.

When I'm close enough to see everything, I stand behind a tall stone cross. SACRED TO THE MEMORY OF JONATHAN ALLBRIGHT WHO

DEPARTED THIS LIFE ON 15 JUNE 1898. FREE FROM LIFE'S CARE, HE RESTS IN THE ARMS OF JESUS.

The priest is still swinging that damn ball on a chain. The breeze carries the burning smell all the way to me. Looks like he's praying, too, but I can't hear the words which are probably in Latin anyway. If Bobbi Jo was here instead of in that goddamn box, she'd probably try to explain what the ball was all about. And why priests talk in a language no one but them and Latin teachers understand. A dead language for dead people.

I notice someone else is watching the funeral, some kid in a black suit a scarecrow might think looked good. He's too far away for me to see his face. I wonder why he's here. Maybe he's the type who likes funerals.

My grandmother read the obituaries every day to find funerals close enough to walk to. Used to drag me along with her when I was too little to get away from her. Of course she was nuttier than a fruitcake. Died at Spring Grove. There's something to be proud of.

I notice a big cloud has covered the sun. I hope it doesn't rain until after Cheryl's funeral.

The crowd's moving toward their cars, the boy's gone, and I hurry toward my car. I hate to leave Bobbi Jo in this place, but I need to be out of here before anyone spots me.

# Cheryl's Funeral

## Nora

THE crowd seems even bigger at Cheryl's funeral, maybe because the Baptist church is smaller. And very plain. No statues of the Virgin Mary, no cross hanging over the altar with Christ's twisted body and anguished face looking down at you. No candles to light if you drop a penny in the box. No holy water, no stations of the cross. No kneelers. No pews. Just wooden chairs.

Cheryl's white coffin is in front of the altar, a table covered with a white cloth. Her flowers fill the church with a funeral-home smell, artificial and too sweet, almost heavy. Beside the coffin is the minister, a slim man in a plain business suit. His glasses catch the changing light.

The service begins. No Mass, no Latin, no incense, no organ. Baptists keep things short and simple. Their hymns are in English and everyone sings them. Even I know some of the words. A pianist accompanies the congregation. She sits in front instead of being hidden away in a choir loft.

I notice Ellie isn't singing, she's gotten out her rosary and is praying. I wonder if it's a sin to sing Protestant hymns, but then I remember I don't believe in religion anymore so why should I care what the Catholic church thinks. Sin or no sin, I go on singing when they get to the chorus because that's the only part I know, and I don't even know why or how I know it.

The minister speaks softly of Cheryl's short life and its tragic end. He begs us not to lose our faith in God, telling us God moves in mysterious ways and everything is done with a purpose.

"'For now we see through a glass darkly,'" he says, "'but then face to face: now I know in part; but then shall I know even as also I am known.'"

I like the way the words sound, but except for seeing through a glass darkly I'm not sure what they mean. I look over at Ellie to see if she understands, but she's still praying the rosary, lips moving, oblivious of the looks she's receiving from two women sitting on her other side. *Bead mumbler,* they must be thinking.

The minister says a few more prayers. The congregation sings "In the Garden," and I join in as if I was raised a Baptist. I find myself wishing Catholics sang hymns like this with a simple tune everyone can sing, not just the choir.

People stand as the pallbearers carry the coffin down the aisle. The Millers follow slowly, hand in hand. Cheryl's brother Davy is about the same age as Billy. It's hard to imagine my brother walking that slowly, so pale and sad. It's not right. It's not fair. Life shouldn't be this sad.

Outside under a cloudy sky, we form another automobile caravan and drive down Wilkins Avenue to Loudon Park Cemetery on the other side of town.

The sky is stormier, full of dark, heavy clouds, but the rain holds off until the coffin is lowered into the grave. I turn away, unable to watch, and see Buddy lurking behind a tombstone. Our eyes meet and he shakes his head—*Don't say anything, look the other way*. He's pale, sad, worn down like an old man. The breeze has blown his hair into his eyes, destroying his pompadour. He looks smaller somehow, thinner. I glance at Ellie, hoping she hasn't seen him, but she's still praying. The rosary beads click as she says each prayer and moves to the next, over and over again just like the nuns taught us.

When I look back, Buddy's gone.

# Cheryl, Cheryl, Cheryl

## BUDDY

DAMN, Nora's looking over here. She sees me. I'm thinking it'll be like that science-fiction movie *The Invasion of the Body Snatchers,* she'll make some signal to the others and they'll come after me. But she just looks at me. And I look at her and shake my head. It's not like a crime show where the killer comes to the funeral. It's me, the dumb jerk who gets blamed for everything. Buddy did it, Buddy, he's the one, he did it. Except he didn't.

I back away, putting a tall gravestone between me and the funeral. That's when I see the kid in the black suit again. What the hell is he doing here? Who is he, anyway?

"Hey," I call, and he runs. I chase him. Damn, there's something strange about him. I almost catch him at the cemetery gate, but he dashes across the street right in front of a truck. Just misses getting hit. The light changes and I'm not risking my life chasing some oddball.

Like I said, maybe he just likes funerals. What do they call it? Morbid, yeah, that's the word. He's morbid. Like my grandmother.

I walk a couple of blocks and get in my car. Somebody told my mother the Millers and the Boyds would be getting together somewhere for a meal. Apparently that's something you do after a person dies. It's like saying life goes on. It seems kind of odd. Almost disrespectful. Like you're gloating.

I read in *National Geographic* there's a tribe in Africa who smear themselves with mud when somebody dies. They don't eat and they do all kinds of rituals to purify themselves in honor of the dead. To me, that makes a lot more sense than wearing black and going to a funeral and then having a big meal.

I drive around for a while, passing places we used to go. No radio. I can't stand hearing the songs we loved. Just the empty car and me.

It's hard to believe I'll never see Cheryl again. Never kiss her, never hear her voice. Never never never. No matter where I go or what I do, she'll always be in that cemetery. Is that why cemeteries have fences? To keep the dead in?

All the time I'm driving, up one street and down another, turning here, turning there, going around the block and back again, I keep thinking I'll see her, walking along ahead of me, swinging that purse of hers. I'll blow the horn and she'll turn around and give me that big grin. Hop in, I'll say, and she'll slide over close. I'll put my arm around her, her hand will stroke my thigh, we'll kiss. Where to, babe? I'll say, and she'll just laugh and say I don't care, wherever you want to go, Buddy, and that will be out by the dam, our favorite makeout place. And it will be just like it used to be. Before Ralph. Before the last day of school.

Cheryl, Cheryl, Cheryl. Your name goes round and round and

round in my head like a song I can't forget. I want to kill the son of a bitch who did this to you.

After an hour or so, I drive back to the cemetery. There's a hearse and a long line of cars ahead of me. Another funeral. More sad people. It's spattering rain now, and I'm thinking it's better funeral weather than the sunshine at Bobbi Jo's.

I pass the mourners. The pallbearers, ancient men in Elk uniforms, carry the coffin and set it down. Behind them old people get out of their cars slowly and hobble over the grass. I want to say, Do you know how lucky your dearly beloved is? He lived to be old, he had his whole life, but Cheryl and Bobbi Jo—they just got started, they were kids. Is that fair?

I'm scared I might actually yell this, so I drive on, keeping my thoughts locked up tight. But it's not fair, is it? Anybody can see that. Some people live to be old and others die when they're hardly more than born. It makes me sick.

I drive past Cheryl's grave. They've filled it in already and covered it with flower arrangements and wreaths and sprays and all that dead stuff people give to dead people. I hate those flowers but at least they hide the raw red earth piled on top of her. I drive a little farther, park the car, and walk back. It's raining harder now, but I don't care. I kneel down beside the flowers, smelling that sick hothouse smell. I can't believe all that dirt is on top of her, holding her down, keeping her there, separating her from me forever.

I tell her I couldn't come to her funeral, no one wanted me there. I tell her I wish it was me that was dead, not her. I tell her I'll always love her, I'll never forget her. Nevernevernever . . .

I try not to think about Ralph, he didn't come to her funeral, I looked for him, he definitely wasn't there. The son of a bitch.

I reach under the flowers and I scoop out a handful of dirt. I dump it on my head, I rub it into my hair, I smear it on my cheeks.

And then I sit there and let the rain fall.

## MISTER DEATH'S BROTHER

H E ought go home now—it's late, almost five, and it's raining—but he's scared of his brother. He knows he shouldn't have gone near the funerals, but he doesn't think anyone noticed him sitting quietly in the back of both churches. Funerals are like weddings, there are always people there that other people don't know but think belong there. Maybe they're relatives or family friends, who knows.

His brother can't understand, but he had to be there, had to see them one last time. He needed to know how he feels about the dead girls. Is he glad they're dead? Or is he sorry? Would he do it over again or would he stand up to his brother and say No I won't, I won't do it and if you do I'll tell. Would that have stopped him? Probably not.

At the funerals, he didn't feel as bad as he thought he would, but he still feels like maybe they shouldn't have done it. Those girls will be dead forever. He and his brother took their lives. Took them. Stole them. They can't give them back. Once you're dead you're dead. And nothing can bring you back to life.

But in a way, they deserved it for laughing at his brother. They made fun of him, they said he was a jerk, they told him he was ugly, they even said he was a fag. Not just that night but other times. Cheryl, especially. She made fun of him at school and made him miserable and didn't even care. It was all a joke to her, something to laugh at.

The other one, though. Bobbi Jo. Maybe she didn't deserve it. She was kind of nice when she wasn't with Cheryl.

His mind spins this way and that way, and he realizes he still doesn't know how he feels. Except for one thing. He wishes they hadn't done it. Him and his brother.

He walks so long, up one street and down another, block after block, always on side streets where nobody will see him. Once or twice he sees Buddy's car and ducks out of sight. He hopes Buddy hadn't recognized him in the graveyard.

Why did Buddy chase him? What would he have done if he'd caught him? Does he know it was him and his brother who did it? He shivers, more scared than ever.

The rain keeps falling, the day ends, dark comes, he's still walking, walking, walking. He doesn't have a watch but he knows it's late.

He wanders down the path and into the woods and stops under the tree his brother hid in. Ahead is the footbridge. He pictures the girls walking toward him, laughing and talking, wearing their pretty summer skirts, swinging their purses on long straps. The sun shines on their blond hair. Pretty girls. Blue-eyed girls.

He wonders if he should have run out of the woods and told them to turn around and go home. "Run," he could have cried, "run for your lives." But they would have laughed at him, and his brother would have shot them anyway and maybe shot him too for messing up.

They were pretty, those blue-eyed girls, but they were mean. No one has the right to laugh at someone because he wears the wrong clothes or combs his hair the wrong way or has pimples. He touches his own cheek, feels the rough skin, the pustules of acne, just like his brother's face. You can't help having pimples.

But still, all those people in the churches crying. So many sad people. He had no idea so many people would care. They'll get over it, they'll forget—but will he?

All that blood, the way they looked and felt, limp and heavy, their eyes looking at him but not seeing him or the sky or anything.

Dead blue eyes, their pretty skirts bloody, their pretty blond hair bloody, their pretty faces bloody, especially Cheryl's. Oh, she looked bad. He dreams about her every night, coming toward him, her face almost gone, her blouse and purple skirt red with blood, she's like a zombie. When he dies, she'll be waiting for him. She'll get him then, she'll drag him down to hell and leave him there. And she'll be laughing. Yes, she'll have the last laugh.

He starts crying. Oh God, let this be a dream, don't let me have done this, let me be sleeping while my brother does it. He paces up and down under the tree. He thinks Cheryl is watching him from the branches over his head, he thinks Bobbi Jo is on the other side of the tree, always moving so he can't catch her no matter how often he walks around the tree trunk.

He pounds his head against the tree until he feels blood run down his face. He's fourteen. How long will he have to live with what he's done? Forty years, fifty years, more?

He could get the gun and kill himself right now. Walk in the front door, go down the basement steps, lift the gun off the wall, and shoot himself. *Bang.* Just like his brother killing the girls.

He could but he won't. He's afraid to die, he's afraid of hell.

He wipes his forehead with his jacket sleeve and walks across the bridge, past the place where they died. His heart pounds, he gasps for breath, he's dizzy with fear. Their ghosts are here, he feels the ice cold touch of their fingers. With one on either side of him he runs, stumbling, stiff legged, sobbing, but they stay with him, laughing, calling him crater face, ugly.

You'll never get away from us, they say. No matter where you go, we'll follow you.

*Tuesday, June 19*
*Night*

---

# At the Reservoir with Charlie

## NORA

AFTER the burials, the Boyds and the Millers sponsor a dinner at St. John's school cafeteria. Ladies from the Sodality serve fried chicken, potato salad, baked beans, cole slaw, string beans cooked with bacon, rolls, sodas, and brownies. Families sit together, mothers and fathers keeping their children close. Safe. The priest and the minister stand in a corner talking softly.

Ellie and I fill our plates and sit at a table with other kids from school. No one knows what to say, no one eats much. The air is heavy with sorrow. It suffocates us, mutes our voices. Everyone is scared.

Ralph should be here, but he's not. He wasn't at the funerals or the burials either. I looked for him. And, yes, okay, it's true, I looked for Don, too. I was hoping—and this is really awful—I was hoping he'd see me in my purple skirt and my white blouse with the little purple flowers and think I looked pretty. It's my church outfit. I've never worn it to school. I feel horrible for thinking about things like that at a funeral.

I can't look at the Millers or the Boyds. I keep thinking Mrs. Miller and Mrs. Boyd wonder why their daughters are dead and not Ellie and me. I wonder about it too. If Ellie and I had been ready when Cheryl and Bobbi Jo came to the door, would all four of us be dead? Or would four have been too many for the killer to shoot? Would all four of us be alive? My mind goes back to this over and over again. Was it fate? Was it chance?

If Cheryl and Bobbi Jo were alive, we'd probably be at the Bijou, eating popcorn and watching *Picnic*. We'd seen it twice already, but it's our favorite movie. Especially the scene where Kim Novak and William Holden dance. That's the part we love. She comes down those steps and oh, I wish I was just like her. Unfortunately I'm more like her kid sister, but there's always a possibility that maybe someday. Some Day. I can hear the song in my head, "Moonglow." I see them clinging to each other, dancing slow and sexy, swaying, like Cheryl and Buddy.

It's hopeless. No matter what I think of, I always come back to Cheryl and Bobbi Jo.

After a while, Paul and Charlie take Ellie and me aside. "Do you want to go for a ride?" Charlie asks.

Ellie and I look at each other. Yes, I think, yes, let's get away from all this death before I go crazy.

Ellie nods. "Okay."

We tell our mothers and then we force ourselves to say goodbye to the Millers and the Boyds. It's hard to look at their faces. Instead, I find myself staring at my feet and the ugly brown linoleum floor.

Mrs. Boyd hugs Ellie. "Don't be a stranger," she whispers. "Come see us. You've always been like one of the family."

"I will." Ellie hugs her hard and slowly backs away. She won't do it, I think. She'll want to, she'll think she should, she'll *know* she should, but she'll put it off day after day until it's too late to go. She'll avoid the Boyds, she'll stay inside if she sees them in their yard. And she'll feel guilty. She'll hate herself.

Or maybe that's what I'd do. Maybe Ellie will be brave and do what she should do.

Outside, the rain has slowed to a misty drizzle, what Mr. O'Brien calls an Irish rain, soft and warm. Paul's car is parked under a streetlight on a side street. The windshield shines with raindrops.

I climb in the back with Charlie, and Ellie and Paul get into the front. We head down Oak Avenue, passing all the places we know so well, including the Bijou. The billboard says PI NIC is showing at four, six thirty, and nine p.m.

"That sign always has at least one missing letter," Paul says.

"Maybe they only have one C," Charlie says.

"There he is again." Ellie nudges Paul and points as a boy in a black suit turns a corner and heads down Chestnut Street toward the park.

"Who?"

"I saw him at Bobbi Jo's burial," Ellie says.

I crane my neck, but he's already out of sight, vanished in the rain.

Paul looks at Ellie, puzzled. "I saw lots of people I didn't know at the funeral."

She shrugs. "There was just something funny about him. You know, not ha-ha funny, odd funny. Like he didn't belong there."

I don't tell anyone I saw Buddy. Who did belong there. Even though no one else thinks so.

"Where are we going?" Charlie asks.

"Where do you want to go?"

"I don't care."

"Not Top's," says Ellie. "I'm not hungry."

"Me, either," I agree.

"Just drive," Charlie says. "We'll know the place when we get there."

So that's what we do. Drive around town until it's dark. Paul heads out into the country. He stops at a liquor store on the edge of Route 40. Veteran's Liquor, it's called. A soldier's face is on the sign. His eyes are electric, they flash off and on, off and on, two bright blue bulbs. WINE AND SPIRITS SOLD WITHIN. It's been there since the war. My dad says they have good prices on Calvert whiskey and National Bo. He should know.

"Why are you stopping here?" Ellie asks. "We're underage."

Paul looks around the parking lot. When he spots a down-and-out guy sitting on the curb, he gets out and walks over to him. They have a short discussion. Paul gives the man money and gets back in the car. A few minutes later, the guy comes out with a case of Rolling Rock and something in a brown bag. He hands the case to Paul and sticks the bag in his jacket pocket. "Thanks, kid," he says, and walks away.

"Piece of cake," Paul says to Ellie.

"Drunks will do anything for a pint of whiskey," Charlie says.

Ellie and I glance at each other. It's a lot of beer for four people, I think, but I don't say anything. She doesn't either.

Paul pulls back onto the highway and heads toward Rockledge dam. It's a famous make-out place. Cheryl used to brag about the stuff she and Buddy did there. Most of the time I wasn't sure what she was talking about. Ellie said she made it up from stories in *True Confessions*.

"Did she cry the next day?" I asked once, and Ellie and I just about died laughing.

Before we turn into the parking lot, Paul cuts the headlights. "Just in case any cops are around."

He finds a nice dark place, far from the other cars, maybe half a dozen, and opens four bottles of beer and passes them around.

We sit there in the dark. Paul lights a cigarette and offers the pack to the rest of us. We each take one. Luckies. Unfiltered. Bits of tobacco stick to my lip, and I puff cautiously. I'm not ready to try inhaling again.

Charlie laughs at the way I smoke. "Oh, Long Tall Sally," he says, "you're the funniest girl I know."

I stare at him, wondering if my feelings should be hurt. After all, I'm not trying to be funny. But the thing is, it's the most normal thing anyone has said since the funerals. So I laugh too. It feels strange. Like maybe I shouldn't.

We drink our beer and talk about what we'll do this summer. Go to the bay beaches, everyone agrees, play the nickel slot machines, maybe win enough to buy lunch. Go to Five Pines swimming pool, go to the quarry up in Rockland, take the boat across the bay to Tolchester. It's like we're trying to convince ourselves we can make this a normal summer, an ordinary summer, just like we'd planned before everything changed.

We talk about movies. The boys have no interest in seeing *Picnic*. "Even though it stars Kim Novak," Charlie says, "it's got a dumb plot."

They want to see *The Searchers,* but Ellie and I hate Westerns and John Wayne. *Carousel* is out because it's a musical and the boys hate musicals. Anyway, Ellie and I have already seen it twice. It's one of our all-time favorites. By the time we run out of movies, we've agreed to go to the drive-in next week and see *Godzilla, King of the Monsters* or *The Invasion of the Body Snatchers,* which I think might be too scary for me but I don't tell them because they might laugh. But not tonight. Tonight we want to stay here in Paul's car and drink beer and smoke and talk.

After we've each drunk two or three beers, Paul says, "Do you think Buddy did it?"

It comes out of nowhere. The murders again. Suddenly nothing's normal after all. We're back to the day, the day, the day . . . the day we all want to forget and can't. Cannot Forget. *Not ever.*

Ellie draws a deep breath and says, "Of course he did."

"Yeah," says Charlie. "Even if they never prove it, I know that bastard did it."

Paul nods. "That's what I think. Why else was he sitting there on the bridge?"

"Maybe he was waiting to kill Ellie and Nora." Charlie slides his arm around me and holds me tight, protecting me from what didn't happen but could have.

"Wait," I say, scared of what I'm about to say. "If he was going to kill us, why didn't he? He had a perfect opportunity."

"Those other kids were coming," Ellie says patiently. She's explained this before.

"But we got in his car," I say. "He could've driven us somewhere and killed us. If that's what he wanted to do."

They all look at me. "What are you talking about?" Paul asks. "Are you saying Buddy didn't do it?"

"Why would he want to shoot Ellie and me?" I ask, kind of losing track of my own argument. "It was Cheryl he was mad at. Not us."

"You saw him on the bridge," Paul said. "At the scene of the crime."

"Yeah," Charlie put in. "You had incriminating evidence."

"Then why didn't he run and hide before we got there?" I ask, back on track now. "Why would he hang around if he'd just . . . if he'd . . ." The word "killed" sticks in my throat like a curse too horrible to say out loud.

Charlie strokes my arm. "What's wrong with you? Buddy did it. He should be electrocuted."

"That's too good for him," Paul says. "Put him in front of a firing squad and let him feel what Cheryl and Bobbi Jo felt."

I drink some more beer. I remember Buddy's face at the cemetery. How sad and lost he looked. How alone. "But what if he didn't do it?"

"What, are you in love with this guy or something?" Charlie asks me.

I know he's kidding, but I feel awkward, like a dumb kid. "I just don't believe he did it. And I feel sorry for him. How would you feel if everyone thought *you* did it?"

"But he *did* do it." Paul sounds angry now.

Charlie and Ellie agree.

And that's when I tell them I saw Buddy at the cemetery. "He looked terrible."

Paul stares at me. "That proves it. Murderers always go to the funerals of their victims."

"I'm surprised the cops didn't take him in for more questions," Charlie says.

Paul shakes his head. "They must not have seen him."

"Why didn't you say something?" Charlie asks me.

"It was a burial," I say. "I couldn't just shout, 'Look, there he is.'" By now I'm about to cry. They're all turning against me.

"Hey." Charlie touches my cheek. "It's okay. You believe what you believe—even if you're totally wrong."

"And she is," Paul mutters.

"Come on," Ellie says. "We've all had a really bad time. Don't make it worse by arguing."

Paul leans back in his seat. "Anybody else want another beer?" He gets out the church key and opens four bottles.

I take one and sip it. My mouth is starting to feel funny. A little numb, like when the dentist gives you a shot of Novocain. Is this my third beer or my fourth?

"I don't know about you guys," Charlie says, "but I could use some fresh air."

"How about a little stroll around the reservoir?" Paul opens his door and gets out. The rain has stopped and the stars are out. We follow Paul carefully down a steep, rocky path, slippery with mud. At the bottom, we stare across the dark water. There's no moon. Just stars. Ellie and I find the Big Dipper and the Little Dipper. Paul points out Orion and Cassiopeia's chair. Charlie thinks he sees the North Star. That's the sum of our astronomical knowledge.

We sit on a ledge of rock. The boys gather sticks and twigs and chunks of logs and start a fire. In the woods behind us, crickets chirp. Somewhere a bullfrog croaks. Paul and Charlie put the rest of the beer in the water to keep it cool.

"Do you believe in God?" Paul asks us.

"Do you?" Charlie asks.

"I asked *you*."

"Yeah, but you can answer, can't you?"

"I do," Ellie says.

I stare at her. "Even now? Even after this?"

"I have to," she says. "Without God there's nothing, and that means they'd be dead and that's all. D. E. A. D. I want to believe they're in heaven, and you can't have heaven without God."

"Or hell," Paul puts in.

"But, Ellie," I whisper, "how could God let them die like that?"

"My father says we can't understand why God does what he does."

I'm thinking my mother said the same thing, but she didn't sound like she really believed it. Does Mr. O'Brien believe it?

Paul laughs. "That's why he's God and we're not."

Charlie opens another beer. "You mean we're not smart enough to be God? Even after eating the apple and all?" He laughs too.

I look at the sky. The universe, world without end, going on and on and on, impossible to imagine. Stars and suns and planets spinning. No God sitting on his throne up there, with angels and cherubim and seraphim praising him. And no souls of the faithful departed basking in perpetual light. Just space. Dark, cold, empty.

Charlie nudges Paul. "So anyway, do you believe in God or not?"

Paul shrugs. "I don't know. I think I'm an agnostic. Especially after what happened."

I surprise myself by saying, "I'm a pantheist." The word pops out of my mouth, and as soon as it does I decide yes, that's what I am. I also think I must be drunk, which makes me laugh.

"What the hell is that?" Paul asks.

"I read about it when I was doing my report on Wordsworth—you know, the poet we studied in English." I wave my arm at the woods and the hills and the reservoir. "God's in the sky and the trees and the water, all nature. He's way too big for churches and priests and ministers. He's just this huge gigantic force in every-thing, and he doesn't give a damn about us. We're just, just—ants. Ants. Stupid little ants. Who cares if we get stepped on?"

"And all this time I thought you were a Catholic," Charlie says. His arm slides around me, hugs me, and I try to relax against him, but I'm all tensed up.

"She *is* a Catholic." Ellie looks at me like she wants to ask, What's wrong with you? Are you crazy, are you drunk?

Yes and yes. Probably both. I lie back on the rock. The sky is spinning now, the rock is spinning, I'm about to break the laws of gravity and fly into outer space. I start to laugh, I laugh until I cry.

Charlie lies down beside me. "Don't cry," he whispers. His lips find mine and we start kissing, real kissing. I love the way his mouth feels, I love the taste of his tongue, I love the touch of his hands, and I don't stop him even when he unfastens my bra and touches my breasts. I know I should, I know it's a sin, but I don't care. I just want to keep doing what we're doing because it stops me from worrying about death and insanity and whether there's a

God or not. I'm beginning to think it's okay if Charlie's shorter than I am. I'm beginning to think maybe I love him.

Charlie's hand slides under my skirt and moves up my leg, past my knee, heading toward my deepest, darkest place. I pull away from him, suddenly scared of what we're doing or about to do. "We better stop," I whisper.

"Yeah, I know." Charlie sits up with a sigh. "I guess I should take you home, Long Tall Sally."

I look at him, scared he's mad, but he smiles and takes my hand, pulls me to my feet, kisses me.

I smooth my skirt, he tucks in his shirt. We cling to each other, unsteady from the beer or something. I don't know. Really woozy. Dizzy, silly. I wonder what he was about to do, what it would have been like. I wish we could lie down and hold each other tight and sleep with each other all night. Not do anything. Just be together while the stars and moon spin round and round.

Charlie picks up an empty beer bottle and hurls it at a rock in the water. It smashes.

Ellie jumps up, frightened. Her blouse is half unbuttoned, her hair has slipped out of her ponytail. We look like two girls from a *True Confessions* story. I hope we won't be crying tomorrow morning.

"I thought it was a gunshot," Ellie whispers.

Paul hugs her, kisses her, comforts her. Charlie throws another bottle. I throw one. We laugh hysterically. The sound of glass breaking is exhilarating. We find bottles left by other people and throw them. *Crash, bang,* it's like the Fourth of July without sparkles.

After all the empties are broken, we stagger up the path to the parking lot, stumbling, slipping, falling. My purple skirt is ruined forever. My favorite favorite skirt, my favorite favorite blouse with the pretty little purple flowers. I'm going to be in so much trouble when I get home.

In the car, Ellie asks, "What time is it?" She sounds sleepy and slurry.

Charlie strikes a match and looks at his watch. "Oh my God," he says. "'It's two o'clock in the morning and we've danced the whole night through'—or is that three o'clock? Can't remember how the song goes. Two o'clock? Three o'clock?"

"Shut up, Charlie," Paul says. "It's late and these girls are in trouble."

"Oh my God," I say, "are we pregnant?"

Everyone laughs. "Not that kind of trouble," Paul says.

"Whew," Ellie says. "*That's* a relief."

While Paul drives me home, Charlie and I make out in the back seat. He French kisses, he touches my breasts, but when I feel his hand moving up my leg again, I pull away. He sighs and looks at me, his face a blur in the dark. We hold each other tight. "Ooooh, baby," he whispers. We start kissing again. It's like we can't help ourselves.

All too soon Paul stops in front of my house. The porch light is blazing bright, casting the railing's sharp-edged shadow across the yard. My father's shadow stretches down the sidewalk toward the car. He's sitting on the top step, his face hidden by the light behind him.

"Goddamn," Charlie whispers. "We're in trouble now, Long Tall Sally." He gets out first and opens my door. Together we walk up to the house. My father's on his feet now, waiting. I don't need to see his face to know how mad he is.

"I'm sorry, Mr. Cunningham," Charlie says, "for getting Nora home so late." He sounds scared, but he stands there facing Dad.

I hang back, reluctant to get too close to my father. I've been in trouble before for little stuff, but this is the worst thing I've ever done. If he smells beer on me, I'll be grounded until I'm twenty-one. How will I explain my muddy skirt, my wrinkled blouse, my scuffed-up shoes?

"Where the hell have you been?" Dad shouts. A light goes on across the street. He's waking the neighbors. I cringe beside Charlie, speechless with humiliation.

"We were just driving around, sir," he says, "and I got a flat and—"

I hear a car door open. Ellie says, "We're really sorry, Mr. Cunningham. Please don't be mad at Nora."

My parents love Ellie. She's the sort of girl they want me to be friends with—in the Honor Society, already applying to colleges, a good Catholic. What I've done can't be too bad if Ellie did it too.

My mother appears on the porch. She's wearing her old blue chenille bathrobe and she has curlers in her hair.

"Where have you been?" she asks. "It's two thirty in the morning. I've been worried sick." She looks at Ellie, still standing by the car. "Your mother and I have been on the phone all night. You need to go straight home."

"We were about to call the police," Dad adds. "They let that kid go, the one who did it. He could have—"

"We were so scared," Mom interrupts. "How could you be so inconsiderate?"

Charlie's backing away now, still apologizing. Paul says, "I'll take Ellie home right now."

"I don't want to see you around here again," Dad tells Charlie.

I watch Charlie get in the car, a short guy with a crewcut. His suit pants are muddy. His shirt is still untucked in the back. He looks back at me, lifts his hand in a little wave, tries to smile.

"Get inside," my father says to me.

A few more lights are on in the neighboring houses. Billy has his face pressed against the screen door, making a hideous face at me which no one else notices.

"Go back to bed," Mom tells him.

"You woke me up yelling at Nora," he mutters. "I just wanted to know what's going on."

"Bed," Dad shouts. "Now!"

Billy runs up the steps so fast he trips and almost falls. I start to follow him, but I'm not fast enough.

"Where the hell have you been?" Dad asks.

"You look like something the cat dragged in," Mom says. She's taking in my untucked blouse, my uncombed hair, my muddy skirt. Her eyes narrow. She thinks the worst, I can tell. "What have you been doing?"

"Nothing," I say, even though I know she knows exactly what I've been doing. "We were just driving around, you know, talking about stuff, and we stopped at the reservoir and the path down to the water was slippery and I fell, that's all."

"You've been drinking," Mom says.

"No," I whisper.

"Smell her breath, Tom."

Dad leans toward me, sniffs. "Where the hell did you get beer?"

I want to say, "At your favorite liquor store," but instead I say, "Paul and Charlie had some beer in the car. Ellie and me had one, that's all, just one. I didn't even finish mine. I didn't like it. I . . ." Finally I stop lying and stand there, silent and ashamed.

My parents stare at each other. Suddenly they look tired. And old. It's my fault. I feel so sad and so sorry. Sorry sorry sorry. Sorry for everything I've done and will do that will make them older and tire them out.

"Go to bed," Mom says in a flat voice. "It's late. We'll talk about this in the morning."

I leave them standing at the foot of the steps, sure they're watching me climb the stairs, taking in my muddy skirt and wrinkled blouse, thinking the worst of me. Disappointed in me. Angry. I'm all alone except for my friends.

*Wednesday, June 20*
2:30 A.M.

———

## MISTER DEATH

HE sees his brother from his bedroom window. It's very late. Where the hell has he been all this time? Who's seen him? Has he spoken to anyone?

He watches him open the front gate and come up the sidewalk. The rain stopped a long time ago, but he can see how muddy and wrinkled his father's suit is, how it hangs on his brother like something a dead man might wear on his way home from the cemetery.

Down the street, Paul's car pulls up in front of Ellie's house. Its headlights sweep across his yard. Luckily his brother is inside already. What if they'd seen the fool?

Ellie's parents rush to the car, both talking at once. Where have you been, we've been so worried, what were you thinking staying out so late, you know Buddy's around here somewhere, your father almost called the police, where's Nora, was she with you, her parents are beside themselves . . . Inconsiderate, thoughtless, shocked by your behavior, do I smell beer, have you been drinking . . .

He smiles, glad Ellie's in trouble. Miss Nice Girl, thinks she's so smart because she's in Honor Society. She's no better than Cheryl, drinking beer, staying out late with Paul. He knows what goes on.

His room is dark, the street lamp casts diagonal lines across his wall. The slanted shadows remind him of black-and-white crime movies, the kind you see on television, cropped and cut up with commercials. Film noir. Dark movies for dark lives. Existential.

Paul drives past the house. Charlie's with him. He hates them both. The way they laugh at everything and everyone—himself in-cluded. He's been in class with them, knows them for what they are: fools. Know-nothings. Scoffers. If he has the opportunity, maybe he'll shoot them, too. Ellie and Nora as well.

But not Buddy. He smiles again. Buddy is safe. He needs Buddy. Someone has to blamed. And Buddy is so obvious. Angry, bellig-erent, stupid. A perfect example of a juvenile delinquent. The type who'd shoot his ex-girlfriend. And all her friends.

The note, though, the quote from E. E. Cummings. Maybe he shouldn't have left it. Buddy sure as hell wouldn't know any po-etry. He shrugs. Everyone has secrets, hidden depths. Maybe the police think Buddy's smarter than he looks. Much smarter.

His brother's coming upstairs now. He opens his bedroom door and steps into the hall, scaring him. He probably thought he'd be asleep. Fool.

He pulls him into his room, shuts the door firmly, leans against it. He doesn't say a word, simply stares, knowing the effect his eyes have on his brother.

"Don't be mad," his brother pleads. "Nobody noticed me, I didn't talk to anybody. I stayed well back and watched, that's all."

"Why did you go?" he asks, keeping his voice cold, his face ex-pressionless. "You put us both in danger."

His brother plucks at a loose button on the suit jacket. "I wanted to see her," he whispers, "one more time. Just Bobbi Jo."

"You said you stayed in the back," he says, "so how could you see her?"

"I went to communion and walked past Bobbi Jo like everybody else. They'd cleaned her up, washed off the blood, combed her hair. Her eyes were closed like she was sleeping. She looked peaceful, like she didn't mind being dead, like she accepted it. I thought what we did might be okay after all."

His brother starts crying before he's finished speaking. He's so weak. How can they have the same blood?

"Pull yourself together." His voice is as sharp as a gunshot in the quiet room. He shows his contempt, his scorn.

"But then I went to the park," his brother goes on as if he hadn't spoken. "They were there—they were waiting at the tree. They hate me for what I did. You, too. They hate us both. They'll never stop hating us."

Jesus Christ Almighty. He's going to have to do something about his brother.

———

# In Trouble

## NORA

THE next morning, my mother and father and I talk. Or actually they talk. I just nod my head when it's appropriate.

Never drink, they tell me, their words running together. Never ride in a car with someone who's been drinking, don't you know how many kids die in car crashes because they were drinking? Stay away from the reservoir, it's lonely and dangerous, kids have drowned there, you don't know who's in those woods. Come home at midnight, that's your curfew.

They also ground me for a week.

I go to my room and sit on my bed, staring at my purple skirt and my pretty blouse lying in a muddy, wrinkled heap on the floor. I kick them under my bed. I'll never wear that outfit again. I'll never drink beer again. Never go the reservoir. Never go to the park. Never take that path through the woods and over the bridge. I'll never see Cheryl, I'll never see Bobbi Jo. Nevernevernever—so many nevers.

I spend the rest of the week talking to Charlie and Ellie on the phone. He's not grounded, of course. Boys never are. He'd come over if my parents would let him but they're still mad at him. Ellie is a prisoner like I am.

When I'm not on the phone, I reread *Catcher in the Rye* and *Member of the Wedding*. I watch television, even in the daytime. I get drawn into *The Edge of Night*. Sometimes I listen to the radio, but most of the songs make me sad because they remind me of doing stuff with Ellie and Cheryl and Bobbi Jo. I get out my watercolors, but I hate everything I paint. I lie awake at night and think about kissing Charlie and wondering what he might have done if I hadn't made him stop. It's hot and horrible and I think my life is ruined. And I'm only sixteen.

## PART SIX

# Doubts and Questions

# Repercussions and Departures

## Nora

SUNDAY finally comes, the end of my jail sentence. Wearily I put on a pale blue sleeveless dress with a full skirt. It has a little white collar with lace trim. My white pumps look good with it, but they're stuffed in the back of my closet with my purple skirt and blouse, muddy and ruined. I find a pair of navy blue pumps and slip my feet into them. They're a little tight, but that can be my penance. Bless me, Father, for I have sinned. For your penance, wear shoes that pinch your toes.

As usual, Dad drops us off at St. John's and heads for the Starlight to meet his brother for a few beers. He's not Catholic, which used to bother me a lot. When I was a kid, I begged him to convert so he could go to heaven with Mom and Billy and me. I believed what the nuns said then. He'd go to hell.

Now I'm not so sure. About that or anything else the nuns and priests say. Or almost anyone, for that matter.

I see Ellie at church. After Mass, Mom stops to talk to Mrs. O'Brien, probably about their wayward daughters, and Ellie and I sit on a bench beneath a statue of St. Francis with a dove on his shoulder. He's my favorite saint—he gave away everything he owned to the poor, and he loved animals. As far as I know, he never preached about hell and damnation.

All around us daylilies bloom, yellow and orange, buzzing with bees, but Ellie looks at me, her face glum.

"My parents are sending me to Boston to spend the summer with Uncle Ed and Aunt Marie," she says. "They're driving me up there tomorrow."

"Is it because of last week?"

"Partly. They were really upset about the beer and staying out late. They're mad at Paul and Charlie. They don't want me hanging out with them."

"Are they mad at me, too?"

Ellie hesitates just long enough for me to be sure they are. "I think it's more like disappointed," she says. "Disappointed in both of us, not just you."

We sit there silently for a minute or two. "The police took Cheryl's diary," she says after a while. "Bobbi Jo's, too."

"Why?" I'm almost too horrified to ask. If anyone read my diary, I'd die of embarrassment. It's full of stupid stuff I wouldn't want other people to know.

"It was in today's paper," she says. "They think maybe one of them might have written something that would shed light on, um, what happened."

I nod. Yes, I can see that. "Will they take our diaries?"

"I hope not. I'm in enough trouble already."

"Yeah, me too."

Billy runs up to us. His face is red with heat and his hair sticks up in funny little spikes. Even Brylcreem can't tame the straw on his head. "Come on, Nora," he says. "Dad's here. Do you want to walk home or something?"

"I'll miss you so much," Ellie tells me.

"I'll miss you, too."

We throw our arms around each other. No Ellie to go places with, no Ellie to talk to or call late at night. My heart is breaking all over again. I need her, she needs me. How will I get through this summer without her?

"I'll write to you every single day," Ellie says.

"Me too," I promise.

"My aunt and uncle are going to Cape Cod for a whole month. It's even better than Ocean City," Ellie says. "Maybe you can come with us."

I hug her again and she gets in her parents' car. I stand at the curb and wave until she's out of sight. Lonely days and weeks stretch ahead. Long, hot summer days with nothing to do and nowhere to go.

That night Charlie calls me. I take the phone in the bathroom and shut the door. My heart beats a little faster. I like his voice in my ear, but I wish we were at the reservoir making out. I feel warm all over thinking about kissing him, his hands on my breasts, his hand on my leg above my knee, creeping up toward—

"Wait till you hear this," he says. "Paul's Uncle Tony owns a pizza carryout place in Ocean City, right on the boardwalk. He's hiring me and Paul to work there all summer. It's like getting a paid vacation."

Something slips inside. He's not going to ask me out—that's not why he's calling. No reservoir. No making out. "Wow," I say, trying to sound enthusiastic. "That's neat, Charlie."

"I'll send you a postcard when we get there and give you my address. Will you write to me?"

"Yeah, sure." I'm picturing all the cute girls he'll sell pizza to and thinking he'll never write to me. But why should I care? He's shorter than I am, and anyway, all we really are is friends who just happened to make out once or twice. No big deal. So why do I have this big lump in my throat? Why do I feel like crying?

"Did you know the cops took Cheryl's and Bobbi Jo's diaries?" he asks.

"Yeah, Ellie told me."

"God," he says, "I hate thinking about cops reading what they wrote. It's an invasion of privacy."

"But if it helps them find the killer," I say, "then—"

"They already know who did it," he says.

I don't say anything. Why start another round of Buddy did it, no he didn't, yes he did.

"I'm sorry you got in trouble last week," Charlie says. "I forgot all about the time."

"Yeah, me too."

There's a little silence and then he says something about the Orioles and the bad season they're having and he hopes they start playing better. No World Series this year. Not a chance. I don't really care about the Orioles. Sports bore me. But I remember the advice column in *Seventeen* magazine and pretend to be interested.

As usual Billy starts banging on the door, yelling he has to pee.

I tell Charlie goodbye and give Billy a dirty look. "Why do you always have to pee when I'm on the phone?"

He makes a face and ducks around me to get in the bathroom.

I go up to my room and sit on my bed and stare at the posters on my wall. Charlie hates me. He thinks I'm cheap because I let him touch my bare breasts and put his hand under my skirt. That's why he didn't ask me out tonight. He could have. If he'd wanted to see me before he left. But I let him do stuff nice girls never let boys do. I've ruined everything. He'll never be my friend again, he'll never kiss me again. It's all over, everything's all over. I can't stand it.

I grab my old teddy bear and cry into his fur. Ellie's leaving, Charlie's leaving, I'm all alone. There's nobody. Nobody. I don't see how I can keep on living.

After a while, I sit up and blow my nose. I feel so empty my insides hurt. Miserable. I am miserable. Elvis Presley stares at me from his picture on my wall, he's smiling that easy smile of his like he's saying life is good, so good. Beside him, James Dean gazes into the distance at something only he can see, his face tragic. Marlon Brando has a kind of sneer on his face. I think I might throw Elvis in the trash can.

I remember what Charlie said about Cheryl's and Bobbi Jo's diaries and I get my diary from its hiding place in my underwear drawer. I haven't written anything in it since the day before the party at the rec center, but I leaf through it, reading an entry here and there, trying to remember what I was like before everything went wrong.

*Jan 10. Saw Don in the hall today. He smiled at me and said "See ya in art class!" He had on a blue shirt that* matched his eyes. He's so cute!!!! But I think he's dating Judy Winograd, she's a cheerleader and a snob and I hate her. She's not even all that pretty. Got a D on my chemistry test. I'm really scared Mr. Haskins will flunk me and I'll have to go to summer school. Boy would that ruin my plans to spend every day at the pool, getting tan and learning how to dive.

Feb 3. Went to the basketball game with Ellie. We beat Windsor Mills by twenty points. Don was high scorer. He's so cute!!!!! Sigh. Got a ride to Ellie's with Buddy and Cheryl. She was practically sitting in his lap, don't know how he can drive with her that close. Ellie and I stayed up late talking about them. She thinks they do a lot of heavy petting. Good thing she's not Catholic. I'd be scared to go to Confession if I did what she does. Ellie also thinks Cheryl has her eye on Ralph, one of Don's friends, also on the basketball team. He's not as cute as Don but who is? Sigh. I thought she was in love with Buddy but Ellie says she told her she's getting tired of him, he's too possessive and he's a sex fiend.

I close my diary and put it back in my underwear drawer. I wonder if the police have learned anything from Cheryl's and Bobbi Jo's diaries.

# CHERYL'S DIARY

*Saturday, December 31, 1955*

*New year's eve, Party at Paul's house. I'm going with
Buddy. I think he's giving me his ring tonight, that's what
everyone says, I hope he is. He's so cute and I really really
like him a lot, maybe even love him, not quite sure yet,
there was this boy last summer in Ocean City, he was a
sailor actually and he was twenty years old so maybe he
wasn't actually a boy anymore but how could I say he
was my man friend, he was my boyfriend for two weeks, I
met him on the boardwalk and he shot these plastic ducks
at the rifle range and won a kewpie doll for me which is
standing on my bureau this very minute. Its just so cute
with its big round eyes and its little curl on its forehead.
The sailor's name was Mike and let's face it he was cuter
than Buddy and taller and a better kisser, especially
French. but he's somewhere out on the ocean now and he
stopped writing to me before Thanksgiving so it was just a
summer love, like that song the autumn leaves by roger
williams. but Buddy's right here in Elmgrove, just a few
blocks away and he says he loves me and he gave me a*

*christmas present, a pretty china horse for my collection, the prettiest and the biggest one of all. It's standing next to the kewpie doll. if her legs were separate instead of stuck together she could ride him.*

*It's almost time to go, I'm walking to Paul's house with Bobbi Jo and Ellie and her friend Nora, this girl who lives in the old part of town, I don't know her real good yet, she seems nice but kind of silly, laughs a lot, kind of immature if you ask me but who's asking, Ellie likes her and so does Charlie even though she's taller than him.*

*My folks aren't real keen about Buddy. they think he's too much of a cat—his ducktail and his pegged pants and his shirt collar turned up, but what do they know.*

*I'm wearing this full blue velvet skirt I got for Christmas and a see through blouse I bought with babysitting money which is hidden under a sweater because even though everybody wears them I know my father would make me change it for something else he's such an old stick in the mud. I also have my pop-it bead necklace that looks like pearls and my pearl earrings, I bought both at the dime store and they look like they cost lots more.*

*oops there's the doorbell—I'll tell ya what happens tonight tomorrow!*

# Bobbi Jo's Diary

*Sunday, January 1*
*New Years Day!!!!! Happy 1956, the best year ever!*

*Last night was the first new years eve I didn't sit at home*
*with my family watching TV in the living room and*
*waiting for the ball to fall at Times Square. I'd love to see*
*that in real life someday, be in that huge crowd, shouting*
*happy new years to strangers, maybe even kissing them.*
*When I'm eighteen, cheryl and Ellie and nora and me are*
*riding the bus up there, we promised each other last night.*

*The party was at Paul's house, this guy in cheryl and*
*Ellie's class. He drives a blue plymouth, sort of souped up*
*but not as much as buddy's ford, but I'll say more about*
*buddy later.*

*Anyway I wore my best red corduroy skirt, it's real*
*straight and has a slit up the back so I think it makes me*
*look older, and a brand new white Orlon sweater I got for*
*Christmas, it's just like cashmere but not as expensive. I*
*tied a new red silk scarf around my neck and borrowed*
*mom's gold clip on earrings. She said I looked beautiful*
*but not to grow up too fast because she wasn't ready for*
*that and daddy said before we know she'll be married and*

*have babies of her own and I said I'm just fourteen don't
be so silly.*

*It will be only neat to get married and have a baby
and I hope I'll be a good wife and mother. If things go the
way I want I'll get married in june 1960, right after I
graduate from Our Lady of Mercy. Ellie wants to go
to college but me and cheryl want to get married and
start our real life. Cheryl hates school and so do I.*

*It was cold outside and Ellie said maybe the lake
would freeze and we could ice skate, she's from
massachusetts where you can skate outdoors practically
all winter. I don't have skates we don't often need
them here.*

*lots of kids came to Paul's party. a guy from St. john's
was there but he wasn't wearing his uniform too bad those
boys look so cute in their uniforms. Paul turned the lights
low and gary brought his records, he has thousands, I
swear. He's fat but nice so he never dances, just plays
records which is nice of him I think, he's kind of cute like
that kewpie doll cheryl has, the one the sailor won for her
at the shooting gallery. He shot twelve plastic ducks to get
it. Bang bang bang, dead duck ha ha.*

*Anyway I danced every dance, some with Paul, some
with Charlie some with Walt and one with Steven from
St. John's who held me way too tight while Unchained
Melody was playing and tried to feel my breasts which he
should know is a sin. So that was the last dance I danced
with him.*

*Buddy and Cheryl danced so close you couldn't put a*

*piece of paper between them. She's not Catholic so*
*maybe it's all right but Sister would kill any girl who*
*danced like that. Well. not kill. Just punish. Kneel and say*
*seven Hail Marys and one act of contrition she'd say and*
*go to confession on saturday. Sister doesn't let you get*
*away with anything. which is why I beg my parents to let*
*me go to public school.*

*Cheryl wore her new see-through blouse. All you can*
*see is her lacy slip underneath but sister would make her*
*say a few prayers for that, too. good thing she goes to*
*Eastern. No matter what sister would say, cheryl looked*
*really pretty. she has the prettiest hair, like the breck*
*shampoo girl or grace kelly, long and blond with a perfect*
*roll under. i might grow mine long and wear it like hers*
*but I think it's too curly. tough break.*

*After a while me and Ellie and nora noticed Cheryl*
*and Buddy were gone. I started looking for them but*
*Steven said, forget it, kid, they're outside in Buddy's car.*
*some girls know how to have fun.*

*Well, I should of guessed that. when I saw them again*
*Cheryl was all rosy and happy and she was wearing*
*Buddy's class ring on a chain around her neck.*

*Somebody yelled happy new year and the lights went*
*out and everybody started kissing and hugging.*

*Then the lights went on and there was Paul's mother*
*holding a big tray of sandwiches and his father had a case*
*of sodas and soon we were all eating and then the party*
*was over, my very first new years eve party. We walked*
*home through the cold night, laughing and talking, me*

*and Ellie and nora. Cheryl had disappeared again*
*with Buddy.*

*That girl better be careful or she'll be getting married*
*shotgun style. I just found out what that means.*

*It's a sin to lose your virginity before you get married,*
*I know that, but if you get married before the baby's born*
*then are you forgiven? say 5 Hail Marys, get married,*
*and everything's okay, you won't go to hell, but you'll*
*probably end up in purgatory for a long time.*

*But I can't help wondering what it's like to be a girl*
*who knows how to have fun. By the time I'm Cheryl's age,*
*I bet I'll know.*

# A Visit to the Priest

## NORA

FOR days after Ellie goes to Boston, I mope around the house. I can't stop thinking about Cheryl and Bobbi Jo and how God, if there is a God, let it happen. I try to pray but I can't. The feelings I had at the funeral come back, even stronger. I'm scared I'm becoming an atheist, which means I'll burn in hell. Or maybe I'm just losing my mind. Which is worse, I wonder, atheism or insanity?

My parents take Billy and me to Druid Hill Park for the Fourth of July fireworks. I want to stay home and read *Peyton Place*, a book I have to hide or Mom will take it back to the library. But Mom says I have to get out of the house.

Why? Where is there to go? What is there to do? All my friends are gone.

While Billy runs around with some of his friends being totally obnoxious, I sit on the blanket and think about last year. We'd come with Buddy and Cheryl, crammed in the back seat of his old car, me sitting on Charlie's lap, Ellie sitting on Paul's lap, and Bobbi Jo and Walt squeezed in between us. Before the fireworks started, we were laughing and joking and talking so loud that some crabby old people on the blanket next to us told us to keep it down. We laughed and laughed and Cheryl gave them the finger. Later when it got dark and the fireworks started, Buddy and Cheryl lay down on the blanket and made out. It was kind of embarrassing. I don't think they saw a single thing except maybe the grand finale, which is hard to ignore.

This year I'm the one who doesn't watch the rockets shoot up into the sky and explode in bursts of red and blue and fall like petals from the sky. I lie on my back with my eyes closed and drift into the past.

Mom notices I'm not enjoying the fireworks. The next day, she asks me if I've thought about her suggestion to talk to a priest.

"Yes," I say, "I've thought about it."

She looks at me, waiting for me to say more. "Well?" she finally asks.

I yawn. "I will."

"When?"

"Stop nagging me. I said I will, so leave me alone." I go to my room and slam my door and pick up *Peyton Place*, but I can't keep my mind on it. Mom is disgusted with me, I'm not acting like myself. Like the self she thinks I am, I mean. Like the self that isn't here anymore.

I can't talk to the priests at St. John the Divine's. Father Bailey baptized me. Father Cahill heard my first confession and gave me my First Communion. How can I tell either of them I'm not sure I believe in God? It would hurt their feelings. You know, after all they did to help me be a good Catholic.

I decide to take the streetcar to Baltimore and go to St.

Alphonsus, this big beautiful church where my grandparents got married a long, long time ago. Grandmother was christened there, too. She wouldn't marry my grandfather until he converted. Mom tried that with Dad, but he wouldn't convert and she married him anyway. Big mistake. Only I wouldn't be here if she hadn't. Funny how easy it is not to have been born.

I know where to get off the streetcar because I've gone there with Mom. She likes to attend Mass at St. Alphonsus on All Souls' Day and light candles for her parents. Afterward, we have lunch at Miller's, her favorite Baltimore restaurant, just Mom and me.

The priests at St. Alphonsus will explain things to me. I'll understand why bad things happen. I'll believe again like I did before, before . . . well, you know, before the awful thing.

I get off at Howard Street. The sidewalks are busy with shoppers coming and going from Hutzler's department store. We always go there to visit Santa Claus and see the Christmas windows. Of course, I don't see Santa anymore. That's gone with everything else from my childhood including thinking I'm safe in Elmgrove. Even Billy's too old for Santa, but we still love the windows. Each one has a different scene from "The Night Before Christmas." The figures move around on little tracks.

I pause at one of the windows. Last December, I stood on this exact spot with Ellie, Cheryl, and Bobbi Jo. We'd come to Hutzler's to do our Christmas shopping. It was a cold, windy day. Cheryl's long hair blew in her face and I wished I'd worn a warmer coat. But Hutzler's was warm inside and crowded and decked out with all sorts of Christmas decorations. It was so beautiful, a winter wonderland, magical, shiny and sparkly. We all bought socks for our dads and scarves for our mothers. Cheryl and I bought cap pistols for our little brothers and Bobbi Jo bought a rubber duck and a coloring book for her little sisters.

The hardest present to choose was Buddy's. It took Cheryl forever to make up her mind. Shirts and sweaters were too expensive. He didn't like to read, so books were out. We ended up going to the record department, where Cheryl bought him five forty-fives, "Midnight Special," "Night Train," "Maybelline," "I Hear Ya Knockin'," and "C. C. Rider." Funny, I still remember the ones she picked. Maybe because we listened to them in a little booth before she bought them. We all squeezed in and got to giggling and the manager told us to leave and Cheryl said, "Humph, maybe I won't buy anything here," but we all groaned and said please just buy the records and let's go get milk shakes. So she did, but she made the guy wait while she counted out all the change she had.

Now I stand here alone. It's a hot July day. Mannequins in summer clothes pose in the windows. They're wearing those long plaid shorts called Bermudas, the new fashion trend, *Seventeen* magazine says. They look awful, I think, but I've seen lots of college girls wearing them. Not me, though. I like short shorts.

I study my reflection in the window as if I'm hoping to see somebody different. A pretty girl, the kind boys like. But it's the same old me. Tall and skinny, short frizzy hair, sleeveless blue dress with a little white lace collar.

Not stylish. Not pretty. Afraid of everything. Hell. Death. Especially death. But also sex. Sometimes I think I'm frigid. Other times, like at the reservoir with Charlie, I worry I'm a nymphomaniac. Maybe I've read too many *True Confessions* magazines where the women are always either one or the other.

I turn away from my reflection, dodging women carrying shopping bags, and keep walking toward Saratoga Street. When I'm in sight of St. Alphonsus, I almost chicken out. Maybe I should go back to Hutzler's and get a chocolate milk shake at the soda fountain. I turn away from the church, take a step, hesitate. I didn't come all the way to Baltimore for a milk shake.

With a deep breath, I open the door and let out the smell of church—musty air, stale incense, dead flowers, candle wax, holy water (which has a smell I can't put into words). At least it's cool and quiet. If nothing else, I'll light two candles and pray for Bobbi Jo's and Cheryl's souls.

But if there's no God, what's the point of that?

My brain spins with doubt and fear, but I force myself to dip my finger into holy water, cross myself, and genuflect. At the altar, I light two candles in a rack at Mary's pale feet and kneel, cross myself, and pray as if I believe. As if God is listening.

Please let them be in heaven with you, let them be happy there, help me to understand why you took them, help me to believe in you.

I cross myself again. In the name of the Father, the Son, and the Holy Ghost, amen. The gestures and the words are so familiar. Why don't they comfort me?

Before I go into the confession booth, I sit in a pew and think about what I'll tell the priest. I can't say I knew the murdered girls, they were friends of mine, I was there when their bodies were found. I'd sound like I was bragging or trying to be famous at their expense. I'm the girl who was THERE. I'm the girl who KNEW the murdered girls.

I look at Jesus hanging on the cross surrounded by angels and saints, all looking up to heaven, not one of them is looking at his twisted body, the crown of thorns pressing blood from his forehead, his side bleeding from the soldier's sword, his hands and feet bleeding from the nails hammered into him. Everywhere I look I see statues and ornate woodwork. The church is like a wedding cake two stories high—no cake, though, just icing over emptiness.

One confessional is open. I push aside the heavy curtain and step inside. As I kneel in darkness, I hear the little panel between the priest and me slide open, I see the shadowy shape of his head.

"Bless me, Father, for I have sinned most grievously in thought, word and deed," I begin, repeating words I memorized when I was seven for my First Communion. Seven years old and a sinner already in the eyes of the nuns. "It's been three months since my last confession."

I stop and the priest whispers, "Yes?"

To delay, I tell him about making out with Charlie.

"How often did you kiss him?" he asks.

The question surprises me. I want to ask him if I was supposed to count, but all I say is "I don't know."

We go on—was it once, six times, more? "Did you let him touch you? Did you do anything you wouldn't have done if the Virgin Mary had been sitting in the back seat, watching you?"

The image of the Virgin Mary in the back seat almost makes me laugh.

Finally I whisper, "I need to ask you something, Father, but it's hard. I don't know what to say, I haven't told anyone because they won't understand, they'll be shocked, but I thought maybe you could give me some advice, tell me what to do, how to . . ." Tripping and stumbling over words, I come to a stop and wait, sure he's guessed what I'm trying to say.

"You must tell your parents first," the priest says. "They'll be disappointed, of course, maybe even angry, but they'll help you."

"I tried to tell my mother, but she doesn't really understand."

"How about the boy, then?"

I'm puzzled. Does he mean Buddy? "He says he didn't do it."

"Have there been others?"

What does he mean—others? "No," I say, "not that I know of."

"Then it must be him." The priest is silent for a moment, thinking, I guess. "Will he do the right thing?" he asks at last.

I'd like to ask the priest what he means by the right thing, but I don't want him to think I'm stupid. "I don't know, Father," I whisper.

"Surely you've discussed it."

"I don't know him well enough to talk to him about the, the . . ."

When I can't finish the sentence, the priest says, "You must ask him what his intentions are."

"His intentions?" Totally confused, I stare at the outline of the priest's head through the mesh covering the window.

"Yes, his intentions." The priest is beginning to sound cross. "You have been a foolish girl, you have sinned against God and the holy Catholic Church, you have given up your treasure to an unworthy boy. Now you must either marry him or enter a home for unwed mothers."

My knees turn to water and I begin to shake. The priest has totally misunderstood me. He thinks I'm pregnant. I have a wild desire to start laughing, but if I let one giggle out, I'll never stop and they'll take me to Spring Grove for sure. It's not really funny anyway.

"N-no, Father," I stammer, "it's not that."

"Then what is it?" He still sounds cross.

"I need you to tell me why God lets bad things happen."

He is silent for a moment. "You're not expecting a child?"

"No, Father." I'm crying now, not laughing. "My friends are dead—they were murdered—and I want to know why God let them die."

"You are very young. Only a child would ask for an explanation of God's will." He pauses. Maybe he's waiting for me to say something. When I don't, he goes on.

"Like everyone, you must accept all that happens in this world, good and evil, as God's plan. You must have faith. You must not question. God's reasons are his own."

He pauses again. When I say nothing, he adds, "Pray for the souls of your friends. You do not know what future pain they were spared by dying young."

I cannot speak. He has said the same thing everyone says. He knows no more about God than my mother does.

"Do not let your friends' deaths weaken your faith in God," he goes on in his pious way. "A Catholic never doubts his faith. Ignore the wiles of Satan. It is he who puts doubt in our minds." He sighs and I hear his robes rustle as he shifts his position.

He clears his throat. "Now, for your penance, make a good Act of Contrition, say three Hail Marys, and accept what you are too young to understand."

Stunned by his dismissal, I automatically say, "O my God, I am heartily sorry for having offended Thee, and I detest all my sins, because I dread the loss of Heaven, and the pains of Hell; but most of all because I love Thee, my God, Who art all good and deserving of all my love. I firmly resolve, with the help of Thy grace, to confess my sins, to do penance, and to amend my life."

I race through the words. They mean nothing to me. When I say "Amen," the priest absolves my sins in Latin and the window between us slides shut. I linger a moment in the dark, and then I leave. If a Catholic never doubts his faith, I must not be a Catholic. Has the priest just absolved me of Catholicism?

Without saying my three Hail Marys, I run from the dark, silent church into the hot sunlight. Cars rush by, horns blow, a flock of pigeons takes to the sky with a clatter of wings. A group of teenagers dash across the street against the light, laughing, daring a car to hit them. At Hutzler's, I stop at the fountain shop and order a chocolate milk shake. I drink it slowly. It's so cold it makes my chest ache. Or maybe it's my heart that aches.

On the ride back to Elmgrove, I wonder if I should tell my mother I've lost my faith and will no longer attend Mass. I imagine her weeping and prophesying my sinful future. My father probably won't care—why should he? He's not Catholic. In fact, he doesn't even like Catholics (why he married Mom is one of life's mysteries), so he might be on my side.

But the thought of Mom's face, her anger, stops me. I'll have to keep going to church. I don't have the nerve to stop. While the priest talks about sin and damnation and the building fund, I'll sit between Mom and Billy and think my own thoughts.

# A Talk with Nora

## BUDDY

AFTER the funerals, I spend a few weeks on my uncle's farm in Virginia. While I'm there, I decide to join the navy. I need to get the hell out of Elmgrove and away from all the goddamn people who think I did something I didn't do.

I come home in July. Not much of a welcome, I can tell you—I think my folks were hoping I'd stay on the farm. While I was gone, they'd gotten dirty looks and crank phone calls like it was their fault I did what I didn't do. They're thinking of selling the house and moving to Florida.

The next day, I head for the navy recruiting office. Since the cops never charged me with anything, I don't worry about them saying I can't join. In fact, they're glad to have me. There's some stuff going on in Egypt about the Suez Canal and I figure the navy's thinking they might have to send some ships over there and that's fine with me. Join the navy, see the world.

I'm walking down Main Street, hoping I don't see anyone, when the drugstore door opens and Nora Cunningham almost bumps right into me. We stop and stare at each other. I think of

*The Invasion of the Body Snatchers* again. She's going to open her mouth and make that noise and everybody will start chasing me.

"Sorry." I'm not sure why I'm apologizing. I didn't actually bump into her or anything. Maybe it's because of what she thinks I did. Maybe I'm saying I'm sorry I exist.

She stares at me and then she asks me if I have my car.

I can't figure out why she wants to know, but I look her in the eye like I'm Sam Spade or something and say, "What's it to you whether I do or don't?"

She looks kind of scared, which makes her freckles stand out like brown blotches on her white face. "I want to talk to you," she says in a teeny tiny voice.

"What about?" I'm getting my pose right, kind of slouching while I light a cigarette. Tough guy. Humphrey Bogart himself.

"Please," she whispers. Her eyes are looking this way and that, everywhere except at me. She must be scared someone's going to see her talking to me. Maybe she'll be tarred and feathered and run out of town.

I shrug and head around the corner to the parking lot behind the A&P. She follows me, not real close, not so we look like we're walking together. Just going in the same direction.

When I open the door, she gets in and slides down in the seat so her head's below the window.

"You don't want anybody to see you with me?"

She shakes her head. She's scared of me, which makes me mad. For a second, I think about telling her to get out of my car and leave me alone. Why should I want to talk to her? I know what she thinks.

But I'm curious, so I get in, slam my door, and burn rubber out of the parking lot. Two old bags pushing grocery carts recognize me. They look like they've just seen one of those guys on the FBI ten most wanted list. The kind I used to study in the post office, hoping to spot one on the street and get a reward.

When we're out of town, I tell her she can sit up, but she stays where she is. "You got any special destination?" I ask her.

"No."

"How about Highland Park?"

"Okay."

So that's where we go. It's a county park along the river, crowded on Saturdays and Sundays but deserted during the week.

I turn off the engine and light another cigarette. Just to be polite I offer her one, and to my surprise she takes it. She makes a sort of pathetic attempt to look like she's smoked all her life, but she doesn't inhale and she purses her lips like she's kissing her cigarette instead of smoking it. I feel like laughing.

"Aren't you scared to be with me?" I ask her.

She looks straight ahead. "Kind of."

She's not bad-looking, I think. Nice long legs. No chest, though.

"Kind of," I echo in a prissy little-girl voice like hers. "You think I'm a murderer but you're only *kind of* scared of me?"

She glances at me and coughs on cigarette smoke. "I don't think you did it," she says slowly.

I stare at her, scarcely believing what she's just said. "You must be the only person in the whole town that thinks I didn't do it."

She nods, her face serious. "You wouldn't have been on that

bridge if you'd done it," she says. "You would've been hiding in the woods or something."

"You don't think I was waiting to kill you and Ellie?"

She pushes her bangs out of her eyes. "If you wanted to kill us, you'd have hidden in the woods and shot us. Besides, you didn't have a gun."

"How about Ellie? What's she think?'

Nora looks embarrassed. "She thinks what everybody thinks."

"Let me tell you something." I look her in the eye. I'm on the level now, there's stuff I need to say and she's the first person who's given me a chance. "I loved Cheryl. I was mad at her, sure. She broke up with me. She liked that dumbass basketball player because he's got a nicer car than me, he's got more money than me, and he's a big goddamn wheel. But I never would have hurt her. Never."

"But you used to hit her," she whispers, her face screwed up like she's scared again. "You gave her a black eye."

"I what?"

"That black eye she had last spring." Her voice has dropped so low I can hardly hear what she's saying. "She told Ellie you gave it to her, she said you hit her all the time."

"Cheryl said *I* hit her?" This hurts me more than I care to admit.

Nora nods. She's hugging her knees tight against her chest like she's protecting herself.

"Listen." I lean toward her and she shrinks away like I'm going to hit her. "Listen," I repeat. "I never hit Cheryl. Not once. That black eye—I can't believe she told Ellie I did that. I brought her home late one night, way past curfew. Her dad was waiting up for her. He opened the door while I was kissing her good night, grabbed her arm, pulled her away from me, yelling and cursing—maybe he was drunk, I don't know. Anyway, he hit her so hard he knocked her down. I saw him do it. He came after me next, but I got the hell out of there before he laid a hand on me."

She sucks in her breath. To her it must be worse to know Cheryl's father, not me, gave her that black eye.

"I should of stood up to the bastard," I say. "I should never of let him treat Cheryl like that."

I turn my head and light another cigarette.

For a while we don't say anything. It starts raining and we sit there listening to it tap on the roof.

Why did Cheryl say I hit her? The question runs round in my head, chasing itself. There's no answer. I can't ask anybody, only Cheryl. Only Cheryl.

"When did she tell Ellie I hit her?" I ask Nora.

She's looking out the window, but she turns and faces me, frowning like she's thinking about my question. "It was around the time you broke up."

"*She* broke up," I correct her, "not me."

"Yeah, well." She drifts off, turns to the window again like she's watching TV or something. "Maybe she wanted a reason, you know . . . to break up."

She might be right. Cheryl always liked people to be on her side. She probably wanted Ellie and everybody else to hate me. She sure as hell got what she wanted, didn't she?

After a while, Nora says, "I saw you at the cemetery." Her voice is still low, but soft. She's not scared of me anymore.

"Yeah, I know you did. I thought you'd tell everybody."

She props her feet up on the dashboard just the way Cheryl used to. She's wearing white moccasins like Cheryl's. I see she's sweating by the dark circles under her arms. It's hot, but I figure that's not the only reason she's sweating.

"What are you going to do now?" she asks.

"I just signed up for three years in the navy. They'll probably put me on a battleship somewhere near the Suez Canal."

"There might be another war, my dad says."

I nod. "Yeah, that's what I hear. I don't even know what it's all about."

"Dad says it's Nasser's fault. He took over the Suez Canal from England, nationalized it or something. Now the English want to fight."

I shrug and light another cigarette. "I don't give a shit one way or the other what happens in Egypt. All I want is Cheryl."

Nora doesn't say anything right away, and neither do I. Just saying Cheryl's name makes me feel sad and crazy and mad all at the same time. I still can't believe I'll never see her again. Never kiss her, never touch her. This empty place opens up inside me. It's huge. And it hurts like all my insides have been ripped out.

After a while, Nora says, "Do you think they'll ever catch the killer?"

"I'd kill the bastard myself if I knew who did it." And I would, I know I would. With my bare hands if I had to.

"They questioned so many people," she says. "They even thought they had him a couple of times. Like that kid who confessed but it turned out he was lying. He just wanted some attention, my mother says. And the crazy man from Spring Grove who also said he assassinated Lincoln. And that guy who killed some girls in Tennessee."

"Don't forget about me," I say. "You got any idea what it's like to spend a couple of days in the lockup with police questioning you, asking the same thing over and over again? Hitting you? Kicking you? Calling you a lying little shit?"

It's raining harder now, like somebody's pouring buckets of water on the windshield. I'm clenching my fists, breathing hard, but she doesn't notice. She's staring out the window again. All I see is the back of her head and her long neck.

"I got a feeling they'll never prove who did it," I say. "Never."

Without looking at me, she asks me a question. Her voice is so low that I have to say, "What?"

She turns toward me. Her face is pale, worried, her forehead wrinkled. "Do you believe in God?"

"What the hell kind of question is that?"

She shrinks back into herself.

"Do *you*?" I ask. "Believe in God?"

She shakes her head. "I used to."

You'd think she was talking about Santa Claus. I study her profile, trying to figure her out. I never heard of a girl saying she didn't believe in God. Cheryl was always praying, Please God let me pass this test, Please God let the Cougars win this game, Please God let me make cheerleaders, Please God let Marlon Brando win the Oscar. Little-girl prayers. Most of them didn't get answered. Except for Brando. He won the Oscar, but I don't think God had anything to do with it.

I think of Cheryl walking to school that morning, I think of her seeing the guy with the gun, I think of her praying, Please God don't let him shoot me, please God don't let me die.

I start the car. I got no time to talk about God and what I believe. Or don't believe. Hell, I'm not even sure.

"Where do you live?" I ask her. She's gone all quiet, sitting up against the door, her knees drawn up to her chest, her head down. All I can see is the top of her head.

"You can let me out on the corner of Grant and Twenty-Third Street, behind the Little Tavern."

"You really don't want to be seen with me," I say.

She shakes her head, her face still hidden.

When I pull into the parking lot, it's still raining. "You sure you don't want me to drive you all the way home? You're going to get soaked."

"I won't melt."

"Yeah, and you're so skinny you can run between the raindrops."

I finally get a little smile. "Thanks for talking to me," she says.

I shrug. "It's nice to know one person in this town doesn't think I'm a murderer."

She opens the door. "Good luck in the navy," she says. Then she's gone, her long skinny self dashing around a corner and out of sight.

---

# A Meeting at the Gas Station

## BUDDY

I REACH for my cigarettes and realize I've smoked them all, so I
stop at the Esso station to get another pack. Just as I drop my
quarter into the vending machine, I hear somebody say, "Look
who's here."

I pocket the cigarettes and turn around. It's Ralph and Don and
a couple of football players. They're dressed all collegiate in those
stupid khaki pants with the crap strap on the back and button-
down shirts and those expensive loafers you get at Hutzler's. Crew-
cuts so short you can see their scalps. They make me sick.

"How does it feel to get away with murder?" Ralph asks.

"I wouldn't know," I say.

The next thing I know, a football player hits me hard, his fist in
my mouth. Caught by surprise, I fall back against the vending machine. The little knobs jab me in the back. Before I can get in a
punch, they all start hitting me, shouting about Cheryl and Bobbi
Jo, cussing me out. I try to defend myself, but they're all bigger
than me. The next thing I know I'm down on the ground and
they're kicking me. Like I'm nothing, like I'm a dog, less than a
dog, something that crawled out of the sewer.

"Leave him alone. It don't matter what he did or didn't do—you got no right to fight on my property. You want me to call the cops?"

It's Joe, the guy who owns the Esso station. He's a big man, fat belly but lots of muscle. The boys back off. Ralph says, "We don't want any trouble, sir." Breathing a little hard, but perfect manners.

"You know who he is?" Ed, the star quarterback cuts in. "You know what he did?"

"He oughta be on death row," Don puts in. "Why do you care what happens to him?"

"Get the hell out of here," Joe says.

They mumble and mutter. I hear Ralph say, "Come on, let's go." From the ground, I watch their shoes step away from me. Swell guys. Honor Society, some of them.

"You okay?"

I look up at Joe. Rain pounds my face. "I'm okay." I get to my feet. I hurt all over, especially my ribs. My nose is bleeding and I can feel my right eye starting to swell. "Thanks."

"Go on," he says. "Get outta here." He spits on the ground and walks away.

I get in my car and light a cigarette, but my mouth is bleeding so I put it out and sit there a while with the engine idling. My mind drifts back to Cheryl and the lie she told Ellie. It really hurts to think she said I hit her. Never, never would I. Not me. Damn it, I loved that girl.

I wonder if she wrote about that black eye in her diary. I wonder if she said it was her father who did it, not me. I wish I could read the whole thing and see if she ever loved me the way I loved her or if she was just faking it all along.

I see Joe looking at me from the office window like he's thinking he might call the cops if I don't leave soon. I ease on out of the Esso station. No place to go but home—where they can't wait for me to leave.

# CHERYL'S DIARY

*Friday, April 6*

*Buddy just won't take no for an answer, what does he think would happen if I get pregnant, rubbers don't always work. He says I'm a tease, he says I just don't know how painful it is for guys, haven't I ever heard of blue balls which is what they call it when a guy's hard for a long time and the girl won't let him do it.*

*I'd like to do it with him, I'd like to know what it's like but my cousin Ruth let her boyfriend get her pregnant when she was my age and she had to drop out of school, that's the law you know, no pregnant girls in school. So they got married real quick and she had the baby and now they're living in this ugly little apartment and she never has fun anymore, they can't even afford a movie and they fight all the time. I don't want to end up like that.*

*I got in big trouble for coming home late. My dad was drunk and he hit me so hard he knocked me down. I'm going to have a black eye tomorrow. And how am I going to explain that? Nobody else has a father as bad as mine. I hate him so much.*

*But I got ahead of myself. Before all that stuff
happened, me and Ellie and Nora skipped school and
went into Baltimore to see On the Waterfront again,
about the 12th time I think. I love Marlon Brando, we all
do, especially when he breaks down the door to Eva Marie
Saint's bedroom and she's just wearing her slip and she
acts like she hates him but you can tell how much she loves
him. Her father hates him and says he's no good. Just like
my father hates Buddy and says he's no good. It's my
favorite movie.*

*I love Rebel Without a Cause too. James Dean and
Marlon Brando are my favorite actors. I can't stand it
that James Dean is dead. He was so cute.*

*Anyway we were talking and me and nora think our
parents don't love each other and probably never did. I
know this for a fact because I heard my mother tell her
sister she married daddy because she thought nobody else
would ask her, and what a mistake that was, it ruined her
life. Yeah, she's stuck with two kids and a husband who
spends every night drinking beer and watching TV and
yelling. That is SAD. Ellie says her mother and father
really do love each other so that's one out of three.
Bobbi Jo's parents seem pretty much okay, so maybe that
makes it fifty fifty.*

*Well, tomorrow's saturday and we're having a
slumber party at Ellie's and I'm going to sneak out and
meet Buddy. No curfew because no one will know.*

# Bobbi Jo's Diary

Sunday, April 8

*Last night we had a slumber party at Ellie's. Cheryl had a black eye, she said she ran into a door but I can't quite see how that could happen. But you could tell she didn't want to talk about it so we all said it didn't hardly show which was a lie, but it made her feel better. Later, Ellie whispered to me maybe it was Buddy, maybe he hit her, but I said no, I don't think so, he loves Cheryl too much to hit her.*

*The first thing we did was go bowling, it was okay with Ellie's parents as long as we were back at eleven which is kind of early but they didn't want us walking home late at night. Mr. O'Brien couldn't come to get us because his car is at the repair shop.*

*I was horrible at bowling—only Nora was worse. We kept bowling gutter balls while Ellie and Cheryl made strikes and spares, I laughed so hard I almost wet my pants. Afterwards we went to Howard Johnsons and these guys we'd talked to at the bowling alley followed us. We ended up at the same booth mainly because the boys just*

sat there without being invited. They were kind of cute.
They lived in Fullerton and they went to Western,
Eastern's biggest rival and enemy. Their ducktails were
longer than Buddy's and they wore tough guy black
leather jackets and talked all this cool slang. One of them
kept saying, meanwhile back at the oasis the arabs were
eating their dates. Then they'd all laugh but I didn't see
what was so funny. In the girls' room, Cheryl tried to
explain it but I still didn't get it. I don't think Ellie and
Nora got it either but they laughed anyway. What's so
funny about eating dates.

They walked back to Ellie's house with us, through the
woods and across the bridge and the baseball diamond.
Then they wanted to come inside and join the party. It
was mainly Cheryl's fault for flirting with them. We were
all getting a little scared then, but Mr. O'brien came
outside and told them to leave, they called him rude
names and cussed and acted like guys in that movie
Blackboard Jungle. One even looked kind of like the worst
juvenile delinquent in the movie, the one who called the
teacher daddyo. When Mr. O'brien said he was calling the
cops, they ran back into the park and that was the end of
them thank goodness.

"That's the last time you're walking home from the
bowling alley," Mr. O'brien told Ellie.

Later after the O'briens had gone to bed, we helped
Cheryl sneak out the basement window to meet Buddy.
"Don't forget to leave it unlocked because I don't know
when I'll be back and you might be asleep," she said and

*ran to his car. On went the headlights and off they went.*
*It was exciting. I think we all kind of wished we had*
*boyfriends to sneak off with. I know I did.*

*Well we stayed up really late waiting for Cheryl. We*
*watched the midnight double feature horror film. First*
*they showed I Walked with a Zombie which was a little*
*corny but still scary, especially the jungle scenes with the*
*real tall skinny zombie. He'd just loom up out of the dark*
*like a dead man. Next they showed The Wolfman and it*
*was scarier I thought. Especially when the actor got all*
*hairy and his fingernails turned to claws and his teeth got*
*long and sharp. I can't figure out how they do things like*
*that in movies and make it look so real.*

*By then it was after three am and Cheryl hadn't come*
*back. We went outside and looked for her, we walked up*
*and down the street and around the block but there was*
*no sign of her. I was kind of worried those guys might still*
*be around somewhere but I guess they'd given up and*
*gone home. I kept watching for them and I was so jumpy*
*they all started teasing me.*

*I don't care if they tease me—it's scary after dark*
*when the streets are empty, no cars even, and all the lights*
*in people's houses are out.*

*Back at Ellie's we drank some more coke and ate*
*popcorn and ice cream but I was getting too sleepy to keep*
*my eyes open so I said wake me up when she comes back*
*and I fell asleep, even though I was worried about her.*

*Well, just as it was getting light, I woke up and saw*
*everybody gathered around Cheryl. Her face was pink*

*and she was laughing. "You really did it?" Ellie asked. "Did what?" I asked, and they all started laughing. "Don't tell," Cheryl told the others. "Bobbi Jo is too young to know about it." and even though I said I was fourteen and not a baby they said they'd tell me about it when I was as old as them, sixteen to be exact. Two years to wait. "It better be good," I said and they all laughed some more and Cheryl said it was very good.*

*Then they all lay down and went to sleep and so did I.*

*And now it's the next day and I'm home and feeling grumpy and kind of sick to my stomach from all the stuff we ate and I bet I'll never know what Cheryl did. If they want to act like that, let them. See if I care.*

# Lonely Street

## NORA

AFTER I get out of Buddy's car, I'm really upset. Why did I ask him if he believed in God? Why did I speak to him in the first place? Why did I get in his car? He must think I'm crazy or something. He's probably right.

All the time I'm thinking this, I'm running through the rain, splashing in and out of puddles. Even though it's summer, the rain is cold and I'm shivering. Maybe I should have let Buddy drive me all the way home. But what if someone saw me getting out of his car? Better to get wet than start a bunch of gossip.

At home, Mom and Billy are doing a jigsaw puzzle at the dining room table. So far, they've put down the puzzle's four corners. According to the box lid, it's a picture of a sunset on the ocean and it has 650 pieces, mostly pink, red, gold, blue, or green.

"You're soaked," Mom says. "Get out of those wet clothes before you catch pneumonia."

I go to my room and strip off my shorts and blouse. Even my underwear is wet. My moccasins are sodden lumps of leather, ruined, I'm sure. I pull on dry clothes, flop down on my bed, and turn on the radio just in time to hear the end of "Heartbreak Hotel."

Damn. I love Elvis and I love that song. Lonely Street—that's where I live.

I lie there hoping they'll play another Elvis song, but instead it's Carl Perkins singing "Blue Suede Shoes." I remember Bobbi Jo singing it one day down in the park, making us all laugh. She wanted a pair of blue suede shoes so bad, but she never found a pair, not even at Hutzler's.

The rain gurgles in the downspout, drums on the roof, and patters from leaf to leaf in the holly tree. The mockingbird sits on his branch, his feathers wet. He looks as sad as I feel.

What does a bird know? Does it know it will die, do dogs and cats know? I think I read somewhere that they don't know until just before, and then they hide and die where no one can see them. Wouldn't it be better to be like them and not know?

Elephants know. They mourn when an elephant in their herd dies. I read that in *National Geographic.*

What's it like to be buried when it's raining? Does the rain seep down through the earth and leak into coffins and run down dead people's faces like tears?

"Nora?" Mom sits down on my bed and touches my shoulder. "Are you all right?"

"I'm fine."

"I'm worried about you."

"I'm *fine.*"

"I know you miss Ellie." Mom goes on as if I haven't said anything. "But maybe you should call some other girls from school. Joan Waters, maybe. I see her around town. She always smiles and says hello. She seems like a nice girl. Or Doreen, that little redhead who lives over on Beacon Street. You and she used to be friends. Maybe if you called . . ."

Mom goes on talking but I've stopped listening. She just doesn't get it. Joan Waters is a stuck-up snob—she runs around with the big wheels. Fat chance she'd want to spend any time with me.

And Doreen is really strange. She walks with her head down and never looks at anybody, like she wants to be invisible or something. A friend like that is all I need.

As for Ellie, I got a postcard from her yesterday, a photo of a sunset on a beach, just like the jigsaw puzzle. *Greetings from Cape Cod*, it said. After I read it, I had a feeling she doesn't miss me as much as I miss her.

> *Dear Nora, wish you were here. Cape Cod is so neat. I met a cute boy yesterday and we talked a long time. I hope I see him again. Guess what. My parents are sending me to St. Joseph's next fall. I don't want to go back to Eastern after what happened. Maybe you can go there too, and it won't be so bad. We'll give the nuns a run for their money. Write soon, Love ya, Ellie.*

I don't want to go back to Eastern either, but I definitely don't want to go to St. Joseph's. Ellie doesn't know I've been absolved of Catholicism. Neither does Mom, for that matter.

"What did you just say?" I ask her.

"I said I've made an appointment for you to see Dr. Horowitz."

"Why? I'm not sick."

"You don't have any appetite, you're always tired, you never want to go anywhere or see anyone. You've lost at least five pounds this summer. You could have mononucleosis."

"You get mono from kissing," I say. "That's why it's called the kissing disease."

"That's not really true, Nora." She starts describing the symptoms. It occurs to me that she's just read an article about mono in *Good Housekeeping* or *Ladies' Home Journal.* Is your teenager listless, has she lost her appetite, have two of her friends been murdered? She may have mononucleosis.

"Mom," Billy yells, "I put some more pieces together. Come and see!"

"Just a minute." Mom pats me on the shoulder. "We'll take the trolley into Baltimore tomorrow morning. After you see the doctor, we'll have lunch at Miller's."

I turn my face to the wall.

Mom gets up, walks to the door, pauses. "Come on downstairs," she says. "We need your help with the jigsaw."

"I'm not in the mood," I say, keeping my back turned.

"No," she says, suddenly angry, "you just want to lie there and feel sorry for yourself. I've tried to be patient, Nora, I've tried to understand, but this has gone on much too long. Think about someone besides yourself for once."

Ah, I think, so it's come to the old familiar You are so selfish, you are so self-centered, you think the sun rises and sets for you and you alone. Well, who do you think you are? Your friends got murdered and no one knows who killed them and your best friend is on Cape Cod and she's going to Catholic school in the fall and nothing will ever be the same but get over it, grow up, think about somebody else for a change. What's more important—your dead friends or the jigsaw puzzle?

Mom stands there for a while. From downstairs Billy calls, "Come on, Mom. Let Nora sulk, see if I care."

She sighs loudly. "Dinner will be ready when your father gets home. Maybe you could give me some help and set the table."

It's Friday, I think, payday. Daddy won't be home until after seven, and he'll be drunk and he'll try to kiss Mom and she'll turn her face away. Then she'll start in about his paycheck: There should be more, have you been playing the numbers, how do you expect us to live on this? I have bills to pay, Billy needs his teeth straightened, yakety yak, yakety yak . . . I can't stand it. My mother hates my father.

I just hope he hasn't brought home a steak. He did that once. Made Mom cook it and all of us had to sit there eating tuna salad while he ate the steak. Truly it was the meanest thing he ever did, but I know sometimes he gets fed up with eating fish every Friday just because he's married to a Catholic.

I don't want my life to be like my mother and father's. I'd rather stay single.

What if I really am sick? What if it's not mono but something worse? I saw a TV show where a girl dies of leukemia. What if Dr. Horowitz tells me I have six weeks to live?

I look around my room at all the stuff I have. The teddy bear my grandmother gave me when I was three, my collection of Storybook Dolls left over from when I was ten or eleven, half a dozen Nancy Drew mysteries, *Lassie Come-Home, The Moffats*—books I loved when I was a kid. *Catcher in the Rye,* the first book I ever read that seemed as true as my own life, *Member of the Wedding,* which spoke to my secret self because Frankie was me and I was Frankie. My diaries, my yearbooks, my sketchbooks and art supplies; photographs of Ellie and me acting silly in the park, hanging upside down on the jungle gym and going down the sliding board; movie stars and posters taped to my wall. And my clothes—a closetful of skirts and blouses and dresses, bureau drawers stuffed with underwear and socks and pajamas and jeans and shorts, my rosary and missal, a palm from Palm Sunday yellowing above my mirror. All the things that will be left behind when I die.

What will Mom do with them? What did Cheryl's mother do? What did Bobbi Jo's mother do? Do you throw them out or give them to the Salvation Army or pack them in a trunk no one ever opens?

I grab my bear and hold him tight. Pooh. I named him after Winnie-the-Pooh because he looks like him, though not so much now with most of his fur loved off and one eye gone and his stuffing leaking out of his paws. I've slept with him almost every night of my life and told him my secrets and cried until he was wet with my tears. When I die, he'll be buried with me.

Sorry for myself, yes, it's true, I'm sorry for myself and sorry for Cheryl and Bobbi Jo and Ellie and Buddy—yes, Buddy, because he didn't do it, I know he didn't do it, and he's living on Lonely Street too.

— PART SEVEN —

# Leaving and Staying

## MISTER DEATH

H E stands at his window and watches two girls walk past the house. He doesn't know them, but they remind him of Cheryl and Bobbi Jo. It's the way their hips sway and their asses jiggle under their shorts. They have the same purses, with long straps and drawstring tops. They swing them casually as they stroll along, laughing and talking. They aren't thinking about dying. Neither were Cheryl and Bobbi Jo that morning. On an otherwise good day, Mister Death sometimes takes you by surprise.

But this is Friday the thirteenth. They should expect something bad to happen.

His brother is in his room as usual, the door closed, listening to Elvis Presley. He himself hates Elvis, who's nothing but an ignorant Southern ex-truck driver who got lucky. He swings his hips, he gyrates, he sneers, he lets his eyelids droop. He has no talent, yet all the girls and their mothers (who should see him for the ignoramus he is) are in love with him.

"Hound Dog," he thinks, what kind of a song title is that? Music for proletarians. The uneducated masses.

Summer vacation is almost half over, and he's uneasy about

returning to school. He has no concerns about himself. He knows how to maintain his invisibility. It's his brother. His behavior is unpredictable. He's lost control over him, he worries he'll say something or do something to give them away. He imagines him writing a report called "What I Did Last Summer": *My brother and I killed two girls. He shot them and I helped him hide their bodies. It was my brother's idea, he made me do it, I didn't want to, I'm sorry now, please don't put me in jail.*

While he's musing, he sees his father's car turn the corner and pull up in front of the house. He's wearing a suit and tie, his shoes are polished, he carries a briefcase. Superficially he's indistinguishable from all the other men coming home on a Friday night. Ah, how deceptive are appearances.

Soon his mother summons him and his brother to dinner. They sit at the table, the four of them, with little to say to one another. Nothing unusual about that. It's a house of silence occasionally shattered by shouts and blows.

After they have begun to eat, his father says, "I've found a job in Texas. Lots of opportunities there. I think we'll leave here at the end of August. Maybe sooner."

No one is surprised. They all know why they're going to Texas. They never stay anywhere for more than a year or two. In the middle of the night, they leave their furniture behind, rent unpaid, and skip town before their father is arrested for embezzlement, writing bad checks, operating a numbers game, or any other of a number of scams and frauds.

He smiles across the table at his brother. It's a reprieve. Once they're in Texas, they'll be safe. They'll know no one and no one will know them.

His brother doesn't return his smile. Head down, he looks at his plate, his shoulders hunched.

His mother goes to the kitchen for another glass of water. She fools no one, except perhaps herself. They all know what's in the glass. When she returns, she pushes her almost untouched plate aside and lights a cigarette.

He helps himself to a slice of meat loaf. His mother sips her drink and smokes. She has nothing to say, but then she seldom does. His brother finally looks at him across the table. He sees the relief in his face.

# Dr. Horowitz

## NORA

WHEN I was little, I used to get carsick every time we took the trolley into Baltimore. The bus was even worse. But now that I'm older I'm pretty much over it if I always ride facing forward and don't try to read anything.

Mom and I don't have much to say. I'm still upset about her calling me self-centered and accusing me of feeling sorry for myself. And I'm not happy about going to see Dr. Horowitz. It's not like he and I are in the habit of chatting. He's the stick-out-your-tongue-and-say-ah sort of doctor. So what am I going to tell him? I'm scared of dying and at the same time I can't stop thinking about it. I can't sleep, I'm always tired, I'm unhappy, I'm lonely, I'm scared that I'm crazy. Look what happened when I tried to talk to a priest. I almost got sent to the Florence Crittenton Home for Unwed Mothers. I don't want to go through *that* again.

I decide I'll just tell him I can't sleep. A doctor can fix that with a prescription.

I glance at Mom. She's looking out the window at an old, run-down Baltimore neighborhood. I wonder what it's like to live in one of those sad little row houses, to spend your childhood climbing chain-link fences like two boys we pass. Nobody has a yard. There's broken glass everywhere. People sitting on their front steps look unhappy. The women have their hair in bobby pins. They wear shapeless housedresses like my grandmother wore. One has on socks and high heels. Every single one of them has a cigarette dangling from the corner of her mouth. They don't even remove them to yell at their kids to get out of the street or leave the cat alone.

"That's where we'll end up someday," Mom says glumly. She's still in a bad mood.

"I thought we were heading for a tarpaper shack."

"Don't be sarcastic," she says. "Tarpaper shack, row house, what's the difference? Your father wastes most of his paycheck on liquor and gambling."

It's one of her favorite predictions. We won't be able to pay our bills because Daddy doesn't give her enough money. So it will be a tarpaper shack or a row house. I wonder what she'd say if I told *her* to stop feeling sorry for herself?

She reaches up and pulls the cord to signal the driver our stop is next. By now we're on Howard Street. It's amazing how quickly neighborhoods in Baltimore change. One minute you're in a slum and the next you're walking past fancy department stores. The women here don't wear baggy housedresses or have bobby pins in their hair or cigarettes in their mouths. They're dressed for shopping—smart little suits, hats, and gloves. Their hair is waved. You can bet they aren't imagining tarpaper shacks in their futures.

Dr. Horowitz's office is in a big air-conditioned building on the corner, right across from Hutzler's. We take an elevator to the third floor. While we wait, Mom and I leaf through old issues of

*Time* and *Life*. The office is full. The woman across from me has a horrible phlegmy cough that I hope isn't contagious. A baby keeps crying no matter what its mother does to comfort it. The baby's big sister whines and fusses and tugs at her mother's arm. The mother looks suicidal.

I count five adults and three children. It will be a long wait.

At last the nurse opens the door to the examining rooms and calls my name.

"Tell him exactly how you feel," Mom says.

"I'm surprised you didn't write a list for me," I say in a voice too low for her to hear. I love my mother, I really do, but when she's in this kind of mood, I can't stand her. One more year until I graduate. Maybe I won't go to college, maybe I'll join the Waves and go to sea like Buddy. Get away from Mom and Dad and Billy and Elmgrove. There's a big wide world out there.

First the nurse weighs me. Jean's been working here as long as I can remember, but she always looks exactly the same. Tight perm, uniform so starched it crackles, glasses, not many smiles.

The scale tells me Mom's right. I've lost almost ten pounds since June. No wonder my skirt feels loose around the waist.

"One hundred and fifteen," Jean says. "Not much for a girl who's five feet ten inches tall."

I shrug. "It's summer. I never eat much when it's hot."

"Well, gain some weight," she says. "You haven't got any reserve. If you get really sick, you'll waste away in no time."

Is she joking? Or trying to scare me? As usual, her face gives nothing away. I decide she thinks I have leukemia. Six months to live. And then off to New Cathedral Cemetery. Nobody would care. Nobody would bother to come to my funeral. After Cheryl and

Bobbi Jo, my death would be anticlimactic. Come to think of it, my whole life is anticlimactic.

Dr. Horowitz comes in and tells me to take a seat. He sits across from me. He wears a stethoscope where most men wear ties. "How are you, Nora?"

I shrug. "Okay."

He looks at me. "That's not what your mother says." He steeples his fingers. I've read that's a power position. I consider steepling mine. But I don't.

"She told me you're depressed about your friends' deaths, you're not sleeping or eating well, you lie around the house all day reading."

"I like to read."

"It's not the reading that worries me," he says.

I want to say it doesn't worry me either, but I shrug and study the floor, octagonal-shaped tiles, endlessly repeating patterns in black and white.

Dr. Horowitz starts talking about how difficult it is to accept death, especially when it's violent and unexpected. "It throws you off-course," he says. "It makes you question everything. Big questions, such as the nature of good and evil, the meaning of life, God's power." He pauses and looks at me over his steepled fingers.

Here is the church, I find myself thinking, here is the steeple, open the doors and see all the people.

"Are you afraid of dying?" Dr. Horowitz asks. "Is that why you can't sleep at night?"

Startled, I look him in the eye for the first time. Is it possible he understands what's going on in my head? I nod. "Why did they die instead of me?" I start to cry before I finish asking the question.

"I don't think anyone can answer that," he says gently. "Through no fault of their own, those girls were in the wrong place at the wrong time. You weren't."

"But I can't stop thinking about it. I feel like I'm crazy. I worry about dying, I worry about my mother or my father dying, I worry about my friend Ellie dying. I used to read about murder in the paper but I never knew anyone who was murdered. Until now." Once I've started talking, I can't stop. "I think about the killer and I wonder who he is and if he'll ever be caught. How can he live with what he did? How can he go on day after day without killing himself?"

"You don't think the ex-boyfriend did it?"

"No." I take the tissue he offers me, I blow my nose, wipe my eyes. "I'm sure he didn't."

"That poor boy," he says. "You might be the only person in Elmgrove who thinks he's innocent."

"Yeah." I blow my nose again, and Dr. Horowitz pushes the tissue box across the desk toward me.

"Have you talked to a priest?"

I nod.

"Was he any help?"

"I don't believe in God anymore." As soon as I say it, I wish I hadn't. Is it normal for a sixteen-year-old girl not to believe in God?

He raises his eyebrows as if I've surprised him.

"Don't tell my mother." I lean across the desk. "Please, don't. She'll get so mad."

He peers at me over his steepled fingers. "Whatever you tell me doesn't leave this office."

Just like a priest, I think. Even if you confess to murder, the priest can't break his vow of secrecy and tell anyone.

I sit back and smooth my skirt. It's full and tan and printed with small pink flowers. My crinoline puffs it out just right. Next to the ruined purple skirt, it's my favorite. Despite the air conditioning, I feel sweat trickling down my back and soaking my underarms.

"Do you think it might help to talk to a psychiatrist?"

Shocked, I stare at Dr. Horowitz. He thinks I'm crazy. *Crazy.* Maybe he's planning to send me to Spring Grove in a straitjacket. I'll spend the rest of my life in a padded cell with barred windows.

"No," I whisper. "No. I'm not crazy." Please don't let me be crazy, please don't let people think I'm crazy, please let me be like everybody else . . . Why am I praying? Who am I praying to?

"Seeing a psychiatrist doesn't mean you're crazy," Dr. Horowitz says. "Sometimes talking to someone can help you straighten things out."

I start to stand up, thinking I might leave now, but he motions me to stay seated.

"How about something to help you sleep, then?"

I nod.

He busies himself writing a prescription. "Try to eat more. You're too thin. And promise to get out of the house. Go to the library, take a walk, call some people and make plans to go to the swimming pool or a movie. It's not good for you to spend so much time alone."

He hands me the prescription. "Your job right now is to put one foot in front of the other and keep going. Trust me, things will get better. Don't worry about God or death or the meaning of life. Just get through each day the best you can."

He smiles at me. I smile back. He doesn't act like he thinks I'm crazy, so maybe, just maybe, I'm not.

He walks me to the door and gestures to Mom to join us. "Nora's going to be fine," he says. "Be patient with her. She's been through a lot."

Dr. Horowitz shakes her hand and then mine. "Try to enjoy the rest of the summer," he tells me.

Ha, I think.

Mom and I step out into the heat of the August day. The ladies in their little suits and hats and gloves look wilted as they trudge along in their high heels and nylons, toting shopping bags from Hutzler's, Hochschild-Kohn, and Stewart's.

"Did you have a good talk with Dr. Horowitz?" she asks.

I nod, but I don't mention the psychiatrist. I know how she'd react to that. Only crazy people need psychiatrists, she'd say, and then she'd get all upset and start thinking that the psychiatrist would blame her for all my problems. I don't tell her about the prescription either. I'll give it to her on the way home and we'll stop at Walgreen's.

We have lunch at Miller's, crab cakes and cole slaw and iced tea, with a hot fudge sundae for dessert. I actually enjoy eating. But I'm still anxious. And worried.

Mom cheers up and acts more like her better self. We stop at Hutzler's to check out the summer sales. She buys me a new pair of moccasins and two Ship and Shore sleeveless blouses. One has a sailor collar and a little navy blue tie. It's white and the other is pink, a good match for the skirt I'm wearing.

I fall asleep on the trolley. Just before we reach our stop, I wake up with my head on Mom's shoulder. I hope I didn't drool.

As we walk home, I think about the prescription folded up tight in my wallet. Suppose one night I took all of the sleeping pills, just did it, an impulse or something. I'd be dead by the next morning. No more worries. No more fear. No more misery. So easy—so, so easy.

I glance at Mom, walking along beside me, talking about the flowers in a yard we're passing. "Aren't they pretty, why can't my daisies look like that, and those marigolds and zinnias, not a droopy one in the whole bunch, she must weed and water every day." Blah blah blah—she's talking about flowers while I'm thinking about dying.

She'd be the one to find me. I can't let myself do that to her. Tiptoe past the medicine cabinet like the little moron, don't wake the sleeping pills.

I decide to throw away the prescription. I don't dare keep those pills in the house.

Not that I want to kill myself. Not that I really think I will kill myself. It's just one more thing to be scared of.

That night, I go up to my room to escape my family. Mom's mad at Dad and she's out in the kitchen, slamming cupboard doors. He's sitting in the living room drinking beer and watching *Gunsmoke*. He loves Miss Kitty. My brother is mad because I won't play checkers with him. They are driving me crazy.

I listen to the radio for a while, but all the songs remind me of how things used to be. After a while, I start writing a long letter to Ellie. I tell her about seeing the priest and what he said and how I've decided not to be a Catholic anymore.

I know she's more religious than I am, but who knows, maybe she's lost her faith too.

It's three pages long, and I end it by saying *Please write soon. I miss you.*

On Monday, the mailman delivers a postcard from Charlie, the first one he's sent. *Hi, Long Tall Sally,* he writes,

> *Ocean City is GREAT. Having a swell time. I got so sunburned my nose almost peeled off but I'm pretty tan now. I burned my hand getting a pizza out of the oven and had to miss work for a couple of days (tough break, huh!) but it's healed up now. Wish you were here. Your friend Charlie.*

It's a good thing I wasn't expecting a love letter.

# Ocean City

## CHARLIE

PAUL and I are staying in a room above his uncle's pizza carryout. At night the neon lights on the boardwalk shine in the window. The colors chase each other across the wall, reds and yellows, greens and blues. It's like living in a Wurlitzer jukebox. I thought it would keep me awake, but after the first or second night I was too tired to notice.

We work from eleven a.m. to ten p.m., selling pizza to pretty girls and other less interesting people. If the girls don't have dates, we flirt with them. Sometimes we get lucky and they meet us after work. I made out with a cute girl from Pikesville two nights in a row, but she and her family went home yesterday. That's the bad part about Ocean City. Girls our age are with their families and they only stay a week or two, so just when you're getting somewhere, they leave.

The waitresses at the hotels are in college and they aren't interested in Paul and me. Just as well—they all wear those plaid Bermuda shorts. I hope they go out of style soon. Lots of college guys wear them, but Paul and I are not about to buy a pair.

Except for the girls and the beach and the boardwalk, the best part about being here is that nobody ever talks about Cheryl and Bobbi Jo. For the first time since they died, I don't think about them every minute of every day. Not that I've forgotten them. Sometimes late at night Paul and I sit on the beach in the dark, drinking beer and watching the waves roll in. We talk about them in low voices, so low we can hardly hear each other over the noise of the surf. We look out into the dark. Sometimes we can see the lights of a ship way out to sea and we wonder if when we graduate next year we could get jobs on a freighter and sail around the world, what would that be like, what kind of things are out there, people and places and stuff we've never seen. Other nights there's so much mist you can hardly see the stars. It seems like there's no sky, just ocean lit by foam when waves crash, going on forever and ever, sea without end, amen.

Sometimes we wonder about heaven—where it is, how big it is, what it's like, is it really there and if it is can Cheryl and Bobbi Jo look down and see Paul and me sitting here, missing them, remembering the stuff we did together.

My thoughts might drift to Nora then. Long Tall Sally and me out at the reservoir drinking beer and making out and how she let me touch her breasts, and then I miss her and wish she was here on the beach and maybe we'd take our clothes off and skinny-dip.

Maybe I should call a Baltimore radio station and dedicate "Long Tall Sally" to Nora like I used to, but she's so far away now, and I don't want to think of her because then I think of Cheryl and Bobbi Jo and I'm in the park again and I see the cop cars and the ambulances and I see them lifting a stretcher and there's somebody on it covered with a blanket and I know it's either Cheryl or Bobbi Jo and I run, I run with Paul and Gary back the way we came, we're cussing and crying and yelling and we see Nora and Ellie and they're standing like statues, pale as stone, clinging to each other, and we shout "They're dead, they're dead, they're both dead," and I want to grab Nora and run away with her deep into the woods and hold her tight and never let her go but she and Ellie are turning away and running in the other direction and they won't stop, not even when we call them. And I glimpse Buddy's car passing Bobbi Jo's house, the goddamn son of a bitch murdering bastard, and I want to kill him like he killed them and that scares the shit out of me.

But sometimes I remember Nora saying maybe Buddy didn't do it and I think, What if she's right? What if it was somebody else? And I wonder how I'd feel if I was Buddy and everybody hated me for something I didn't do. The poor bastard. No wonder he joined the navy.

I never mention this to Paul because he'd get mad and call me a dumbass jerk. Let him think what he wants about Buddy—me, I'm not so sure anymore.

So we've been here five weeks and all I've sent Nora is one stupid postcard. She must think I hate her, which I definitely do not—I really really like her, but I just can't think about her right now.

Anyway, there's this cute girl staying with her family at the Beach Plaza and Paul and I are meeting her and her friend at the arcade Tuesday afternoon, our one day off. Paul's uncle promised to loan us his car so we can go to Junior's for shakes and burgers and then head out to the Shore Drive-In, where we might get lucky. The girls are from Pennsylvania and you can bet they've never heard of Cheryl and Bobbi Jo.

# ELLIE'S DIARY

*Saturday, July 21*

*Dear Diary,*

*I owe Nora a letter, but I don't know what to say. She wrote me she can't imagine going to Our Lady of Mercy because she doesn't want to be a Catholic anymore. She has a bunch of reasons, mostly having to do with what happened to Cheryl and Bobbi Jo, but I can't understand it. Doesn't she realize she's damning herself to hell? How can she throw away the only true religion? Is she going to be a Baptist or a Methodist or something really strange like a Unitarian or a Quaker? Or does she mean she doesn't believe in God at all? I've actually been praying for her to realize how wrong she is, but I can't tell her that—she'd be mad probably. What would I do without Jesus and Mary and all the saints? How could I get over what happened without them?*

*She told me she talked to a priest and he said a true Catholic never doubts his faith and she seems to think that means she can give it up. Just like that. Everything she's believed since she was little. Communion and* confirmation and confession, the Mass, the Virgin Mary, novenas and retreats, the rosary, holy water. When I come home, I'll talk to her about it, even if it makes her mad.

I'll tell her no one understands why God allows bad things to happen. But you can't let it weaken your faith because that opens the door for Satan to enter your heart. And I'll keep praying for her—and Cheryl and Bobbi Jo, because if there's no God there's no heaven which means when you die, there's nothing, and I will not believe that.

I guess I just don't understand Nora. I never in a million years dreamed she would turn against God. I remember the retreat we went to and we cried while we sang Mother dear, oh pray for me, whilst far from heaven and thee. The church was filled with incense and we lit candles and prayed for the souls of all the faithful departed and said the Stations of the Cross and went to confession and took holy communion and then we got scared we might get a calling to be nuns and as much as we loved being Catholics we didn't want to spend our lives in convents. So far I don't think that's what God wants for me, but at least you're safe in a convent. You spend your days in peace, praying and worshiping God, you're married to Jesus, you even get a sort of wedding ring. Nothing bad happens in convents. If I get the call, maybe it won't be as bad as Nora and I thought last fall.

Okay, though, there's this. I'll be safe from Buddy in a convent, but what about boys in general? I really like making out with Paul. I went to confession and the priest *told me to avoid the occasion of sin (which means being alone with a boy in a car or someplace) and not to have impure thoughts and to remember if I dressed in a way that gave a boy impure thoughts I was responsible for his sin. Which seems a little unfair, but I think I see the logic of it. Nora and I talked about that once and we decided Marilyn Monroe was responsible for lots of guys' impure thoughts. Ha ha.*

*Maybe Nora thinks it's too hard to be a Catholic. Sometimes I think that too, but like I said, I can't imagine giving it up. It's like physics or calculus—you keep struggling till you get it. When Nora finished plane geometry, she was done with math. And now she's done with religion.*

*At confession, I told the priest what Nora said and he said I shouldn't be friends with her anymore. He said she'd be a bad influence, I should make new friends at St. Joseph's. He also said not to worry about Bobbi Jo and Cheryl, they're safe in heaven with Jesus and I'll see them again someday. Someday—after I die, that's what he meant.*

*Well, I'm starting to get sad again, so it's good I have a date tonight with Andy, this cute guy I met at the swimming pool. We're going to see Invasion of the Body Snatchers—it's supposed to be really scary! I remember Cheryl talking about it—she and Buddy saw it last winter and she told me she almost sat in Buddy's lap, she was so scared. Darn. Why did I have to think of that?*

*Aunt Marie is calling me for dinner, so that's it for now, dear old diary.*

# Ready to Leave Town Except for One Thing

## BUDDY

I'LL be shipping out for basic training tomorrow, so I went to the barber this morning and got my head just about shaved. Since my hair's getting cut off anyway, I figured I'd rather take care of it myself.

I never realized how big my ears are and how skinny my neck is. I look like Dopey, the bald dwarf who wears the brown nightgown in *Snow White*. The one who can't talk. It figures. My teachers always thought I was dumb. Or lazy. Or had a bad attitude. Shit, who cares what they thought? I'm done with all that.

I can't wait to get away from this place. Every time I go anywhere, people look at me. I know what they're thinking: *There he goes, Buddy Novak, the boy who killed those poor girls and got away with it, I hope he burns in hell. What's wrong with the police—why isn't he in jail where he belongs? Just look at him. I don't feel safe with him on the loose, no telling who he might shoot next.*

I light a cigarette and give them an evil look and they turn and scurry away like cockroaches.

The thing is, I want to talk to Nora before I leave. I keep thinking about her. Not in a let's-go-park-and-make-out way. She's not my type. Too skinny, too tall, too flat. It's just that she's the only person I know who doesn't think I killed them, the only person I can talk to. Not one of my old friends will come near me. If they see me, they look the other way. They cross the street, they turn their backs, they get in their cars and burn rubber getting away from me. I'm a disease no one wants to catch.

Even my parents are nervous around me—they hope I didn't do it but they're not absolutely sure. Mainly I guess because nobody's been arrested and charged. The cops have run out of leads, they've never even found the gun. The newspaper prints a paragraph now and then, but it's not a big story anymore. The Suez Canal business is on the front page now, not Cheryl and Bobbi Jo.

So the night before I leave, I call Nora from a phone booth in front of the Little Tavern. Traffic whizzes back and forth. I can hardly hear when someone answers.

"Can I speak to Nora?"

This kid yells, "Hey, Nora, phone—it's a boy!"

I hear her rush downstairs from the sound of it and I wonder who she's hoping it is. Charlie, probably. She was with him that night in the park, the night I messed things up with Cheryl forever, the night before she . . .

Nora says hello like it's a question, and I say, "It's me. Are you doing anything tonight?"

Dead silence on the other end. "Who?" she finally asks.

"Buddy Novak," I say. "I was just wondering if maybe you, I mean, yeah, you and me could get together and talk. You know, just talk." Damn it, I sound like a thirteen-year-old kid who's never talked to a girl on the phone.

"What about?" she asks. Worry comes hissing down the phone line from her to me. I can just see her, standing in some room I've never seen, clutching the phone, scared pissless.

I say, "Just stuff," but what I want to say is, You know what stuff, goddamn it, there's only one kind of stuff for me and you to talk about.

"I don't know," she says slowly. "I don't think . . . I mean, well—"

"I'm leaving for Norfolk tomorrow," I cut in, "and, well, hell, I don't have anybody to say goodbye to, this whole town hates me, they can't wait to see my ass go down the road and out of sight. So I thought maybe me and you . . . Oh, hell, never mind."

I'm about to hang up but I hear her say, "No, wait a minute. Maybe for a little while, not long. I mean . . ." She's stumbling over her words. She doesn't really want to see me, I can tell, but she doesn't want to hurt my feelings either.

"I'm at the Little Tavern," I tell her. "I'll wait for you inside. If you don't show up in half an hour, I'll find something else to do." Like go down to the reservoir and drown myself or something.

"Okay," she says, still not sure she really wants to see me. What a bad idea this was. I feel like telling her to forget the whole thing, but she's already hung up.

I go inside and take a seat at the counter. The grumpy old man who's worked there as long as I can remember is frying up some death balls for a couple of guys. College kids from the look of them. One of them's wearing those ugly plaid shorts, Bermudas or something. They probably go to Towson State.

While they wait, they talk about some girls they know. The

girls are lucky they can't hear this conversation, which is about how all you have to do is buy them a couple of beers and they'll put out. They remind me of that son of a bitch Ralph.

After they leave, the cook turns to me. Well, I guess he does. He has this eye that doesn't work with the other one, like he's looking in two directions at once. You can never be sure if he's looking at you or somebody else. Wall-eyed, my father calls him. I order a cup of coffee and a cheeseburger.

"Coming up." He turns to the grill, black with grease, and drops a burger on it. "You're the kid the cops took in for questioning," he says.

"Yeah." I light a cigarette.

"You think they'll ever solve it?"

"I hope so."

He sets my coffee down in front of me. "Almost everybody I talk to thinks you done it."

"Yeah." I look at him, suddenly curious. "How about you?"

He shakes his head. "If I killed somebody, I sure as hell wouldn't stick around at the scene of the crime. Might as well hang a sign around your neck saying you done it."

"Yeah, that would be a really stupid thing to do." I swallow a mouthful of coffee and nearly scorch my throat. Tastes like it's been sitting in the urn since morning, strong enough to walk out the door and black as tar. "And I'm not stupid."

He flips my hamburger and slaps a slice of Kraft cheese on top. It bubbles over and burns on the grill. "Onions?"

I nod and he scrapes a mess of brown slices off the grill, dumps them on top of the cheese and levers everything into a grilled roll, brown on the edges and yellow in the middle with melted butter.

Or maybe grease. Tops it off with a pickle and hands it to me. "Fifteen cents," he says. I drop a nickel and a dime in his hand.

"So what are you doing now?" he asks.

"I leave for naval training tomorrow."

"I'd have left this dump long ago," he says.

A couple comes in and the girl puts a nickel in the jukebox. Cheryl's all-time favorite song comes on, Elvis singing "I Want You, I Need You, I Love You." For a second, I feel her in my arms, dancing slow and close, I smell the perfume she wore, I hear her voice singing the words in my ear, her breath warm and tickly.

I get up, leaving half my hamburger and most of my coffee.

When I'm at the door, the guy asks, "Don't you like my cooking no more?"

I shrug and step outside into the heat and humidity of the August night. I see Nora walking toward me. I really didn't think she'd come, but there she is, long legs and all, no smile, holding herself too straight like she's still wishing I hadn't called her.

# Another Secret Meeting

## NORA

I TAKE the receiver from Billy, hoping to hear Charlie's voice, but it's Buddy. I swallow, too surprised to say anything. What could he want?

He sounds nervous, not like his usual self. He wants to talk to me. I almost say no but he's leaving tomorrow and he's got nobody to talk to except me, which is so sad. He's lived in Elmgrove as long as I have, which is all his life, and he hasn't got one friend. Not since the murders. So I say okay, I'll meet him at the Little Tavern. I don't want to go but I feel sorry for him, I really do.

I tell my parents that Susan Allen, a girl in my class, wants me to meet her at the Sugar Bowl for a sundae.

"Do you want me to drive you there?" Mom asks.

I say it's a nice night and I feel like walking.

"It's dangerous after dark. You don't know who's out there," she says. I say there's nothing to be scared of. She says, "That boy is still in town, Myrtle Atwood saw him yesterday."

I wonder what she'd say if I tell her that's who I'm really meeting.

"You're always saying I should go out more," I tell her.

At last she and Dad decide it's okay, I can go, but I have to be home at nine thirty. A baby's curfew, I think, but I don't dare argue. And anyway, I don't want to stay out with Buddy any later than that.

It's five blocks to the Little Tavern, and even though I told Mom and Dad there's nothing to be scared of, I find myself almost running from one streetlight to the next. The yards are so dark, the trees cast such big shadows. I pass a few houses where people sit on their porches talking softly, but no one is out walking, not even the Clements totter past with their dog. Television sets flicker behind living room windows. *The Ed Sullivan Show* is on in almost every house I pass. Cars drive by, some with loud radios. A boy yells at me from an old Studebaker, "Hey, Legs, wanna ride?" I walk faster and I hear him laugh as the car speeds away.

Main Street is a relief. Stores are open, people come and go, and I feel safe.

I see Buddy coming out of the Little Tavern. I almost don't recognize him. He's gotten a really short crewcut. To be ready for the navy, I guess. He looks like a kid with a skinny neck and big ears, not like himself anymore.

"Your hair," I say.

He runs his hand over his stubby scalp. "Yeah," he says. "Saved the navy the trouble."

I picture him sitting in the barber's chair. Mr. Bellamy stands over him, his scissors snip, snip, snipping while Buddy's hair falls on the floor. I don't know why this makes me so sad. It just does.

For a while, we drive around the dark streets like we're on a tour of Elmgrove. Buddy stares straight ahead, smoking one cigarette after another. Neither of us says anything. The radio is silent.

I ask if I can turn it on. Buddy shakes his head. "I hate the music they play."

I nod. I understand. Here and there, the headlights pick up somebody walking a dog or a bunch of kids on a corner.

We pass Eastern, a big block of brick in the moonlight, its windows dark, its parking lot empty. "God, I hate that place," Buddy mutters.

"It was fun sometimes."

"Maybe for brains like you and Ellie."

"Ellie's the brain," I say, "not me. I almost flunked geometry and chemistry and I scraped through Latin with straight Cs."

He looks at me. "Yeah, but you're going to college. Teachers love that. They think kids like me are losers, going nowhere."

He hits the steering wheel with his fist. "I bet every one of them thinks I killed Cheryl and Bobbi Jo."

I shake my head. "I'm sure—"

He cuts in. "Two people in this town think I'm innocent. You and the cook at the Little Tavern. And you know why he thinks I didn't do it? Because I never went in there and laughed at him like Ralph and his friends. They'd make fun of him, cross their eyes and stuff, act like he was a moron. Jesus H. Christ. Those are the kind of guys teachers love."

What Buddy says about Ralph is true. Once I saw him making fun of Raymond, the janitor at Eastern. He's kind of retarded, I guess, and he has a harelip, which makes him talk funny. Ralph did a perfect imitation of him, and all the other basketball players laughed, even Don, and so did the cheerleaders. Poor Raymond just stood there, holding his broom. He knew they were laughing at him but he wasn't sure why. It made me so mad, but instead of saying something, I just walked away. The gym teachers saw it all. They didn't do a thing about it.

"You know what I think?" Buddy asks. "That son of a bitch was using her. Sally Smith dumped him and he was looking for somebody to make out with."

We're in the country now and it's dark. He speeds up, swerves around a curve. A Deer Crossing sign zooms past. What if we hit a deer?

"You saw her dancing with him," he goes on, "acting so sexy, wearing that low-necked blouse, you could practically see her tits. She looked like some cheap slut. And that's how he saw her—all he wanted was to get in her pants."

I've never been around a boy who talks about tits and getting into a girl's pants. I'm so embarrassed I can't even look at him.

Suddenly he swears words much worse than *tits* and pushes the gas pedal to the floor. The car speeds up, the tires squeal on a curve. Out of the darkness, telephone poles rush toward us, lit for a second, pale and straight, then gone again. Trees lurch past, here and gone in a sweep of the headlights.

He's going to crash, he's going to kill us both. I imagine the *Sun*'s headlines—MURDER SUSPECT DIES IN CAR CRASH ALONG WITH FRIEND OF VICTIMS. Everyone will think he was going to kill me, why else would I be in his car?

Why can't I say "Slow down"? I'm too scared. I've lost my voice. My face is paralyzed, I can't open my mouth.

The car swerves around a sharp curve, it crosses the center line, it heads straight at a huge tree, a killer tree. There's no escape. I'm going to die. I clench my teeth, shut my eyes, brace myself. Buddy struggles to control the car. We miss the tree, but we go off the road, skid through mud, slide sideways to a stop.

He turns off the engine. The sudden silence is like an explosion.

I sit beside him shaking, my heart pounding. So close, we were so close to dying.

Buddy doesn't look at me. In a quiet voice, almost a whisper, he says, "Cheryl was my girl. I loved her, I wanted to marry her after she graduated. She's all I ever wanted."

He presses his forehead against the steering wheel and grips it with both hands. I can't see his face, but his shoulders shake.

Very slowly, almost fearfully, I touch his shoulder. "I'm sorry," I whisper.

Without lifting his head, he nods.

We sit there silent again. The car windows are down. All around us, cicadas buzz and shriek. Lightning bugs glimmer in the trees. And the air smells sweet like cut grass. The night is cooler, not so humid.

I prop my feet on the dashboard. My new moccasins almost shine in the moonlight. I lean back in the seat, my head turned toward the window and the dark woods beyond.

# Nora, Nora—What the Hell

## BUDDY

I GOTTA say one thing about Nora. I almost wreck the goddamn car, I go to pieces on her, and she just sits there, nice and quiet. She even pats my shoulder and says she's sorry.

It means a lot to me. After I pull myself together, I tell her so. She gets all shy and hugs her knees to her chest like she's locking herself up tight. Against what? Me maybe. Like maybe she's just realized what a great makeout place this is, the side of a country road way out in the middle of God knows where and maybe I'm going to try something.

In the moonlight, I decide she's kind of pretty, not cover girl pretty, not sexy pretty like Cheryl, but pretty in a sort of sweet way. I wonder what she'd do if I tried to kiss her, a thought that surprises me.

I light a cigarette and look at her profile while I smoke. She has a nice mouth, full and definitely kissable.

We talk for a while about ordinary things. I ask her if she ever got a better camera but she says no, she's still got that Kodak Hawkeye. I tell her I drive around sometimes and take pictures of places Cheryl and me used to go. I don't say I always hope I just might see her wading in the spillover at the reservoir like she used to or walking along the road swinging her purse or sitting at the counter in Walgreen's drinking a cherry Coke or playing the jukebox at the Sugar Bowl or sitting on her front steps waiting for me to drive by. I can see her in those places so clear, I can't believe I'll never see her anywhere again. It's like a dagger in my heart carving me to pieces.

I tell Nora I'd like to be a photographer for *National Geographic* and travel all over the world—Africa, the South Pole, India, the Amazon, Japan and China and Easter Island where those heads are. I've never told anybody this, not even Cheryl, but Nora doesn't laugh or say guys like me don't get jobs like that.

Instead she says, "Maybe that's why you enlisted. To see the world. You should take lots of pictures and when you get out of the navy you can show them to *National Geographic*."

Like it's that easy. For a smart girl, Nora doesn't know much about how the world works. But still you can never tell. I could get lucky or something.

She tells me she wants to go to Maryland Institute, this art school in Baltimore, but her parents say they can't afford to send her there. She has to go to Towson State and live at home and take the trolley to class like she's still in high school. Her mother tells her she'd meet the wrong kind of people in art school—wild, Bohemian, no morals. She'd be ruined.

I tell her that's bullshit. She's a really good artist (and she is, I've seen some of her pictures in the art display case) and she should go to a real art school. But she just sighs and looks sad.

"The trouble with you is you got no backbone," I tell her. "You got to fight for what you want."

We look at each other and laugh because neither one of us knows how to get what we want. Never have, never will.

After a while we run out of stuff to talk about. She goes back to looking out the window, even though there's nothing to see in the dark. I go back to thinking about kissing her.

I look at the key in the ignition. I should start the car and take her home—yes, that's what I should do, what I ought to do, but I keep sitting there, smoking and thinking about kissing her. I never expected this. It wasn't on my mind when I called her up, it wasn't on my mind when she came walking out of the dark on those long legs of hers, it wasn't on my mind till she touched my shoulder and said she was sorry.

"Do you know what time it is?" she asks. Even though her voice is low, it's like a shout in the silence.

I check the glow-in-the-dark dial on my watch, a birthday present from Cheryl so we'd always know what time it was, even in the dark. "A little past ten," I say.

She draws in her breath. "Oh my God. I promised my parents I'd be home at nine thirty. They'll be worried to death—they think I'm at the Sugar Bowl with Susan Allen. Shit!" She says it in a cute way, like a kid who's just saying it out loud for the first time.

"Shit," I say like a goddamn echo. "How come you have to be home so early?"

"They're scared something will happen to me." She hesitates, bites that sweet lower lip. "You know, I might be killed by a maniac or something."

I feel like laughing, only it's not funny. "What do you think they'd say if they knew you were out with the killer himself?"

"They'd send me to the looney bin in a straitjacket." She tries to laugh like she's joking, but she means it. That's what her parents think of me. A girl would have to be crazy to get in my car. It's what they all think.

Nothing to do but drive her home now. It's probably just as well. She's not really my type. Cheryl was in Commercial like me—she was planning to go to secretarial school. This one's academic, maybe not in the Honor Society with the other brains, but going to college for sure. No sense starting something with her.

I turn the key and the engine starts. Maybe I was hoping it wouldn't, that we'd be stuck here and I'd take a chance and kiss her.

# Secrets

## NORA

Buddy stops the car around the corner from my house. He looks at me and I get this strange feeling he'd like to kiss me good night. I jerk the car door open. "I've got to go," I say and then add, "I hope you like the navy." Boy, does that sound dumb.

He shrugs. "It can't be worse than high school."

"Yeah." I hesitate, one foot outside the car but the rest of me inside. Do I want him to kiss me?

"If I write to you, will you write back?" he asks.

"Yeah, sure." But I'm thinking how will I explain when Mom notices I'm getting letters from him?

"I'm a lousy writer," he says, "almost flunked English more than once. Can't spell. So don't laugh when you read my letters."

He's still got that look in his eyes. I'm still more in the car than out. Part of me wants to lean over and kiss his cheek, which is crazy.

"I really should go," I say. "My parents . . ."

"So go," he says. "I'm not forcing you to stay."

"You know something?" I've got both feet on the sidewalk

now, but I'm leaning in the open door. "You're much nicer than I thought."

Suddenly he reaches over and pulls me closer. His lips bump against mine.

Startled, I let him kiss me again. His mouth is soft and warm, his teeth hard. I kiss him back.

Suddenly a car passes us, and I jump away, caught in the headlights.

We stare at each other, surprised. I remember laughing the first time Charlie kissed me. I don't laugh now. Buddy's not joking around. And neither am I.

"Take care of yourself, Legs," he says.

"You, too."

We stare at each for a long moment. I want to get back in the car and come home when the sun rises. Like a girl in a story. A doomed girl maybe. But I don't even touch the door handle. I stand there in the dark and memorize his face, scared of my own thoughts.

"I'll write," he says.

"Me, too," I whisper.

Then I turn and run around the corner toward home. Behind me, I hear him drive away. I touch my lips with my fingers.

Mom and Dad are watching *What's My Line?* and laughing at Bennet Cerf's attempts to guess the identity of the show's mystery guest. Taking advantage of their good mood, I apologize for being late and make up a lie about meeting some other kids and forgetting about the time. Since it's obvious I haven't been drinking or making out, they say good night and I go up to bed.

Alone in the dark, I hug my old bear and worry about what happened between Buddy and me. What if Ellie finds out I let him kiss me? She'll hate me. But maybe she hates me anyway for writing all that stuff about the Church.

Downstairs I hear Mom and Dad talking. Their voices are soft, but I can pick out a few words. "Seems happier . . . Susan . . . Sugar Bowl . . . just what she needs . . ." They must think I'm getting over Cheryl and Bobbi Jo, I'm going to be my old self again, I won't be moping around the house all day. They're happy because I lied to them.

I've never had a secret life before, and I'm not comfortable with it.

I'm not comfortable with my feelings about Buddy either. Truthfully, I wish he'd kissed me while we were parked in the woods, I wish I'd stroked his fuzzy head, I wished we'd made out. I wish I'd gotten back in the car and we're driving through a dark wood with honeysuckle and lightning bugs and the moon gliding along beside us. He's so much nicer than I thought. He's so sad. So haunted, so tragic . . . Oh, I don't know what it is about him. I like him, I just do. I can't help it.

My life is in danger of becoming a *True Confessions* story.

# CHERYL'S DIARY

*Friday, May 11*

*Guess what? I broke up with Buddy tonight. He's been
getting on my nerves really bad, always kissing me and
hugging me and touching me, even in school down by the
gym he tried to feel me up. He's like that joke about
foreign boyfriends—russian fingers and roman hands and
a french tongue. Ha ha. I told Bobbi Jo that but as usual
she didn't get it, said she thought he was an american.
That girl needs to get out of catholic school, and get away
from those nuns. What a load of crap they put in her head
about sin and hell and stuff. You just can't take religion
all that seriously. I mean I believe in God and all but I
don't think I'm going to hell for the stuff Buddy and
me do.*

*So anyway he begged me not to break up, I swear he
almost cried. I gave his ring back and he threw it out the
car window. If I didn't want it what good was it? I got out
of his car and ran inside and told my dad he wouldn't
leave me alone so he went out and cussed him out and
Buddy drove away so fast I was scared he might wreck the*

*car and kill himself. I saw him the next day and he tried*
*to talk to me but I was with Bobbi Jo and Ellie and they*
*didn't let him near me. I told them I was scared of him*
*which was a lie but I figured it was good to have them on*
*my side. I also told them he gave me the black eye my*
*father gave me last month.*

*Here's the reason I broke up with Buddy. I'm in love*
*with Ralph Stewart. He broke up with his girlfriend, that*
*stuck-up Sally Smith the cheerleader queen, and I think*
*he likes me. He's been hanging out near my locker and*
*talking to me before and after school. I'm scared Buddy*
*will see me with him and ruin everything, but so far he*
*hasn't. Now it doesn't matter what Buddy sees me do, I'm*
*not his girl anymore.*

*Ralph's so cute and he's on the basketball team and*
*the baseball team and he drives a brand new fifty-six*
*Chevy convertible his parents gave him cause he's*
*graduating this year. It's got these big fins and it's*
*turquoise and white and the seats look like leather but*
*maybe they're just vinyl, I can't tell. Anyway it's*
*beautiful and guess what???? He asked me out!!!!!. We're*
*going to the drive-in Saturday night to see The Searchers.*
*I saw it with Buddy but I pretended I hadn't seen it. It's a*
*western, not my favorite kind of movie, and it stars John*
*Wayne, not my favorite actor, but who watches the movie*
*at a drive-in? Ha ha.*

*My mother is really glad Buddy's finally out of the*
*picture. She says he'll never amount to anything, no*
*ambition or anything, just like my father. She told me it*

*was just as easy to fall in love with a rich guy as a poor guy. Smarter, too. It's practically the first thing she's ever told me that makes sense. She's right. A guy like Buddy won't get me out of a life like hers—no money, fighting all the time, trapped in a crummy little row house. But a guy like Ralph. His family's loaded, they must be if they live in Dulaney in one of those big houses. Besides, he's going to college, he plans to make something of himself.*

*Please God, let Ralph like me as much as I like him. Let him give me his class ring and ask me to go steady. Let me ride around in his car all summer with the top down and the radio playing loud. And when he leaves for Penn State, let him ask me to parties there. I'd love to see what college parties are like.*

*That's all, dear diary, wish me luck Saturday night!!!!!!!!!!!!!!!*

> *Ralph and Cheryl, Cheryl and Ralph,*
> *Mrs. Ralph Stewart, Cheryl Stewart*
> *Ralph and Cheryl 4-ever*

# Ellie's Letter

I DECIDE to write Nora and not say anything about religion. I'll just tell her what I've been doing and all. Maybe by now she's forgotten she wrote that stuff. Hopefully she's changed her mind, gotten over her doubts, back in the fold as the sisters say.

*Dear Nora,* I begin. *Hi, how are you? I'm fine.*

I sit and stare at the paper. My room is hot. My hand's sweaty. It sticks to the paper. Perspiration rolls down my back. I don't know what to say next. It's like I don't know Nora anymore.

I bend over the paper and try to picture Nora's face, her freckles, her smile, but she's blurry, like a snapshot out of focus. I frown and hold the pen tighter. I decide to tell her what I've been doing. Like we're talking on the phone the way we used to.

*It's not as boring here as I thought it would be. A few weeks ago, Uncle Ed and Aunt Marie invited some kids from church to a cookout in the backyard. Lou Ann's our age and Barb's a year younger. They go to Sacred Heart Academy and they're really nice. You'd like them. A boy*

*named Wayne also came. He reminds me of Paul,*
*always joking but much cuter. Too bad he goes steady*
*with Barb! It was kind of awkward at first, but after we*
*had soda and hamburgers we all kind of warmed up and*
*soon we were talking about movies and songs and stuff.*
*They like the same things we do. Louise saw Picnic three*
*times and On the Waterfront twice, just the opposite of*
*you and me! They love Elvis just like we do, especially*
*"I Want You, I Need You, I Love You." Except for*
*Wayne. He says it's corny. His favorite is "Hound*
*Dog" because you can jitterbug to it. He hates slow*
*dancing. Boys!!!*

*Tomorrow we're going to the swimming pool.*
*Wayne has a friend named Hank he wants me to meet.*
*Lou Ann tells me he's a makeout artist, she says I better*
*keep my buttons buttoned and my zippers zipped.*
*Ha ha.*

*I have to say, it's really great to be with kids*
*who don't know anything about Cheryl and Bobbi Jo.*
*No questions, no funny looks. I'm not scared here*
*either. Buddy's far away. I hope he's in jail*
*by now.*

*Aunt Marie's house reminds me of your house. It's the*
*same style. It's not as hot here though and the nights are*
*lots cooler.*

*How do you like my lavender stationery? Doesn't it*
*go well with this green ink? I bought it at the five and*
*dime just to write to you.*

*Write soon and tell me what you're up to—nothing I wouldn't do, ha ha.*

*Your friend forever,*

*Ellie*

The letter sounds dumb, but I don't know what else to say, so I put it an envelope and mail it. A dumb letter is better than no letter, I guess.

# PART EIGHT

## Changes

# The Bookstore Beatnik

## NORA

I FINALLY get a letter from Ellie. After I read it, I stare at the green ink looping cheerfully across the lavender paper. She's made circles over the *i*'s instead of dots. When did she start doing that? I read it again—she's got new friends, maybe a boyfriend, she's going places, doing things. She's glad nobody up there knows about Cheryl and Bobbi Jo. She seems to be having fun, though, definitely more than I'm having.

I shove the lavender paper away and stare out my bedroom window at the leaves of the maple sighing and rustling in the morning breeze. It's the kind of letter you write to someone you don't know very well. She tells me what she's doing, but she doesn't say anything about what she's thinking. Or feeling. And that makes me sad. Really sad.

There's nothing in her letter about religion. Not one word. That probably means she doesn't feel the same way I do. Maybe she hates me for what I told her. Maybe she thinks I'm going to hell. What if she's right?

What if I told her about Buddy? She'd really hate me.

I decide not to answer her letter right away. Mainly because

I don't know how to say what I need to say. Such as does she still want to be my friend? Is she mad because I don't believe in God?

What if she tells her mother what I said about God and church and all that? Suppose her mother calls my mother and tells her?

I look at my clock. Ten thirty. I decide to go to the used book store in Fullerton. It's a long walk, but I need something to read. I don't want to go the library because they all know me there and they'll ask about Cheryl and Bobbi Jo. I wonder how long I'll have to avoid people who ask questions about the murders. Lucky Ellie.

I take the path along the streetcar tracks. It dips through a patch of woods and I hesitate at the edge. The woods are full of shadows and splashes of sunlight and birdsong. I feel uneasy when the trees close in and I walk faster, looking over my shoulder, tensing at every rustle and snap in the underbrush. Anyone could be hiding in the shadows, waiting, finger pressing a trigger. My heart beats faster. I'm almost running when I leave the trees behind.

In Fullerton, I keep an eye out for dogs and mean kids. It's got some tough neighborhoods. One night last winter, Cheryl and Bobbi Jo and Ellie and I had some trouble with a few boys from there, they followed us back to Ellie's house from the bowling alley and Mr. O'Brien had to chase them away. If Cheryl hadn't been such a flirt. God, she just had to go after every guy she saw, even though she was with Buddy then. She'd toss her hair and smile and give them the eye and before you knew it they were expecting a makeout party.

I realize what I'm thinking and I feel awful. I'm sorry, I'm sorry, I tell Cheryl. But does she hear me?

By the time I get to the bookstore, I'm melting. I must look awful—my blouse is sticking to me and the hair on the back of my neck is damp. I'm sure my bangs have curled up like I have a home permanent and whoever did it left the stuff on too long.

The bookstore's not air conditioned. An old fan whirs away, but it's just moving hot air around and making my hair look even worse. Not that it matters.

I wander between rows of tall shelves, crammed tight with books. Surplus books are stacked in piles on the floor. The store smells like old paper turning to dust, ink evaporating, glue dissolving. I breathe it in, loving it. I wonder how long it takes books to get this particular smell.

I come across a bunch of Kathleen Winsor's books. Ellie and I read *Forever Amber* last year, even though it's on the Index of books Catholics aren't supposed to read. According to the Church, it has too many sex scenes, which is why, of course, we read it. *Gone with the Wind* is on the list, too, because of Scarlett and Rhett's divorce, a sin in the eyes of the church. We read it, too. I had to hide *Forever Amber* from Mom and read it under the covers at night, but she didn't even know *Gone with the Wind* is on the list.

Near *Forever Amber*, I find a copy of *Marjorie Morningstar*, the story of a teenage girl who wants to be an actress. It's pretty new and I'm surprised to see a used copy. I think it's still number one on the *New York Times* bestseller list. Everybody's reading it. Maybe it's here because the person who bought it didn't like it after all. Their loss, my gain.

In the S's, I pick out the English edition of *Bonjour Tristesse*. It's supposed to be very romantic (in other words, it has lots of sex in it), and I'm pretty sure it's on the Index, but what do I care about the Index now? Or what the Church thinks? I'll read what I want to read, and I want to read this book because the author, Françoise Sagan, is French and about my age, which is amazing. I can't imagine writing a novel, let alone finding someone to publish it. The title means *Hello, Sadness*. Even I know that much French. It suits my mood perfectly.

I decide I can buy both books and still have enough left for a cherry Coke at Walgreen's.

The guy at the cash register looks like a beatnik. Pale and thin, longish hair, a beard, but handsome in a mysterious way. He's wearing a black T-shirt and black slacks. And sandals. I've never seen a boy wearing sandals. I'm kind of scared to talk to him, so I put my books on the counter and wait for him to look up from what he's reading.

"Seventy cents," he says. His eyes are a brilliant shade of green.

Still speechless in the presence of so much sophistication, I hand him a dollar and he counts out my change. While he's busy, I peek at the book he's reading. *Poems: 1909–1925*. It's an old book. I guess he found it here, among dozens of musty books in the poetry section. I can't quite make out the author's name.

He catches me looking and turns the book toward me. "Have you read T. S. Eliot?"

I shake my head slowly, aware of the sweat trickling down my spine and soaking my underarms. The name sounds familiar, maybe I've heard of him but I'm not sure. Feeling hopelessly stupid,

I just stand there and wish I was smart and sophisticated and wore my hair long and straight and dressed in black and knew who T. S. Eliot was.

He closes his eyes and recites poetry unlike anything I've ever read, dark and strange and unsettling. Hearing it, I want to do things with words I've never done. I want to know what the poem means, I want to read it myself.

Suddenly he stops and opens his strange green eyes. "*That's* T. S. Eliot. *The Wasteland.*"

"It's neat," I say, blushing with embarrassment. *Neat*—is that the best word I can come up with?

"Neat." He smiles. "Yeah, it's neat, all right."

"I never heard poetry like that."

He comes out from behind the counter and beckons me to follow him. He's tall and lanky and his T-shirt is slowly fading from black to green. I notice a few holes in it. I can see his white skin through them. His shaggy dark hair clings to the back of his neck. I wonder what Dad would say if he showed up at our front door. Nothing good, that's for sure.

In the poetry section, he looks for T. S. Eliot's poetry. He has long slender fingers and his nails are short and jagged. He must bite them.

"Nothing here," he says. "Too bad."

He looks at me and turns back to the shelves. "How about Walt Whitman? Have you read him?"

The name sounds familiar. "Didn't he write a poem about lilacs or something?"

"That's him." He smiles and hands me an old paperback. "*Leaves of Grass,*" he says.

I look at the price. Thirty cents. If I buy it, I won't have enough left for a Coke. "I can't afford it."

He leads me to the counter. "Put *Marjorie Morningstar* back. It's a crappy bestseller. Plus Wouk's a crappy writer. Don't ruin your mind with junk like that."

I nod. Up until now I hadn't been sure I had a mind to ruin. "Okay."

"And look, you get ten cents back." He slides a dime across the counter. "How old are you?"

"Almost seventeen."

"Still in high school."

For the first time I wish I was older instead of shorter. "I'll be a senior this fall."

He smiles again.

"Do you go to Towson State?" I ask.

"Towson State? Me?" He laughs like I've said something funny. "I'm home for the summer. I go to NYU."

"What's that stand for?" I know I should know, but I ask anyway.

"New York University."

"You live in New York City?" I'm awestruck.

"Yeah." He shrugs and studies me with those green eyes.

"Have you ever been to Greenwich Village?" I ask.

"Only almost every day. You been there?"

I shake my head. "My friends and me—and I," I correct myself, "are going to Times Square on New Year's Eve when we're eighteen." And then I remember two of them are not going.

He's grinning like I'm the funniest person he's ever met. "Times

Square—God, that's as bad as reading *Marjorie Morningstar*," he tells me. "Go to the Village, find a coffeehouse, hear some beat poetry, try some reefer."

"Reefer?" I don't know what he's talking about.

He laughs. "On second thought, go to Times Square. Save the Village till you're older. Like twenty-one or something." He puts my books in a bag and hands it to me. "You're a gas," he says.

I blush again. Is he complimenting me? Or insulting me?

"Come back and tell me what you think of Whitman," he says as I turn to leave.

"Okay." I trip over a pile of books and they tumble across the floor. I stoop to pick them up and *Leaves of Grass* falls out of the bag. The bookstore beatnik comes over and hands me my book. He's laughing.

"I'll clean up the others," he says. "At the rate you're going, you'll destroy the whole store."

"I'm sorry, I didn't see them. I—"

"Don't apologize. The store's a booby trap." He looks at me with his electric eyes. "My name's Larry Brownstein, what's yours?"

"Nora Cunningham."

He nods. "Well, Nora, it was nice to meet you."

"You, too." I back away, clutching my bag. "I'll see you later."

As I walk down Center Road, I realize there's a whole world out there, places I haven't been, places I haven't heard of. There are books I haven't read, writers I don't know. Paintings, poems, plays, movies, music. Oddly excited, I don't notice the woods closing in around me, the stillness, the green shade. One more year of high school. And I'll be free.

At Walgreen's, I sit at the counter and sip my Coke. I want to make it last so I can bask in air-conditioned comfort as long as possible and think about Larry. How long will it take me to grow enough hair to pull back in a ponytail? Do I dare to wear black clothes to school? How much does a train ticket to New York cost?

"Nora, I haven't seen you all summer. Where've you been?"

Startled out of my thoughts, I spin around and see Susan. She's with Julie Ferguson and Nancy Browne, girls I hung out with before Ellie and I became best friends.

"We thought you'd gone away like Ellie," she goes on. "Somebody told me she was about to have a nervous breakdown because of what happened in the park and her parents sent her to stay with her aunt or something."

"Did you know Buddy Novak joined the navy?" Julie asks. "My father says he can't believe the navy accepted him. God, he murdered two girls."

"The police never charged him," I say.

"Everyone knows he did it," Julie says. "My father's a policeman and he says if they find that gun Buddy's fingerprints will be all over it."

"Somebody told me you and Ellie saw him on the bridge," Susan says. "He gave you a ride to school—you must've been really scared when you found out why he was there."

I shrug. I don't want to talk about that day, I want to forget it, pretend I wasn't there, it didn't happen. Before anyone can say anything else, I ask Julie where she got her lipstick. "I love that color."

"It's Revlon," she says, "Cotton Candy Pink. They sell it here." She gestures at the makeup section.

"We're going to the pool tomorrow," Susan says. "Do you want to go?"

For some reason I say sure, yeah, I'd love to, when all I really want to do is get away from them and go home and read Walt Whitman so I can go back to the bookstore and talk to Larry.

# Five Pines Swimming Pool

## NORA

Susan, Julie, and Nancy pick me up the next day. Mom is happier than I am. You'd think I was going to the senior prom or something. I tell her it's no big deal, but she keeps on smiling. My daughter will soon be her old self, she must be thinking. Normal. No need for a psychiatrist after all.

I haven't been to the pool all summer and I look like it. My legs are as white as a fish's belly. My arms are almost as white as my legs, and my face has more freckles than suntan.

If it had been a normal summer, Ellie and I would have lain out in our backyards building up a good burn in hopes we'd eventually turn tan. We'd have gone to the pool at least twice a week, bumming rides with Buddy and Cheryl or Paul and Charlie. I'd planned to practice diving. I wanted to learn flips. And I wanted to swim the length of the pool underwater and sit on the bottom and hold my breath for so long a cute lifeguard would dive in to rescue me.

All that seems stupid now. In the little changing booth, I tug down my bathing suit, hoping to cover my rear end without revealing my breasts. I can never find a suit that fits right. I'm just too tall.

"Hey, Nora, whatcha doing in there?" Julie calls.

I push the curtain aside and follow her to the mirror. "You want to borrow this?" Julie holds out the tube of Revlon and I put some on.

Next to her, I look so plain. Freckles and hair that needs cutting, a bump in my nose that I hate, long neck, collarbones that stick out like my skeleton is working its way out of my body. Julie is short and cute, dirty blond pixie haircut, tan, perfect figure. I like her black and white plaid bathing suit. It's elasticized cotton like mine, but it fits her the way mine doesn't fit me.

Susan and Nancy are combing their hair. They both have bouncy ponytails.

The three of them come up to my shoulder. Why do I have to be so tall? It's not fair.

"Look what I've got." Nancy pulls a bottle of peroxide out of her purse. "We're going to bleach streaks in our hair. You want to do yours?"

"I guess so."

I follow them outside, taking care to step in the foot bath of disinfectant at the door. It's cloudy and sort of gray, like old dishwater. Is it for athlete's foot? Ringworm? Best not to wonder why it's there and what it's preventing—or not preventing.

The noise of the pool slaps me, kids shouting and laughing, splashing water. The smell of chlorine and Coppertone. I see Ralph on the high dive, bouncing lightly, making sure everybody's looking. Sally the cheerleader is perched on the edge of the pool, looking up at him and smiling. She claps when he dives, a perfect jackknife.

"Wow, did you see that?" Nancy asks. "God, he's so damn cute."

While the others go on about Ralph's tan and his patch of blond peroxide hair and his build, I watch him sit down beside Sally and give her a kiss. She's wearing his ring on a chain around her neck again. I remember Buddy saying he was after one thing from Cheryl and I hope he didn't get it while they were down in the woods the night before, before . . . Oh, how I hate him.

Beside me, Nancy is opening the peroxide bottle. While we watch, she wets a cotton ball and dabs at the wave of hair dipping across her forehead.

"How much do you put on?" Julie asks.

Nancy shrugs. "I've never done it before." She wets the cotton ball and dabs more on her hair.

"Don't put on too much," Susan warns. "It can turn your hair orange."

Nancy holds out the bottle. "Who wants to try some?"

Julie takes it. Instead of bothering with a cotton ball, she bends her head and pours it right on her hair. She's not out for one streak.

Susan screams. "Are you nuts?"

"My hair's almost blond anyway," Julie says. "It's only brunettes who turn orange."

Susan reaches for the bottle. "Give me a cotton ball, Nancy. I just want to try a little. If it doesn't work, I can always put more on."

While we watch, she touches her hair lightly, dabbing the peroxide on like it's iodine or something.

"Here, Nora, you try."

I take the little brown bottle from her and wet a cotton ball. I'm

a little more daring than Susan but not quite as daring as Nancy—
and certainly no way near as daring as Julie.

"How long do you think it will take?" Julie asks.

"I don't know." Nancy lies down on her towel and shuts her
eyes. "We shouldn't go in the water right away. You know, the chlorine might do something to it."

We lie in a row, feet toward the pool, eyes closed, and wait to
see what happens.

The pool's loudspeaker plays old songs. Nat King Cole sings
"Nature Boy." Next it's "Mona Lisa." It must be Nat King Cole day
at the pool.

My mind drifts away on that soft, sweet voice to last summer.
Ellie and me in the pool turning somersaults underwater, standing on our hands with our feet sticking out of the water, seeing
who can sit on the bottom longest, trying to talk to each other
underwater and then popping up, laughing. *Did you understand
what I said? Sure: Bubble bubble bubble.*

Cheryl and Buddy kissing underwater, Bobbi Jo flirting with
the lifeguard—*I told him I was sixteen and he believed it! He asked me for
my phone number—do you think he'll really call me?*

Ellie and me diving off the low dive, trying to improve our
style, getting in line for the high dive and jumping off, hitting the
water feet first, daring each other to dive but both of us scared
to try.

It's like watching a movie in my head, a story that happened to
some other girls in some other time and place.

I roll over on my stomach and hide my face in my arms so nobody will see me cry. I want to go back to last summer, I want

Cheryl and Bobbi Jo to be here. I don't want to be confused and scared anymore. I wish I were still a Catholic and believed in God and thought the world was a safe place and nothing bad happened to people you know. Only strangers in the newspaper got murdered and raped and died in car crashes and drowned when ships sank.

That Nora, the one who went to Catholic retreats with Ellie, is gone, the one who went to confession and prayed to be forgiven for impure thoughts is gone, the one who believed she was unworthy to receive the body and blood of Christ, the one who wept over the hymn "Mother dear oh pray for me" and said the rosary and the Stations of the Cross and followed the Mass in her missal and gave up candy for Lent—she is gone and she will never come back.

That Nora is as dead as Cheryl and Bobbi Jo. The bullets hit her, too. They hit Ellie. They hit Charlie. The bullets hit all the kids in Ellie's neighborhood, they hit mothers and fathers and little sisters and little brothers.

They hit Buddy, too, maybe hardest of all, but nobody noticed, nobody cared.

I lie there and watch an ant crawling through the blades of grass. Rosemary Clooney is singing "Come On-a My House." Another old song but a good one. I wonder what Buddy's doing and if he thinks of me. I hope he likes the navy. I hope he's made some friends.

"God," Julie mutters, "why can't they play Elvis? Next it'll be Johnny Ray singing 'The Little White Cloud That Cried.'"

Susan laughs. "Followed by Patty Page singing 'How Much Is That Doggie in the Window?'"

But they're both wrong. It's Tennessee Ernie Ford singing "Sixteen Tons." We all groan. I think the pool should hire Gary to play his record collection.

"Who wants to go swimming?" Nancy asks.

The pool is packed with people, mostly little kids, screaming and splashing and ducking each other, cannonballing into the water. We jump in the deep end, where there aren't so many kids, and paddle around. We check each other's hair but don't see any blond streaks.

While we're sitting on the edge of the pool, I see Ralph making out with Sally.

The others see them too. Julie scowls at Sally. "Lucky duck," she says. "Wish I had a boyfriend like that."

"I heard he was dating Cheryl on the sly," Susan says to me. "Is that true?"

I shrug.

"That's why Buddy killed her," Nancy says. "He was jealous."

"Why did he kill Bobbi Jo, though?" Susan asked.

"Because she was with Cheryl," Nancy says. "If she hadn't walked to school that day, she'd still be alive."

"It's so sad," Julie says. "Poor Bobbi Jo."

"That's right, isn't it?" Three pairs of eyes turn to me.

I shrug again. Will they ever get tired of talking about it?

"God," Julie says. "If you and Ellie had been with them, you'd be dead too."

I'm saved from answering by Nancy's scream. "Oh my God, Julie—your hair."

"What's wrong with it?" she asks.

"It's green!"

Julie gasps and jumps up. We follow her to the dressing room and peer over her shoulder at the mirror. "Oh, no." She starts to cry.

"It's the chlorine," Susan says.

"My parents will kill me."

"I told you not to put so much on," Nancy says.

"Stop crying, Julie," Susan says. "A beautician can fix it. My cousin did that to her hair once and she got it bleached or dyed or something and it looked fine."

"Really?" Julie wipes her eyes and blows her nose.

We get dressed and leave the pool. My hair has a blond streak, not green and not orange. It looks really good, I think. Natural. Nancy's is like mine but wider, more noticeable. Susan's doesn't even show. She must not have put enough on.

"I hope Mom will give me the money to fix it," Julie says. "If she won't, I'll die."

Nancy laughs. "You can always wear a grocery bag on your head, you know, with holes cut out for your eyes."

"Oh, that's really funny." Julie glares at Nancy. "I could die laughing."

"Geez, what's wrong with you? Can't you take a joke?"

The radio plays "The Great Pretender" and the others sing along. In the back seat with Julie, I look out the side window. We're in Elmgrove's oldest neighborhood; big Victorian houses three stories high line both sides of the street. Towers and cupolas and huge porches—or would they be called verandas? Tall oaks, shady yards, new cars with tail fins like rocket ships in the driveways, the sort of places lawyers and dentists call home.

I try not to listen to the Platters, but they get in my head anyway. Julie and Nancy and Susan sing along the way Ellie and I used to, but I just sit there silently, hoping no one can tell how lonely I am. Lonely for my old life, lonely for Ellie and Charlie, for Cheryl and Bobbi Jo, for Buddy. Yes, for Buddy. Poor lonely Buddy with his big ears and sad little fuzzy head.

Pretending, pretending, pretending. Sometimes I think my whole life is pretending.

Nancy lets me out first. They say goodbye and promise to call me and wave and smile and drive away. I watch the car disappear. They won't call me. I scarcely said a word all day, didn't crack a joke or laugh or even smile much. What a drag I am. What a boring girl. Why would anyone want to be my friend?

Avoiding Mom, I sling my bathing suit and towel on the clothesline, go to my room, lie down on my bed, and spend the rest of the afternoon reading *Bonjour Tristesse*. If only I lived in France. Life would be different there. I'd be different there. Sophisticated. I'd never trip over things or drop them. I'd wear black and my hair would be long and straight—there must be something you can do to make curls go away. Maybe I'd have a lover on the Left Bank. He'd look like Larry from the bookstore only he'd be French. Somehow I'd learn French and read *Madame Bovary* in a café while I drank black coffee in one of those little cups and smoked Gauloises, a cigarette they smoke in France.

## PART NINE

# The End of Summer

# What Is the Grass?

## NORA

To my surprise Susan calls me a few days later. I go to the movies with her and Nancy and Julie and see *Guys and Dolls.* I fall in love with Marlon Brando all over again. We all do. We love his pinstriped suit and his gangster accent. I think he's sexier as Terry Malloy in *On the Waterfront,* but the others go for him as Sky Masterson. Maybe because he's in technicolor.

We go to the pool two or three times a week, and I actually learn how to do a flip off the diving board, even though I almost kill myself. We rent skates at the roller rink and I fall down a lot, but a sailor asks me to skate in couples. We bowl and I still excel at gutter balls. I laugh more than I've laughed for a long time.

I start to feel a little more comfortable around them, especially now that they've given up asking about Cheryl and Bobbi Jo. It's not like being with Ellie, of course, but it's kind of nice to go places again. And it makes Mom happy.

Julie goes to a beauty salon and has some kind of expensive treatment to get the green out. Her mother made her pay for it, which means she had to use all the babysitting money she'd been saving for fall clothes. We all think that was really mean of her mother.

My hair has one little blond streak, but since I need to get it cut, I expect it will be gone soon. Mom doesn't like it and Daddy got mad and said did I want to look cheap and I said everybody does it. They said I wasn't everybody. It's as if they have a button and when they push it that's what comes out of their mouths. When I have kids, if anybody ever marries me, that is, I hope I can come up with something better than "You're not everybody."

When I'm not hanging out with Susan and Julie and Nancy, I read. Now that I'm going out more often, Mom isn't always nagging me to get my nose out of a book. She lets me lounge around on a blanket in the backyard and work on getting a good tan while I read. With ants crawling on my legs and bees buzzing in the clover, I read *Leaves of Grass*. I savor it, I let the words roll round in my mind until I can almost taste them, until they flow through me like blood in my veins. Walt Whitman is unlike any poet I've ever read—the rhythm, images, and words he uses, the pictures he makes in my mind. At night, I spend hours trying to draw what I see when I read, but throw most of them away. Why is it so hard to move a picture out of your head and onto a piece of paper?

Parts of the poem make me feel the way I do at Mass when the priest reads the last Gospel. There's mystery in the words, things I don't understand with my mind but feel with my heart. I decide *Leaves of Grass* will be my Bible and Walt Whitman will be my God. I study a picture of him, an old man with a beard. He looks like a prophet or even God himself.

I want to memorize the whole poem but that's impossible. Bits and pieces of it stick in my mind, though. When no one is around to see or hear me, I sometimes whisper to the lawn, "'What is the grass? . . . it must be the flag of my disposition, out of hopeful green stuff woven.'"

At church, I say to myself, "'Why should I pray? Why should I venerate and be ceremonious?'" It's a good thing the priest can't hear my thoughts.

I write these and other quotations in my diary, but I don't copy down the parts that disturb me and excite me and make me feel like I'm bursting out of my body. Things like the wind brushing your flesh and young men bathing naked and the beauty of their bodies. Things that remind me of making out with Charlie and how much I liked kissing him. And Buddy, too. Sometimes I think about kissing him the way I kissed Charlie, of letting him touch my breasts. And Larry—how would it be to kiss him?

These things are too private to put in a diary your brother might find. Or your mother.

One day I finally get the nerve to walk to the bookstore. I'm going to tell Larry I love Walt Whitman, I'm going to say he's changed my life, he's made me think things I never thought before.

Mr. Long, the owner, is sitting at the counter. He's an old guy and sort of scruffy. Always needs a shave and a haircut and a bath— *You use Dial, don't you wish everybody did?*—but he's really nice.

Anyway, he smiles when he sees me. I've been coming here since I was ten and looking for Nancy Drew books.

"I haven't seen you for a while, Nora," he says. "I just got in a set of Agatha Christie's Miss Marple books—are you still reading those?"

I shake my head. "After you read a few they're all the same. The killer will be the really charming person, the one you'd never guess."

Mr. Long grins. "Too true, too true."

Yeah, too too true, I think. In real life, murder isn't like anything Agatha Christie ever wrote about. Sometimes the killer gets away with it.

"Maybe you should try a different writer," Mr. Long goes on. "You might like Edmund Crispin. *The Moving Toy Shop* is one of my favorites."

I nod, but while he's talking, I'm looking for Larry. I hear someone moving around in the back and hope it's him. Please let it be him. I have to see him.

Finally I ask, "Is Larry here?" I blush and trip over my words. I must sound like I have a crush on Larry. Maybe I do.

Mr. Long shakes his head. "He went back to New York last week."

"Oh." I shrug like it doesn't matter, it isn't that important.

"I miss him," Mr. Long says. "He was a good worker. Loved books. Poetry especially."

I struggle to hide my disappointment. "If you see him, will you tell him I really love Walt Whitman?" My face feels so hot I must be on fire.

"I should have known it was you." Mr. Long reaches under the desk and comes up with a book of T. S. Eliot's poetry. "He couldn't remember your name, but he said if a tall girl came in and said she liked Walt Whitman, I was to give her this." With a smile, he hands the book to me. "And here I am thinking you still liked Agatha Christie."

The phone rings and he turns away to answer it.

"Thanks," I whisper. Clutching the book, I leave the store and find a shady place. I sit down on the grass and slowly open the book. On the title page, there's a scrawl of handwriting: *To the tall girl whose name I forget—sorry sorry sorry—I'm glad you liked Walt Whitman, I knew you would. When you're older, come to Greenwich Village and look me up. We can talk about Whitman and Eliot.* "Missing me one place, search another; I stop somewhere, waiting for you." *Larry Brownstein.*

Is that just a line he likes in *Leaves of Grass,* or does he really mean he's waiting for me? I wish I could get on the train to New York tomorrow and find him and escape this town, this place, these people forever. I think I might be in love with him.

I read the first lines in *The Wasteland,* the ones Larry recited, and I hear his voice. I see his dark hair straggling down his neck and his electric eyes and his pale skin and his black clothes and his sandals. He's everything I don't know about. Which makes him scary and attractive at the same time.

I go back to the store and tell Mr. Long to thank Larry for me. I ask if he ever comes home, maybe at Christmas or something, and Mr. Long shrugs and says, "With Larry, who can tell?"

With anyone, who can tell?

# A Talk with Ralph

## NORA

A COUPLE of days later, I run into Ralph in the drugstore. I've been avoiding him all summer, but this time I almost bump right into him, which forces us to look at each other.

We say hello and I start to turn away but he stops me and says, "Can I talk to you for a minute?"

"About what?" I ask him, though I know damn well there's only one thing for us to talk about.

"Just some stuff that's on my mind." His face is red and he fumbles for words.

The next thing I know we're sitting at a booth in the back of the drugstore drinking cherry Cokes and he's saying, "Look, Nora, I know you must hate me for not going to her funeral."

"*Her* funeral?" I look at him as if I don't know who he's talking about. He doesn't want to say her name, I think, but now he has to.

"Cheryl." He says her name in a low voice and looks at the table as if he's talking to it instead of me. "Cheryl's funeral. I didn't go."

"Yeah," I say, "I noticed."

"I couldn't," he says. "I got up that morning, I put on my suit, but I couldn't get my tie right. I looked at myself in the mirror and I knew I should go, I really did, but somehow, somehow . . ." He shrugs.

"Somehow you just didn't," I say.

"I've never known anyone who died," he says as if this is a valid excuse. He swallows hard. "I was scared," he whispers, still studying the scratched tabletop. "I didn't want to see her—or Bobbi Jo either."

I lean toward him. "Do you think *I* wanted to see them? Do you think Ellie or anybody else wanted to see them?"

He shakes his head. His glass has left a wet ring on the table. He traces it with his finger.

"I was scared too," I tell him. "We all were, but we went to the funerals anyway."

He keeps on tracing the ring, smudging, smearing, altering it.

"It was the first time I went to a visitation or a funeral." I look at the top of his head, streaked even blonder now, at the crisp collar of his blue shirt, at his wristwatch with the luminous dial on a chrome stretch band. "I didn't want to go, but I had to," I tell him. "They were my friends."

"I liked her," he mutters. "She was, well, she . . ." His voice trails away as if he can't come up with anything to say about Cheryl. Like what a good dancer she was or what she and he did down in the woods all that time. Or if Buddy was right when he said guys like Ralph only wanted one thing from girls like Cheryl.

So I suck up the last of my Coke and say, "I notice you're back with Sally now." It's kind of nasty, but the longer we sit here, the more I hate him.

He nods. His fingers have found the ashtray and he's sliding it around the table. "Well, I just wanted you to know, wanted to say, uh, I mean, I wanted . . ." He stalls again. "Look," he says, "I have to go. I'm supposed to meet my mother at the dentist's office—in fact I'm already late."

I watch him leave. He's in such a hurry to get away from me, he almost knocks a kid down on his way out of Walgreen's. God, I am so glad he's leaving for college soon. I won't have to see him when school starts. Or Don either. Good riddance.

# BUDDY'S LETTER

*Friday, August 24*

Buddy finally writes to me. It's embarrassing, but my heart beats a little faster when I see the envelope. It's not as if I'm in love with him or anything, at least I hope not. Mom hasn't seen the mail yet, so I run up to my room and read it there.

*Dear Nora,*

*I bet you didn't think I'd write but here I am. It's been a while since I left but you have no idea how tough the Navy is. When I get off duty I'm usually too tired to pick up a pen, I either fall asleep or go out with some of the guys and get a beer. Tonight though I thought I'd write you a letter which I hope you answer because so far I haven't gotten any mail, not even from my folks.*

*I gotta say I don't much like the Navy. Officers boss you around all the time and you have to salute and say yes sir and no sir and act like you respect them, even if their jerks, especially if their jerks. They make you swab*

*decks and clean the heads and eat crappy food and obey*
*hundreds of rules most of which are stupid but I signed on*
*for three years so I'm stuck, it's not the kind of job you*
*can quit.*

*I'm at sea now, I can't say where but there's lots of*
*water as far as I can see. Ha ha.*

*I think about Cheryl every day and night. I write*
*letters to her in my head, I tell her what I'm doing and*
*how much I miss her, sometimes I forget she's dead. Out*
*here away from everybody it's easy to think of her*
*hanging out with you and Ellie and Bobbi Jo, and I'll see*
*her when I come home on leave, she's just so real to me. I*
*keep her picture in my wallet and sometimes I show it to*
*guys and tell them she's my girl and they all think she's*
*really pretty and I'm a lucky SOB. So far, nobody here*
*knows anything about what happened in Elmgrove. If I'm*
*lucky it'll stay that way.*

*One night when I was drunk I got her name tattooed*
*on my arm. The guy did a nice job, put it inside a*
*heart. It's on my bicep which is bigger now from all the*
*work I do.*

*I hope you're having a good summer, better than*
*mine. Maybe when I come home on leave we could go*
*to a movie or something but it's okay if you don't*
*want to.*

*Well write soon and tell me how you are and what*
*your doing.*

*As Ever,*
*your friend Buddy*

I read the letter a couple of times. The parts about Cheryl are so sad I feel like crying. Poor Buddy, I think, oh, poor Buddy. I wish I could stroke his fuzzy head and make him forget Cheryl.

If he asks me to a movie when he comes home, should I go? I start worrying, My parents will have a fit. Ellie will hate me. Susan and Nancy and Julie will think I'm crazy. I feel like I'm breaking out in a rash just thinking about it. Prickly heat maybe.

But I also know I will go if he asks me, even if I have to lie. And if he kisses me again, I will kiss him back.

# Ellie Comes Home

## NORA

THE week before school starts, Ellie calls. She's back, she's sorry she hasn't written more often, she wants me to come over and spend the night like I used to.

"Why don't you come here?" I ask.

There's a heartbeat of silence. "I asked first," she says with a laugh.

How can I tell her I don't want to go to her house? I don't want to see Bobbi Jo's mother or her little sisters or her father, I don't want to see the park. I just don't, don't, don't. I try to think of something to say, but nothing comes to mind. Except Cheryl and Bobbi Jo and this is the first time I've thought of them for days, maybe even weeks, and I feel terrible. Awful.

"You don't want to come here, do you?" Ellie sounds a little mad, a little sad.

I twist the phone cord. "It's, I, well. I really want to see you, I've missed you so much, but, well . . . it's just . . ." My face burns with embarrassment.

Ellie doesn't say anything for a while. I breathe, she breathes.

Finally she says, "School starts next week. I'll be at St. Joseph's. We'll never see each other."

When Ellie starts crying, I cry too. If we could just go back to the night before they died, if we could just figure out what was going on and change something, maybe everything would be the way it used to be. But deep down inside, I know we can't go back. No matter how much we want to.

# Nora's Second Dream

## NORA

THAT night I sit up late reading *A Certain Smile* (or, if you know French, *Un certain sourire*), Françoise Sagan's newest book, which I checked out of the library despite a disapproving look from Miss Snyder, who knows my mother and probably thought if I were her daughter I wouldn't be allowed to read French novels.

When I'm too tired to read, I turn out the light and stare into the darkness. I wonder what it's like to be twenty years old in Paris and have an affair with an older man. I wonder if my life will ever be that passionate. Somehow I doubt it.

I want to sleep but my room is hot and the cicadas are thrumming and the more I try to relax the tenser I get.

I think about Ellie's phone call. I should go over to her house. Maybe I'd get used to being there, maybe I'd stop thinking about the murders. After all, we've been best friends since tenth grade—two years. In and out of each other's houses, going to parties, hanging out with kids in her neighborhood. I'll miss her when school starts and she's not there. I'll miss her parents, too. I'll miss eating dinner at her house and spending the night there, sharing secrets in the dark, wondering what we'll be like when we're grownups.

Will we get married, will we have kids, will we still love Elvis. What if a war starts, what if the Russians drop the bomb, what if the world ends.

But deep down inside I know we can't go back to the way we were. Neither can Buddy. Neither can Charlie or Paul. What happened in the park has changed us. The things we know now are things we can't forget.

I turn on my side, I flip over on my back, I curl up, I stretch out. I lie on my stomach. But I can't sleep.

Downstairs, Mom and Dad are arguing. I hear her say, "You never think about the future, you never take any responsibility for this house or your children. I'm at my wits' end." Dad mumbles something that sounds like, "Oh, honey." A door slams. The bathroom, I think. The only place in this house anyone has a speck of privacy. The kitchen screen door creaks open and slams shut. He's gone out in the yard to sit in a lawn chair and smoke, drink a beer or two. He probably hopes she'll go to bed and wake up tomorrow in a better mood.

I hug my old bear and try to imagine myself in Paris, walking down the Champs-Élysées, passing sidewalk cafés, buying pastry, meeting a tall, handsome Frenchman. I wonder if you can buy Gauloise cigarettes in America.

Just before I fall asleep, I think of Buddy. Why, I don't know. He's about as far from a romantic Frenchman as you can get. But there he is, his hair shaved off for the navy, leaning across the car to kiss me. I wonder where he is right now and what he's doing.

A few hours later, I wake up with a jolt, stunned, not sure where I am or who I am. Slowly my room comes into focus. It's still dark, but I make out the Virgin Mary on my bureau, my collection of china dogs at her feet, pictures on the wall, no more than dim outlines of faces, moonlight spilling through my window. My room, my place, my things, everything as it should be but dimly seen, colorless.

The dream comes back to me, far more vivid than anything in my bedroom.

It's dark and rainy. Two girls are standing in an empty parking lot facing a rundown diner. Most of the lights in its sign are missing. Behind the girls is a dark road with a traffic light blinking red. The only building besides the diner is a boarded-up gas station. Not a car in sight. No noise but the rain and the wind.

I can't see the girls' faces. It seems to me I know them, but I'm not sure. For some reason, I'm glad their backs are turned. I don't want to know who they are.

The younger girl looks at her friend. "Where are we?" she asks.

The other girl seems as puzzled as she is. "I was hoping you could tell me." She starts rummaging in her purse and pulls out an empty cigarette pack. "Damn, I could use a smoke."

"Should we go in there?" The younger girl points at the diner.

"It looks deserted."

"The lights are on."

I know the younger girl wants to go inside. Her hair is wet, her full skirt drips water. She's cold. She'd like something warm to drink. Coffee, maybe. Hot chocolate. Tea. Something to cup her hands around and sip slowly. Something to warm her. Something to comfort her.

"They'll have a cigarette machine," she tells her friend, "right by the door. Diners always do."

I don't want them to go into that diner. I want to stop them, but I know this dream won't let me interfere. It's like a movie. You know the heroine shouldn't do something—open the door, go down in the cellar, get into the stranger's car—but you can't stop her. She's in a movie. She can't hear you. Her role is written and can't be changed.

So I watch the girls I may or may not know run across the parking lot. They jump over puddles, swinging their purses on long straps, eager to get out of the rain. Why do they look so familiar? Why do I think I've seen them do these things before?

The older girl gets to the door first. The glass is steamed up, but when she pushes it open, the bluish light inside makes her blond hair glow white.

They don't know it, but I'm right behind them, scooting through the door before it closes.

There's no cigarette machine. The diner is silent, but all the booths are filled with people. Their heads are down. They neither move nor speak. No motion. No force. Under a harsh light, the waitress scrubs the counter.

How did the people get here without cars? They must have walked, but from where? I didn't see any houses. They watch the girls seat themselves at the counter. Their faces are sad. As they whisper to each other, the diner fills with the dry, rustling sounds of their voices.

The waitress doesn't look up. Her hair is bleached. I can see her dark roots.

Without looking at the girls, she asks what they want. Her voice is gruff. The words sound like she's been chewing on them.

"Do you sell Winstons?" the older girl asks. Why is her voice so familiar?

The waitress shakes her head.

"Marlboros?"

She shakes her head again. She still hasn't looked at them.

"Well, what kind of filter cigarettes do you have?" The girl's voice has an edge I've heard before. She gets mad quickly. How do I know that?

The waitress lifts her head and scowls. She reminds me of my aunt Joan's Boston terrier. She's got the same broad face with droopy jowls, a short flat nose, a wide mouth, and bulging eyes. It wouldn't surprise me if she barked.

"Are you stupid or something?" the waitress asks the girl. "We don't have any cigarettes. Not with filters. Not without filters. Not mentholated either. None as in none. Zero as in zero."

"How about coffee?" the younger girl asks. Her voice has a desperate edge. "Do you have that?"

The waitress shakes her head and gives the counter another wipe. "No coffee. No tea. No sodas."

"What *do* you have?" The girl is close to tears.

"Water." The waitress fills two glasses and sets them down in front of the girls. "That'll be twenty cents each."

"Twenty cents for *water*?" The girls stare at the waitress.

She shrugs. "Take it or leave it."

"At home, water's free."

"Well, you're not home. Are you?"

The girls open their purses and pull out their wallets. "I could have sworn I had a dollar," the older one says. "How about you?"

The younger girl shows her an empty coin purse. "I thought I had fifty cents from babysitting for the Morans, but it's gone."

The waitress snatches up the glasses, dumps the water in the sink, and moves away from them.

"My God," the older girl says. "I can't believe this. Is she crazy or just plain rude?" She sounds angry and scared. Before she does it, I know she's going to give the waitress the finger.

The waitress is too busy scrubbing the counter to notice.

"Let's get out of here," the younger one says.

A woman who's been sitting silently at the counter turns her head to face the girls. "If you leave," she asks, "where will you go?" Her voice is soft and kind.

The man beside the woman says, "Don't get involved, Stella. Let them figure it out for themselves."

"But they're so young," she says. Her eyes linger on the girls, taking in their wet skirts and blouses, their soggy white moccasins, their rain-soaked hair. "Almost children."

He shrugs. "Have it your way. You always do."

"Where are you girls from?" the woman asks. She's not ancient but too old to call by her first name. She has the same sad look everyone in the diner has.

"Elmgrove," the older girl says, "near Baltimore."

I must know them, I *know* I know them, but I can't remember their names.

"How long have you been here?" the woman asks the girls.

"In the diner, you mean?" the older one asks.

The woman nods.

"We just came in."

"From the rain," the younger girl adds. "We were in the parking lot and we were cold."

"Do you remember how you got here?"

Without looking at the woman, they shake their heads.

Why can't they remember? Why can't I remember?

The younger girl looks down to hide her tears, but they splash on the counter, one drop after another.

"What were you doing before you found yourselves in the parking lot?" the woman asks.

"There was a party," the younger girl says slowly. "And we danced and—"

"No," her friend says. "That was the night before. This morning we walked to school together."

Yes, that's what they did, I remember now. They walked to Eastern High School. Ellie and I were supposed to walk with them but we overslept.

"Yes," the younger girl says, "that's right, and it was already hot and the sun was in my eyes."

"But something happened." Her friend frowns. "Something horrible."

I'm scared now, so scared so scared so scared I can barely breathe. I know why, I know everything, but I don't want to know.

"It was dark all of a sudden," the younger girl says. "Dark like an eclipse."

"Yes," her friend agrees, "that's just how it was. Then there was roaring all around us and I was reaching for you."

"Me too, I was reaching for you because, because if we, if you and me . . . I'd be alone in the dark."

The woman reaches over and pats the girl's arm. The younger girl shivers as if the woman's hand is cold. "Were you in a car?" she asks the girls.

"We could have been," the younger girl says. "We might have been. Maybe we got a ride."

"No," her friend says, "we were in the park, we were walking across the ball field, we were laughing, you were swinging your purse and the sun was in our eyes and there was someone in the woods but we couldn't see who."

I put my hands over my ears. I don't want to hear any more. I want to wake up.

"And then we were running," the younger girl says. "Running and running and running."

"Did we run all the way here?"

"We must have."

"No," the woman says, "you were running from something you couldn't escape. Don't you see? Don't you understand?"

"Stop it," the man says to the woman. "Let them alone. You're making it worse."

"Yes," another woman says. "You're scaring them, Stella."

"I want to go home." The younger girl stands up and pulls her friend's arm. "I want my mother."

"Poor baby," the woman says. She puts her arm around the girl.

The girl pulls away, as if the woman's touch has chilled her bones.

She tugs at her friend and begs her to come along, but her friend just sits there shaking her head. "For God's sake, don't you get it?"

"These people are crazy," the younger girl shouts. "We have to get away from them."

"Dumb kid," the waitress mutters.

"Shut up!" the younger girl cries to the waitress. "You're the meanest, rudest person I've ever met. What's wrong with you?"

The waitress shrugs, wipes her hands on her dirty apron, and goes back to scrubbing the counter.

"Please, please," the girl begs her friend. "Don't just sit there, do something."

"There's nothing to do," her friend says. "Nothing as in nothing. Zero as in zero. Zip as in zip."

The younger girl runs to the door. Everyone watches her. Their sadness fills the diner. It's suffocating me. If only I could reach out, put my arms around her, comfort her.

She looks outside. It's still dark, it's still raining. Puddles in the empty parking lot reflect the diner's neon sign. The traffic light swings in the wind, blinking red, staining the sky a dull pink. No other lights. No cars. Not a dog. Not a cat.

Nothing as in nothing. Zero as in zero. Zip as in zip. Nada as in nada.

Suddenly, I see what she sees. Not the empty parking lot, not the rain, but a different place, a place I know well. A path through the woods, a bridge just ahead. No one is sitting there.

I hear what she hears. Gunshots. Bobbi Jo turns toward me and I see her face. She's scared, so scared. She runs, she runs, she runs, and I run with her, trying to pull her away, trying to save her, but she can't escape the bullets. And I can't save her, I can't change anything.

She falls. Behind her, Cheryl lies broken, her full skirt streaked with blood. Dead. They are both dead. Nothing can change that.

No, no, no, I try to scream, but I can barely whisper. No, no, no.

Two boys come out of the woods. One has a rifle. They begin to drag the girls away. I don't recognize them, but I know that the one with the rifle is the boy they laughed at, he's the one, he did it, he shot them because they laughed at him.

Then Bobbi Jo and I are in the diner again and Cheryl is sitting at the counter, her face as sad as the other faces.

Bobbi Jo runs to Cheryl. She grabs her hands. She's crying. "What's going to happen to us?"

No one answers. The woman with the cold hands and the kind face sighs. The man beside her mutters a cuss word under his breath. The waitress scowls and wipes the counter.

I lie in my own bed, safe in my room but scared to move, breathing hard. A breeze rustles the leaves and shadows dance on my wall.

This is the true dream, I think. Not the one both Ellie and I dreamed the night after they died. This dream is the truth.

The boy they laughed at in the picnic grove. The one whose name I can't remember, whose face I can't remember. He did it, he killed them.

Nothing as in nothing. Zero as in zero. Zip as in zip. Nada as in nada.

I wish Buddy were here so I could tell him about my dream.

## PART TEN

# Winter

# Memories

## NORA

I'M sitting at my desk reading my e-mail. Among the dozens of messages is one from Eastern High School. The class of 1957 is planning our fiftieth reunion.

I stare at the screen. Fifty years—is that possible?

I've been to only one reunion. The twentieth. Paul and Charlie didn't come. Ellie graduated from St. Joseph's, so she was absent too.

The cheerleaders, the athletes, the class officers, and the popular kids sat together just like they used to. The rest of us were lucky if they spoke to us. I must confess, it was gratifying to see how much weight Ralph had gained and how much hair Don had lost. They both were married to cheerleaders in my class. Ralph to Sally, of course, and Don to Denise McCarthy. The girls looked like the boring housewives they'd become—overweight, hair in out-of-date beehives, too much makeup.

I didn't talk to either Don or Ralph, but once I noticed Ralph looking at me across the room. As soon as our eyes met, we both looked away.

In his opening remarks, our class president read the names of the dead. Not many then. After all, we were in our late thirties. He didn't mention Cheryl, maybe because she didn't graduate. That really bothered me. We'd been together in tenth and eleventh grade. He should have said something about her. Whether or not we knew her, we all remembered her. Of that I was certain.

At dinner, I was sitting with Susan and Julie and Nancy and four or five other people. Just as I feared, someone mentioned the murders. All the other people at our table still believed Buddy did it. They asked me to tell them about the party in the picnic grove and what it was like to be there when the bodies were found and why Buddy wasn't ever convicted when it was obvious he did it. I remember thinking, people will never tire of talking about the murders. Never. Even those who barely knew the girls consider themselves part of the story. The legend. The ballad of.

I gaze at the invitation on my computer screen and let my thoughts drift back to 1956, a long-ago day in June, the last day of school. I see us sitting on the footbridge in the park—Ellie, Charlie, Paul, and me. It's the day the bodies will be found by a boy walking his dog, but we know nothing about that yet. Ellie and and I wear full skirts puffed out with crinolines, Ship and Shore blouses, collars turned up in the back. We both swing our feet, white Keds with the little blue tags on the back to show they're the real thing, not Thom McAn imitations. Our bobby socks are thick-cuffed. Paul is next to Ellie, his arm around her, khaki pants pressed, plaid shirt, crewcut. Charlie's beside me, wearing pretty much the same outfit, his arm around me. We're smoking cigarettes and laughing. Summer stretches ahead—picnics, swimming pools, car rides, movies, parties. The four of us together, always together.

But things happen. Things change. What you plan doesn't happen. What you don't plan almost kills you.

After Ellie transferred to St. Joseph's, we saw each other a few times, but the murders were always there when we got together. They defined us somehow. We both wanted to stop thinking about them. The easiest way to do that was to drift apart.

I haven't seen her for years now, but we still exchange Christmas cards. She lives in Missouri, she's married, has three sons, teaches high school chemistry. I still miss her.

In our senior year, Charlie and I had a few classes together, Problems of Democracy and senior English. We joked and laughed, but we never kissed each other again. He stopped dedicating "Long Tall Sally" to me. I worried he might think I was cheap because of the things we did at the reservoir.

In February he started going steady with Judy Spencer, who was short and cute. By the time we graduated, we were almost strangers. He signed my yearbook *To Nora, keep drawing—see you at Towson! Your friend Charlie.*

I forget what I wrote in his yearbook, but I never saw him at Towson. It was a big campus. He majored in electrical engineering and I majored in fine art.

Buddy wrote to me a few times, but after a while I stopped hearing from him. He never took me to the movies. As far as I know, he didn't come back to Elmgrove.

I wonder what happened to him, where he is, what he's doing. It's a shock to realize he's almost seventy, a year or so ahead of me on the dark path. Retired, probably. Old like all of us who have lived this long.

I've been to Greenwich Village many times now, but I still

haven't watched the ball fall in Times Square, except on TV. Although I used to look for Larry when I was in the Village, I never saw him, but I have the copy of T. S. Eliot's poetry he gave me, and I often lose myself in *Leaves of Grass*. I still know Wordsworth's "A Slumber Did My Spirit Steal" by heart, as well as the words to lots of songs. Funny what you keep.

I click WILL NOT ATTEND and shut down the computer.

Then I gaze out my window at the trees blowing in the wind. It's late December. Twenty-three degrees, cold for Maryland.

A few weeks later, I pick up the morning paper and stare at the headlines: POLICE HOPE TO CLOSE 1956 DOUBLE MURDER.

Stunned, I set my coffee down and spread the paper out on the kitchen counter. A woman in Montana has called the police and told them her brother-in-law shot Cheryl and Bobbi Jo. He was sixteen at the time, she said. He lived on Twenty-Third Street, about a block from Ellie's house. He went to Eastern High School. So did his younger brother, the woman's husband.

Just before he died, her brother-in-law told her he killed the girls because they made fun of him, especially the older one. He said the girl had a sharp tongue and mean eyes. He was never sorry he shot them. Never. Now that her husband was also dead, the woman had decided to inform the police.

I study the woman's last name. I don't remember a boy with that name.

The killer told his sister-in-law two things the police had never revealed to the public. He'd climbed a tree and shot the girls the way a hunter shoots deer. His younger brother had helped him hide the bodies. Before he disappeared into the woods, he'd covered Cheryl's face with a sheet of notebook paper. On it he'd written *and what i want to know is how do you like your blueeyed girls, Mister Death.*

The reporter identified it as a quotation from a poem by E. E. Cummings. He didn't need to tell me. I knew the poem well enough to recognize that the killer had changed one word. In the original, Cummings had written "blueeyed boy," not "blueeyed girls."

Blueeyed Girls, yes, they'd been blue-eyed girls, both of them. I remember. Blue eyes, blond hair, hardly more than children.

After the woman hung up, the police tried to find her, but she'd dropped out of sight. According to her relatives, she and her husband were scam artists and grifters who traveled all over the country, masters of false identities and quick disappearances. Unfortunately, the killer and his brother were both dead, and there was no one to corroborate the woman's story. No witnesses. No gun.

So, even though the police are satisfied with the woman's story, the case is still officially open.

But not for me. I *know* this is the true story. It has to be. How else could the woman have known about the poem? And the tree? What more do the police need?

I look out the patio doors and watch the snow. It shows no sign of stopping. The trees behind my house are almost hidden by blowing veils of white.

Slowly a dream takes shape, one I've had many times since that summer. I'm following Cheryl and Bobbi Jo, not sure who they are at first. We go into a diner where nothing seems right. The waitress is rude; the customers are strange. Bobbi Jo runs outside. I'm scared, but I follow her into the woods. I know what's about to happen. I want to save her, but I can't. I hear shots. This time I know what they are. Bobbi Jo turns, runs toward me, falls. Behind her, Cheryl lies crumpled and broken and bloody. They're dead and I can't change it. No one can.

Then the boys come. Somehow I know the one with the gun was the one they laughed at. That's why he shot them. They laughed at him. Laughed.

I pull myself out of the dream and fold my arms tightly across my chest. The room is cold. The wind is leaking in everywhere.

I continue reading the newspaper. Using a 1956 Eastern yearbook, the reporter had contacted people from our high school class. Although he talked to several people, they all said the same thing. They didn't remember the brothers. Not even a girl named Bonnie, who lived in Ellie's neighborhood, even though that boy probably cut through the park every day on his way to school and back home. We all must have seen him and his brother in Ellie's neighborhood, at school, here and there in Elmgrove.

Puzzled, I get out my 1956 yearbook and find him and his brother. Their faces are small and blurry, not quite as big as postage stamps. Ordinary boys with unsmiling narrow faces and dark hair. Nothing warns you, nothing cries out danger.

He might have been in my chemistry class, he might have sat in front of me in English, but I could swear I've never seen him. Never heard his name.

My mind drifts back to the night before the killings. It's hot, humid. There's no breeze. Heat lightning flickers across the sky stained pink with neon light from the shopping center. We're in the picnic grove. Little Richard, Fats Domino, Elvis Presley, Shirley and Lee sing in my head.

While Ellie and I are laughing and dancing and probably drunk, a boy comes along. It's dark, no one sees his face, no one notices him. He talks to Cheryl and Bobbi Jo, tries to flirt with them. They laugh at him. They insult him. He walks away. Disappears into the shadows.

Such a little thing to them, not worth talking about. Forgettable.

But not little to him. Not forgettable. No, not to him.

But how could we know? How could anyone?

I think of Columbine, of Virginia Tech. Today the brothers wouldn't have stopped with Cheryl and Bobbi Jo.

I cry. Not the huge gulping sobs that almost choked me then, but silent sobs and slow tears, the way Niobe wept for her dead children. Cheryl and Bobbi Jo have been dead much longer than they were alive. They've been held fast in darkness by rocks and stones and trees day after day, night after night, season after season.

Yet the killer lived to be almost seventy. He was never sorry. He was never caught. He was never punished. To me, it's proof you can't count on God to redress the sins of the world.

So I hope his time on earth was racked with pain and guilt and failure. I hope he suffered. I hope he died a miserable death. Not very charitable, I know, but it's how I feel.

I turn to my yearbook's senior section and look for Buddy's picture: *Harold Novak, a.k.a. Buddy. Photography Club, Rifle Club. Ambition: To be successful.*

He's smiling and his eyes look directly into the camera. He's combed his hair into a carefully constructed pompadour. His face is sweeter than I remembered—young, untouched. He had no idea what was waiting for him.

I read his autograph and smile: *To Nora, the nice gal I met at Ellie's house and fellow photography sufferer, good luck, Buddy.*

His handwriting sprawls across his face. In a fancy curlicue under his name he's written *Class of '56.*

I touch his face tenderly with one finger. Sad, I think, it's all so damn sad.

On a whim, I check Facebook for Harold Novak—a very popular name, it seems. One is a nuclear physicist. Another is a neurosurgeon. Yet another is a professor of economics at Tufts. I think I can rule them all out. None of their faces looks right.

Come to think of it, why would Buddy join Facebook? I doubt he wants to find old friends from high school.

I sit and watch the snow fall. Five inches on the ground already and more to come. In the tree outside my window, a bluejay hops from branch to branch, his feathers plumped against the cold and the snow. I should fill the bird feeder, but I hate to leave the warm house.

I try the phone book. Fifteen Harold Novaks live in the Baltimore area. I have a load of laundry in the washing machine, an unfinished painting to finish, a driveway to shovel, but finding Buddy suddenly seems more important than any of these.

I call the first Harold Novak. I can tell by the voice on his answering machine he's not Buddy, not with that New York accent. The second one tells me he's on the no call list and hangs up. He doesn't sound like Buddy either. The third one says he wishes he was the Buddy I'm looking for and asks me if I'd like to meet him for coffee at the Starbucks on Reistertown Road, across the street from a Shell station. I say no thanks and go on to the next. And the next and the one after that until I get to the thirteenth Harold Novak.

When I tell Harold number thirteen who I am and why I'm calling, there's a long silence.

"Hello," I say again, "are you still there?"

"Yeah," he says, and a jolt goes through me. It's Buddy. I know it is.

"Buddy?" I whisper.

"Yeah." His voice is flat, lifeless.

"It's me," I say, "Nora Cunningham."

"I know. You already said."

I'm sixteen again, a girl calling a boy, something I never did in 1956. Awkward, clumsy, disappointed that he's obviously not happy to hear from me, I stumble on. "Did you see the *Sun* this morning?"

"Yeah, as a matter of fact I did."

"Well, what do you think? Do you remember those boys?"

"Nora, it's been fifty years. What the hell difference does it make who killed them? It's not going to change a goddamn thing."

I hear bitterness in his voice, anger. I wonder what kind of man he is. I press the receiver to my ear and wish I hadn't tried to find him. A bad idea, like tossing a lit match into a gasoline can that might not be empty after all. "I'm sorry I bothered you," I say.

He's silent again. Should I hang up? The bluejay cocks his head at me and flies away, a flash of color in the snow.

"You still live in Elmgrove?" he asks.

"Federal Hill," I say.

"In the city, huh?"

"Yes."

"You're not worried about crime?"

"Crime can happen anywhere."

"Yeah."

Silence stretches between us. I'm in Federal Hill, he's in Pikesville, but we're both in the park again, the day we can't escape.

The bluejay returns. My cat sees him and makes a chittering sound. His tail lashes back and forth. He sings softly to the bird, invites him inside, lies about his intentions.

"I wanted to be sure you knew someone confessed," I say. "I thought you'd be glad."

"There's no proof that woman told the truth," he says. "Remember, two or three crazies confessed back in the fifties."

"But Buddy," I say, "the poem, how about the poem? How could she know about it if the real killer didn't tell her?"

He sighs so loudly I can almost feel his breath in my ear. "Just ask anybody—Ellie, Charlie, Paul—they'll say I did it. Even now, even today, no matter what the *Sun* says, no matter what the cops think, those SOBs made up their minds in 1956 and they'll believe it till the day they die. They have their teeth in me like a dog with a rat. They'd break my neck if they could."

His voice has come to life. He sounds like Buddy now, eighteen years old, scared and mad.

"I haven't seen or heard from any of them for years now," I tell him. "They all drifted away. Or maybe it was just me. Maybe I did the drifting." I shrug and stroke the cat, who has scared the bird away and needs comforting.

After a short silence, Buddy says, "We never went to that movie." He laughs, maybe to show it's not a big deal.

"No," I say, "you never called me." I laugh, too. No big deal here either.

"While I was in the navy, my parents moved to Florida. What was the point of going to Elmgrove?"

There's another silence.

"Are you married?" Buddy asks.

"Twice," I say. "And twice divorced."

"Got you beat," he says. "Married three times, divorced three times." He says it lightly. Even laughs. Three divorces. What the hell. No big deal.

"What do you do now?"

"I ran a linotype machine for the *Sun* until they computerized everything. Lucky for me it was just about time to retire." He pauses and I know he's lighting a cigarette. I can see it dangling from the corner of his mouth in that tough-guy way of his. It's hard to believe he doesn't still wear his hair in a ducktail. Even harder to believe he might be bald, he might be fat, he might have a beard or need a shave.

"Now I take pictures," he says, "just a hobby, but some are pretty damn good. My daughter framed a bunch of my best ones and hung them all over her house. It's like a goddamn museum or something."

He takes a puff on his cigarette and coughs. "But what about you? Did you go to that art school in Baltimore?"

I shake my head and say, "Towson State." I wonder if he can tell I'm still disappointed. "I ended up teaching art at Eastern." Another disappointment, but after a while I got used to it, and being a teacher wasn't so bad. "I'm retired now." Something that still surprises me when I say it. How can I be old enough to retire?

"I haven't seen Eastern since I joined the navy," he says.

"It's changed a lot."

"Not enough for me. It could look like the Taj Mahal and I'd still hate it." I hear him inhale, exhale. "Do you still go around asking people if they believe in God?"

Surprised he remembers, I laugh. "I keep things like that to myself now." I think of telling him I'm a lapsed pantheist, but only Charlie would get the allusion.

He coughs again. "You want to get together sometime, meet for coffee maybe, see that movie?" He might not look like he did then, but he certainly sounds the same. A little hesitant, a little unsure.

I gaze into my cat's wise eyes. He blinks slowly and stretches, extending his claws for a moment. Then he settles into my lap as if he has no intention of ever leaving. The snow is still falling, coming down thick and heavy, blanketing the house.

"Sure," I say.

We agree on the Daily Grind, a coffee place in Fells Point. A week from today. At ten a.m.

After I hang up, I stroke my cat's side. His body is warm, strong, relaxed. He purrs softly. "I wish you'd bring me a cup of coffee," I tell him.

His ear twitches but he remains where he is.

The snow continues to fall, six inches, seven inches, they've given up predicting how much to expect.

# Afterword

O N a June morning in 1955, two teenage girls were shot and killed in a suburban park near Washington, D.C. Because of my friendship with a girl in the neighborhood, I knew them both. I was at my friend's house when the bodies were discovered. Hearing sirens, we went outside and saw police cars and ambulances speeding into the park across the street. My friend talked me into following them to find out what was going on. Just as we reached the edge of the woods, a group of neighborhood kids ran toward us screaming and crying, "They're dead, they're dead."

I am returned to that moment every time I think about it. I feel the fear I felt then. I remember the screaming kids, the sirens. The world spins, my knees turn to water, my friend and I run away from her house toward mine, a mile or so away. We see a boy we know and he asks what's wrong, we look like we've seen a ghost. My friend says, "If we've seen a ghost, you know whose it is."

Bewildered, I run after her. I ask her why she said that and she tells me he did it, he killed them, she saw him in the park on her way to school. She had overslept that morning, and her friends went on to school without her. Ten minutes later, she met the boy on the bridge near the place where the bodies had been hidden. He drove her to school.

She shudders. If she'd been on time, if she'd been with her friends, he would have killed her, too.

The police took the boy in for questioning. They held him for more than forty-eight hours without charging him, they gave him lie detector tests (which he passed), they interrogated him about the gun. This happened in 1955, eleven years before the Miranda Warning was enacted in 1966.

Reluctantly, the police let him go. There was no evidence. The gun was never found. However, most of the people in his community believed the boy was guilty. He joined the navy and left town.

The unsolved murders dominated the front pages of the *Washington Post* and the *Washington Evening Star* for the rest of June. World news was elbowed aside. Important events moved to the second and third pages. As the investigation dragged on, the story slowly receded from the front pages and eventually disappeared from the news, but not from people's memories. Every now and then, as the years passed, follow-up stories appeared, including one in which a woman claimed her dead husband's brother had murdered the two girls.

At my fiftieth high school reunion, the subject came up. No one believed the woman's story but me. The people I was with still believed the boy did it.

The murder, like all murders, made a profound impact on everyone who knew the girls, and even on those who didn't know them. I'm not the only one who has never forgotten a single detail of that morning in the park.

That's what has made it so hard to write this novel. I've been struggling with it for more than thirty years now. How do you fictionalize an event that was extremely painful for people close to the victims? How do you avoid presenting characters in a way their families might dislike?

Finally I decided to begin with the actual event but fictionalize the story surrounding it. The characters do not reflect actual people. They spring from my imagination, as do many of the story's events. Although I'd been to parties in the neighborhood, I was not at the party the night before the murders. I'm still ashamed that I was too scared of death to go to either funeral.

My main connection with the neighborhood was my friend. She knew both girls much better than I did. It's her story far more than mine.

Before the murders, the boy and I took a high school photography class together. He signed my yearbook. I saw him at parties. I never talked to him after the murders, not then, not now, but I saw him once at a high school homecoming dance in the fall of 1955. Word spread around the gym— "He's here, the boy who killed them." Everyone rushed to the doors, faces ugly, full of anger, looking for him, hating him. I glimpsed someone in a sailor suit, a mob of kids following him, yelling at him to get out. How does it feel to be accused of a crime you did not commit?

In creating Buddy Novak, I've tried to explore the impact of being accused of murder.

I've been truthful about my memories of my own teenage life and the thoughts and fears and worries the murder aroused. It was definitely the beginning of my religious doubts. Nora's experience with the priest is based on a similar experience of my own.

Like Nora, I kept my doubts from my mother until I was in college and could no longer pretend to believe.

*Mister Death's Blue-Eyed Girls* is an attempt to exorcise some of my ghosts. I sincerely hope no one thinks the characters in this story are meant to be anything but fictional. They are simply teenagers in a story that has haunted me for many years.